I0717101

Praise for Deputy #714 Is Down

"*Deputy #714 Is Down* puts you smack dab in the middle of the action, solving two major crimes right alongside the brave and compassionate officers of Oak Lea and Winnebago County. You get the scoop on police procedure while the story whisks you along on the trail of a deadly gunman." D. M. S. Fick, Author of *Lewis Sinclair and the Gentlemen Cowboys*.

"The latest from Christine Husom is truly a late-night page turner. What a ride! *Deputy #714 Is Down* kept me wide awake and turning the each page a little faster. It's a heart-pounding race against time. A fascinating game of cat and mouse where the lines blur -who is hunting who? It's a winner!" Timya Owens, Author/Editor, Killer Nashville Silver Falchion Finalist.

"Once again, Corky Aleckson takes us behind closed doors, so we can experience the authentic difficulties faced by law enforcement to solve a murder. Even though she's very competent and a team player, she's often overlooked by male colleagues---until she comes up with the critical solutions. And like real life, the "plot thickens," forcing Corky to dig deeply and come up with her best. You'll love the ending!" Colin Nelson, Author of *Flashover, The Amygdala Hijack, The Inca Code, and just-released, Ivory Lust*.

"When one of their own becomes a mark, only to discover he's on a list, things start moving really fast. Even the FBI gets in on this one. The most intense of the series yet." Rhonda Gilliland , Editor and Author of the Cooked To Death Series.

"When a Winnebago County, Minnesota deputy is shot and a deputy in another county is killed, the reader is drawn into an investigation to find the killer before they can strike again in Christine Husom's latest thriller, *Deputy #714 Is Down*. Husom's own law enforcement experiences ensure an accurate portrayal of the deadly cause-and-effect this all too familiar situation has on everyone involved." Thekla Madsen, Co-Author of The Detective Nicholas Silvano Crime Thrillers.

"*Deputy #714 Is Down* is a fast-paced, engaging mystery, a worthy addition to the fine series." A. W. Powers , Author of the Psychic Guardian Angel series.

"*Deputy #714 Is Down*, starts with a bang, kept me breathless in anticipation with the twists and turns, and made it a "can't put down read." Christine Husom weaves a mystery you won't soon forget." Julie Seedorf, Author of the Fuchsia, Brilliant, and Whistle Stop, MN Cozy Mystery Series.

Titles by Christine Husom

<u>Winnebago County Mystery Series:</u>

Murder in Winnebago County, 2008

Buried in Wolf Lake, 2009

An Altar by the River, 2010

The Noding Field Mystery, 2012

A Death in Lionel's Woods, 2013

Secret in Whitetail Lake, 2015

Firesetter in Blackwood Township, 2017

Remains in Coyote Bog, 2019

Death to the Dealers, 2021

Deputy #714 Is Down, 2023

<u>Snow Globe Shop Mystery Series:</u>

Snow Way Out, 2015

The Iced Princess, 2015

Frosty the Dead Man, 2016

Cold Way To Go, 2022

DEPUTY #714 IS DOWN

Tenth in the Winnebago County Mystery Series

Christine Husom

The wRight Press

The wRight Press edition published December, 2023.

Cover photo by Magna Ehlers
Cover design by PrecisionPrints
Buffalo,Minnesota.

The wRight Press
46 Aladdin Circle NW
Buffalo, Minnesota, 55313

Printed in the United States of America

ISBN 978-1-948068-17-8
ISBN 978-1-948068-18-5

Dedication

To the dedicated law enforcement officers who put their lives on the line to keep us safe. When they report for duty, they don't know where their calls for service might take them. They need to be astute, prepared, vigilant, and have servants' hearts. In addition to enforcing the law, they help people in many other ways, with positive results and impacts. Without order, we would have chaos, and I thank each of you for your service.

Acknowledgments

My humble thanks to my faithful beta/proofreaders and editors who gave their time, careful reading, and sound advice: Arlene Asfeld, Judy Bergquist, Barbara DeVries, Rhonda Gilliland, Ken Hausladen, Elizabeth Husom, Thekla Madsen, and Edie Peterson. Also, thank you to all the respected authors who read the manuscript and wrote reviews. I greatly appreciate each one of you and your talents.

And again, with deep gratitude to my husband, and the rest of my family, for their patience and understanding when I was stowed away for hours on end, researching and writing.

And to all my faithful readers. I couldn't do this without your support!

Thank you all from the bottom of my heart.

1

I clicked the call button on my Winnebago County Sheriff's radio. "Six oh eight, County. I'm clear the traffic stop."

"Sergeant Aleckson, you're clear at nine twenty-three," Communications Officer Robin confirmed.

The person I'd stopped drove away at a reduced speed, as per usual. I glanced at Whitetail Lake beyond the safety barrier. Waves rippled across the surface, and it appeared the lake teemed with spawning fish. Not the case that gray November morning. I entered the stop time in my log and pulled back onto County Road 35.

Robin was back on the radio before I'd gone a mile. "Winnebago County and Oak Lea police, go to channel three." Her voice sounded panicked, and my body tensed as I switched from channel one to three.

"Officer down," she said. "Seven fourteen's been shot. Brookings Café, Oak Lea. Suspect fled, unknown direction, or if he's on foot, or left in a vehicle. Tall. Wearing a long black robe with a hood over his head and face. And gloves. Seven twenty-eight's onsite, multiple witnesses, ambulance en route." Robin was mute for a moment then said, "Keep channel three open for. . . this."

Vincent Weber shot? No, no, no, no, no, no, no.

I pulled onto the shoulder. My vision tunneled, the periphery blurred, my heart hammered against my vest, and my respirations puffed faster than I dared count. My arms and legs felt like they were encased in concrete.

"Three twenty, County. Shooter's point of entry?" Detective Smoke Dawes asked.

"Front door, Detective."

"Copy. All responders use the café's east side entrance," Smoke ordered. "On my way from the office." He'd get there ahead of me.

Oak Lea Police Officer Casey Dey responded next. "Ten four. Two thirteen's en route from the station."

"Seven ten, en route from a mile south of Little Mountain." Todd Mason.

"Seven twenty-three, ETA in three." Brian Carlson.

"Oak Lea PD, and Winnebago County deputies, the County copies," Robin said.

It sounded like Smoke was running when he said, "Two thirteen, preserve the scene at the front entry. Seven twenty-three, you'll be the first deputy there. Assist Seven twenty-eight inside."

"Ten four," Dey said.

"Copy," Carlson said.

"Be on the lookout for the shooter. Seven ten, start canvassing the neighborhood, ask residents and business owners if they saw the suspect running from, or getting into a vehicle, near Brookings," Smoke said.

"Ten-four," Mason said.

"Communications, get a statewide alert out to all Minnesota law enforcement agencies," Smoke directed.

"Copy that, Detective," Robin responded.

"All available units, report to the area, meet with Seven ten to divide up the search efforts," Smoke said.

"Seven ten copies." Mason again.

More radio chatter. Each voice held urgency. An army of officers responded. Communications officers repeated Smoke's directives, and instructed them where to report.

A fog surrounded and entrapped me. I had to push through it. *Respond.* Seconds ticked by before I hit the call button. "Six oh eight, County. ETA in four." So near, yet way too far away.

"Ten four, Sergeant," Robin said.

"Sergeant, report inside the café," Smoke said.

"Copy that, Three twenty," I said.

Deputy Amanda Zubinski was with Vincent Weber. I prayed for them both and for mental clarity as I activated lights and sirens and accelerated east on County 35 at the fastest speed possible. The weekday mid-morning traffic was light so few vehicles had to pull over to clear my path. I was in Oak Lea in a minute and at Brookings—a brick structure built in the 1950s, located a block south of the Highway 55 and Highway 25 intersection—in another three. Weber's, Zubinski's, Carlson's, and Smoke's squad cars, along with Officer Dey's Oak Lea police car, sat in the half-empty lot. Smoke was parked near the entrance. The ambulance had not yet arrived.

I parked in the nearest stall, snatched my work cell from the dashboard, and radioed Communications my location. Oak Lea Police Chief Bud Becker drove into the lot and lifted his pointer finger as I climbed from my car. We exchanged a quick glance and a brief sense of calm washed over me. Oak Lea was "his town" and he meant to keep everyone in it safe. Officer Dey was stringing a yellow "Crime Scene Do Not Cross" banner between two front posts.

I entered the café's east side entrance and did a trained visual scan of the area. Booths sat on either side of the café with three picture windows on the walls above them. Round and square tables filled the center area. A group of around a dozen people—staff and patrons—huddled in the back across from the side entrance. Their faces displayed bottled up emotions: shock, fear, uncertainty, disbelief.

A crack of thunder and bolt of lightning tightened my muscles and drew an array of audible gasps and words from the crowd. One woman screamed. Chief Becker touched my elbow on his way toward the witnesses.

My focus went to the crime scene as I moved forward to join the team. Nothing about it seemed real. Weber was sprawled face up on the floor next to a booth, eyes closed, his ruddy complexion pale. His uniform shirt and bulletproof vest were open, the flaps pushed aside.

Smoke had his hand and forearm positioned under Weber's left shoulder and the other gloved hand pressed on his upper chest area. Blood circled around the outline of Smoke's hand and spread on Weber's T-shirt. Smoke glanced up at me and said, "Bullet entered his chest under his armpit, just outside of his vest."

Amanda Zubinski knelt beside Weber, one hand under his chin to keep his head tilted back and his mouth open. Her opposite index finger and thumb pinched his nostrils shut as she delivered life-giving breaths.

Brian Carlson knelt on Weber's other side. An open AED case was on the floor beside him. When I moved in beside the team, I spotted a small hole in the back of the booth.

"Carlson, we've gotta get his duty belt off. Sergeant Aleckson, can you assist?" Smoke said.

Carlson unbuckled the belt. We worked together and slid his service weapon and taser holsters off the belt, followed by cases that held his radio, ammunition, freeze-plus-3 mace, flashlight, knife, keys, memo pad, and work cell phone. We left his personal cell phone and wallet in his pockets.

Smoke called out to Becker, "Chief, get folks into the kitchen until we're clear here. And see if you can locate a bag for Weber's equipment."

My eyes locked with Smoke's. "Has a pulse, stopped breathing." His voice was a hair above a whisper. "Talked to the emergency room doc, asked him if Weber's heart stops beating if chest compressions would be safe, given this." He glanced down at Weber's wound. "Doc said to go ahead if that happens."

Oh, dear God, please no.

I dropped down next to Mandy Zubinski. "Let me spell you."

She gave a quick head shake and delivered the next resuscitation as her tears fell on Weber's cheeks. I needed to stay strong and not fall to pieces like I feared might happen.

"Mandy, let Corky take over till EMS arrives," Smoke said.

She sniffed and shifted. I used the cuff of my sleeve to blot her tears as I moved into position. My mouth had never touched Weber's before, and it felt both natural and unnatural to deliver respirations that inflated his lungs. His skin was cool next to mine, and I prayed it was because my body had heated to about a hundred degrees; not because life was leaving his.

I kept my focus on Vincent Weber as Smoke and Carlson exchanged words. Chief Becker came over with a paper bag, and Smoke and Carlson put Weber's belt and contents into it.

Mandy sucked in a loud, ragged breath as I delivered another lifesaving one to Weber.

"Carlson, secure his equipment in my trunk," Smoke said.

"Copy." Carlson left and returned in short order.

"I'll stay with the folks in the kitchen," Becker said.

"Good," Smoke said.

Mandy let out a few coughs then said, "I'd just joined Vince. He got here a few minutes before me, had a cup of coffee in front of him. I hadn't ordered. No clue what was happening at first. I saw Vince glance up and frown at what turned out to be the shooter. My back was to the door. And I almost *never* sit with my back to the door. Vince kind of turned to the right as his hand went for his gun. Before he drew, before I could react, there was a loud shot.

"People started screaming. Vince jerked backwards then fell sideways. I rolled out of the booth, drew my gun, but the shooter was gone. That's when I saw the blood on Vince's shirt, and moved to catch him so he didn't fall head first to the ground. A guy helped me lay him on the floor."

"Dear God," Smoke said.

I continued to deliver breaths, and when the emergency medical technicians arrived, a heavy weight lifted from my heart. EMT Max pushed in the gurney with a tank of oxygen and IV drip bottle attached to its rail.

"We'll get him on the gurney, cover the wound, and assess," EMT Lisa said. I stood, helped Mandy to her feet, and we backed away to give the EMTs the space they needed.

Max lowered the gurney, removed a backboard from the top, and laid it on the floor next to Weber. "Let's slide him on."

"Aleckson and Carlson will assist," Smoke said as he continued to apply pressure on Weber's wound.

We moved into position. The EMTs took Weber's upper body. Carlson and I slid our arms under his hips and legs.

"To the board on three," Lisa said.

We moved him on the third count. "Now to the gurney. One, two, three." And we lifted the board onto the gurney.

Max tore the wrapper from a hemostatic gauze patch, designed to stop bleeding in gunshot wounds and other traumas, and applied it to Weber's chest while Lisa clipped an oximeter on Weber's finger, put an oxygen mask on his face, and slid the straps around his ears. She placed two fingers on one side of his neck then slid them to the other side. "No pulse," she uttered.

Mandy grabbed my arm with both hands, and it felt like everything slid into slow motion. Max pointed at the defibrillator. Carlson picked it up and set it next to the gurney.

"Start chest compressions," Max said as he removed the oxygen mask. Carlson sprang into action. He located the spot beneath Weber's breastbone, locked his elbows, laced his fingers, and with the heel of his bottom hand pushed and released, pushed and released. The tune "Stayin' Alive" played through my mind, in sync with the tempo of Carlson's compressions.

Max pulled a pair of scissors from somewhere and cut through Weber's T-shirt, exposing his bared, broad, and hairless chest. Lisa ripped the covers from the AED pads and attached one underneath his collar bone on the right side of his chest, and the other on the lower left side of his rib cage below the wound area.

I kept count as Carlson delivered the chest compressions. I was up to a hundred and fifteen when the voice in the AED said, "Do not touch patient, analyzing."

Smoke and Carlson removed their hands and took a step back.

"Do not touch patient, analyzing heart rhythm. Do not touch patient. Step away. Shock will be delivered in three, two, one . . ." I felt my heart jump into my throat when Weber's body jerked.

"It is now safe to touch patient. Start CPR," the voice said, and Carlson resumed. He did thirty compressions, and I moved in to deliver the two breaths as directed by the AED voice. "Do not touch patient, analyzing heart rhythm. Do not touch patient." After a long moment it said, "No shock advised. It is now safe to touch the patient."

Thank you, Lord.

Lisa and Max removed the AED pads, attached the gurney straps to secure Weber, placed the oxygen mask back on his face, and raised the gurney. All in about forty seconds.

"Let's roll. Give him an epi shot on the way if need be," Max told Lisa, as if she needed the reminder.

I ran ahead, glanced up at the threatening sky wondering when the rain would fall, and opened the rig's door for the EMTs and their precious cargo. Smoke, Carlson, and Zubinski fell in behind. Smoke helped Lisa and Max roll the gurney into the rig. Lisa hopped in the back, followed by Mandy who turned to us. "I need to go with."

Smoke nodded. "Sure."

Mandy's eyes met mine. Her face was drawn and flushed; her mouth downturned. I managed a half smile and a few nods. Max closed the ambulance doors, hustled to the driver's door, and climbed in. Seconds later, lights flashed and sirens blared as the ambulance sped away at 9:44 a.m. with our friend, the victim of a heinous crime.

Smoke pulled off his gloves inside out. He withdrew a plastic bag from his pocket, stuffed the gloves inside, opened his trunk, and tossed it inside. We looked at the paper shopping bag that held Weber's equipment. "It'll be okay in my trunk till I get back to the office and secure it in a locker. We'll need to check his work cell phone for any suspicious calls or text messages."

"Yes," I agreed.

Smoke rubbed the back of his neck, turned his head from side to side, and pulled out his phone. "I gotta call Chief back. We talked for a couple seconds on my drive here." He connected with Chief Deputy Clayton Randolph, filled him in on the details then said, "I know it's very early in the morning in Hawaii, but the sheriff needs to be apprised a-sap. . . .You did? Good . . . . No, we'll hold off on bringing in the crime scene team until we've finished interviewing witnesses."

A-sap was Smoke's condensed version of ASAP, the acronym for as soon as possible.

Smoke continued, "There were eleven people besides Weber and Zubinski in the cafe, and given how fast everything went down, it shouldn't take thirty minutes between the four of us. Meantime, can you ask Doug Matsen to go to Holiday, the closest business with cameras, ask for their video footage thirty minutes before and thirty minutes after the incident. . . . Yep, we'll keep each other in the loop."

Sergeant Matsen was in charge of Winnebago County's Crime Lab and oversaw the four crime scene teams. Each team had two deputies, on call twenty-four seven for one week at a time. Joel Ortiz and Bruce Holman made up the current team.

After they'd disconnected Smoke said, "Sheriff's in Hawaii, Chief's sicker than a dog, Lieutenant Armstrong's out on medical leave, Weber is down, and his shooter is loose out there in the world. Chief said he'll have Communications send a 'we have nothing to report yet' message to all the media outlets."

"The media," Carlson muttered.

Smoke took a moment to look at his text messages and shook his head.

Chief Becker and Casey Dey came out the café's east side door.

Becker pointed at the café. "I got a hold of Pete, the owner here. He was up at the restaurant supply store in Saint Cloud and will be on his way. Didn't get into details with him, but said there'd been an incident here, and told him to drive safely, and concentrate on the road.

"Officer Dey and I strung tape across the front half of the dining area to preserve the scene. The café's phone rang a few times. We turned off the volume so the calls will go to voicemail for now. I let the witnesses back into the dining area, asked them to stay back by the kitchen and not to make any phone calls till we'd gotten their statements. If family members call, I said send a message back that you'll call 'em soon."

"Good advice, Chief," Smoke said.

"Reminds me, when we were in the kitchen the witnesses started going over what happened. I instructed them not to discuss what they saw until we'd interviewed them. Didn't want 'em to start comparing notes, maybe get false memories planted. Something along those lines," Becker said.

Smoke's eyebrows lifted. "Or start doubting what they saw, maybe think the other guy's right, they're wrong."

"Happens," Becker agreed.

"Okay. Let's gather our thoughts, then get to the interviews," Smoke said.

I patted my front pocket. "My memo pad's in my car."

Smoke, Chief Becker, and Carlson headed toward the east side door, and Dey to his guard post.

2

On the way to my car I noticed a satiny black cloth on the ground next to the front entrance. "Detective, Chief, Carlson, Dey?" They turned, and I moved my fingers in a 'come here' gesture. "You need to see this. "This may be a piece of evidence."

Smoke's brows lifted when his eyes landed on the cloth. Becker frowned. Carlson and Dey both shook their heads.

"Carlson, will you take a photo?" Smoke asked, and he did.

I withdrew a pair of gloves from my back pocket, pulled them on, and bent over. "Ready, Detective?"

Smoke said, "Yep, go ahead and pick it up."

I used the pointer finger and thumb of each hand to lift the cloth from the ground. It was a face mask hood with holes for eyes and mouth, or nose. Carlson took more photos.

"How'd you spot it there, your sixth sense again?" he said.

My shoulders lifted. "Maybe."

Smoke shook his head. "I sure didn't see it when I ran by there."

"None of us did," Becker said.

"When the call went out, Robin said the suspect was wearing a long robe and with a hood over his head. I imagined it as a robe with a hood, one piece," I said.

"Pretty much the image I had," Carlson said.

"If this belongs to the shooter, it makes me think he shed his cover before he fled the scene and accidentally left this behind," I said.

"A credible theory. The atrium only has a what, three-by-three-foot window in the outside entrance door, and a two-by three-foot window in the inside door."

"Yep," Becker agreed.

"And the bottom edge is at the top of my eye level," I added.

"So it's possible the shooter slipped off his garb without being seen by the folks inside. I suspected something along those lines from the text message updates I've gotten saying our cops haven't located a single soul who spotted a man running away in a long black robe with a hood. Nor did anyone see him walking up to the café dressed in that garb," Smoke said.

I nodded. "Someone dressed like that would've gotten peoples' attention for sure. The atrium could've served as a good quick-change spot before he stepped into the café, and when he stepped back out. But what a huge risk to dress and undress in there. Somebody could've gone in or out. Or tried to." The thought made my stomach tighten.

"Downright brazen. One good thing, there'll be body fluids on the hood, so all we'll need is for his DNA to be in the system," Smoke said.

"I'll get a paper evidence bag for the hood from my car," Carlson said.

"And I'll get my memo and join you shortly," I said.

As I slid onto my front seat, *Mother* popped into my head. She had a shop in town, and when word got out she'd be among the first to hear about it. I lifted my personal phone from its holder on the dashboard and stared at it. I'd break down if I heard her voice so decided to text her instead. It took a second to gather my thoughts, figure out how to phrase it. *One of our deputies was injured in a shooting. Keep it quiet till it's public. Can't talk now but wanted you to know it wasn't me.* I couldn't tell her it was Vincent Weber.

She was quick to reply. *Oh no! I heard all the sirens and wondered. Call me as soon as you can.* She ended with a folded hands emoji. I slid the phone in my pocket, snatched my memo book from the center console, and headed to the café's side entrance.

Chief Becker, Smoke, and Brian Carlson stood in a makeshift triangle outside the door and moved into a circle when I joined them.

Becker nodded at me. "Spotting that hood was a godsend, Sergeant." Then he turned to Smoke. "Detective, this is a bigger case than our PD's got the resources—the people power—to handle."

"The sheriff's office can take the lead on this, but we'll work together, pool our resources. After we get the statements, we'll see where they lead and take it from there. Chief Deputy Randolph has already contacted the BCA. Per Communications, other sheriffs' offices and agencies have reached out, offered to help with whatever we need. And we may tap into their services."

Becker nodded. "One step at a time."

"Brian, will you send the hood photos to me?" I asked.

"Sure," he replied.

Smoke pulled on the café's door handle. "Let's get 'er done. The witnesses are free to leave after their interviews, and ask them to use the kitchen exit out back. Also, if members of the press contact them, tell them not to talk to them. Not until we make an official announcement later."

We filed into the café and I gazed at peoples' faces. My eyes met with some, and my heart hurt for all. They'd experienced and lived through a nightmare.

Everyone was silent, yet the air was alive with apprehension and tension. Some people were seated. Others milled around. An older gentleman stood behind a chair and grasped the rail so tight his knuckles were a yellowish white from the pressure. Another man on a chair looked like he had restless leg syndrome the way his knees bounced up and down at a fast tempo.

My favorite server Cleo, a classic old hippie baby boomer, sat at a table, her long gray hair knotted on top of her head, her face in her hands. The cook, another boomer as bald as his palms, stood in the back and rebounded his body back and forth against the wall.

The food and coffee odors intermixed with a variety of stress-sweat smells, a phenomenon when apocrine glands were activated by psychological stress or fear and produced a strong odor. It could be a metallic or sour or bitter smell, or akin to something rotting. I had smelled variations on myself and others over the years and detected at least three separate ones present in the room. A dab of mentholatum under my nose would've been welcome about then.

My first stop was the restroom. Once inside, I scrubbed my hands then turned from side to side in front of the mirror, and checked my uniform for blood, surprised there wasn't any. I patted cool water on my face and breathed in some mist to help calm my nerves and tap into some inner strength needed to conduct the interviews.

When I returned to the dining room I saw Smoke, Becker, and Carlson had wasted no time. Each was with a witness, notebooks open, pens in hand, recording statements. Besides the two people with officers, eight others waited in the wings.

My eyes met a teary elderly woman's. I raised my eyebrows, waved my hand, and she followed me to a table. She groaned softly as she sat down, like my gramps often did.

"I'm Sergeant Aleckson and am truly sorry for what you've been through here this morning."

She nodded and sniffed.

I withdrew my memo pad and pen, asked for her name, birthdate, address, and phone number. Opal Reynolds, age eighty-one. She was petite, her white hair cut in a stylish, short pixie. The aquamarine ring on her finger matched the color of her keen eyes. I asked for her account, where she was when the crime occurred, what she'd witnessed. Her frown lines deepened as she pointed at a side table, about eight feet from the booth where Zubinski and Weber had been, to the right of the entry door.

"Right over there, table number eight. I was about to take a bite of my muffin when a tall man came in and that got my attention. He was dressed in black from head to toe. It was like a judge's robe with a hood." She dabbed her eyes with a wadded-up tissue.

I recorded her words. "Can you describe the hood?"

"Like I said, it was black." Opal touched her cheek. "It covered his face and had openings for his eyes and nose. Or maybe his mouth."

"You said 'his'. You didn't see the suspect's face, but you thought it was a man."

"Yes. He was *very* tall. I'd say well over six feet, maybe six seven, even. He had broad shoulders, built like a man." She stopped for a breath. "My first thought was, why is he here wearing a costume? You know, seeing that Halloween was over a week ago. Then he lifted his arms, straight out, not bent. Like cops do in the movies when they point their guns. He was wearing black gloves and holding something, but for some reason I couldn't see what it was. I didn't know it was a gun." It wasn't unusual for a person's brain to not register something they didn't want to see.

It took her a moment to go on, "Then there was the loudest blast. It made my ears pop. That's when I *knew* it had to be a gun, but still couldn't see it. It was over in seconds but it didn't seem real at all. Like it hadn't really happened." She shook her head. "You know the saying, 'all hell broke loose?' Well, that's exactly how it felt.

"When I realized the officer had been shot, I was too shocked to move. Terrified, really. People were screaming and throwing themselves on the floor. I heard someone yell, 'Call nine-one-one,' and another yelled, 'The shooter's gone.' Others were screaming things I didn't catch."

Opal looked around. Smoke stood next to a young, muscular man around thirty-five. She lifted her hand and discretely pointed at him. "That one with the detective, he was the one who helped the lady deputy get the wounded one to the floor. Then I saw the lady deputy start mouth-to-mouth resuscitations."

"Opal, did you see the suspect leave, which way he went?" I asked.

She shook her head. "I guess I couldn't take my eyes away from the officers."

I laid my hands on hers for a moment then gave her my card. "That is completely understandable. I appreciate your help, all the details you provided. Is there anything we can do, assist you in any way?"

"Thank you, but no. I'm going to have my daughter pick me up after we're done here—even though she'll be a nervous wreck when she finds out I was here when all this happened. But I'm too shaken up to drive home myself."

"It's a good idea to get a ride. Give me a call if something comes to mind later, all right?" I passed her another card. "Here's a list of resources, professionals you can talk to."

Opal nodded then narrowed her eyes. "I just pray that officer will be okay."

That's my prayer too. "He's in good hands," I said.

I interviewed two others who gave reports similar to Opal's.

Chief Becker was at a table with Cleo, the last witness left in the café. They were a study in opposites. At six-four and three hundred pounds, Becker was over a foot taller and close to two hundred pounds heavier than Cleo. If she wasn't a smoker, she would have no problem beating him in a foot race. But given the way she often struggled to take a good breath they would likely cross the finish line about the same time. Becker's short gray curls were often disheveled. Cleo kept her long white hair in either a ponytail or a bun. One's face was as somber as the other's.

Becker closed his memo pad. "Thank you, Cleo."

She nodded then turned at a snail's pace, a little lost child's expression on her face. When our eyes met she sidled over to me.

Cleo's wrinkled face twisted and made her look like she was in pain. "Sergeant Corky, this is probably my last hurrah here at Brookings. I'm not getting any younger you know, and I don't think I can ever come back here again. Even to eat. What poor Pete is gonna do with the place remains to be seen. You hear about shootings all the time, but unless you're part of one yourself, you have no clue."

"No, you do not. It's way more terrifying." I drew her in for a hug. "Did Chief Becker give you a list of professionals you can connect with?"

She held me tight a minute then pulled back and lifted her tear-stained face. "He did. And I'll give one of 'em a call. I've been living alone since my husband died and was never afraid until now."

I lowered my voice. "You need a place to stay for a while?"

"Ed already invited me to crash at their house, sleep in the spare bedroom, at least until that a-hole is caught." She and Ed were longtime employees at Brookings.

"You'll feel safe there. Take good care, Cleo."

She nodded and disappeared into the kitchen.

Smoke, Chief Becker, Carlson, and I gravitated to a center table. Smoke put his phone in its holder, and said, "I let the crime scene team know we were clear so they could head our way."

We compared notes on what the witnesses had told us. Ed the cook and the dishwasher had been in the kitchen and hadn't seen the shooter, but heard the shot, the shouts, and screams. The eyewitnesses had much the same report on the shooter, the way he entered the café, his actions. After he'd stepped back into the atrium, no one saw him after that, which way he went. And not one of them had noticed him outside the café windows.

"You'd think if he got into a vehicle in the parking lot, or ran past the west side café windows, it would've caught someone's eye. But maybe not," Carlson said.

"From their reports they were either seeking cover or had eyes on Weber and the rescue efforts. But we're bound to find video coverage of him. No one can disappear into thin air. Although at the moment it seems like he did. We don't yet know who the shooter is, but it's obvious this was a planned attack. A *well*-planned attack," Smoke said.

"And the question is *why* did he do it?" I said.

"Say he was targeting cops, maybe he'd seen deputies here at some point. A lot of us take our coffee breaks, eat our meals here. Some every day," Carlson said.

"No doubt, a lot of us do." Smoke tapped his fingers on his chest. "Consider that he was looking to kill a cop, he could've staked out the place, watched for one to show up. He saw Weber, and then Zubinski drive in, or saw their squad cars in the lot."

"The other thing to consider, anyone with a scanner could've heard them tell Communications when they arrived here," I said.

Smoke frowned. "Right. That raises another question. Did the shooter know who they were by their numbers, or their voices? Or didn't it matter to him who they were? Does he live nearby, was he somewhere close, waiting for the opportunity?"

"That thought just sent chills down my arms. He shot Vince, but not Mandy. Thank God for that much. But again, why Vince, and not Mandy?" I said.

"Nothing about what he did is rational in my book. And damn frustrating there are no cameras outside the café, either at the entrance, or in the parking lot." Smoke waved at a camera mounted in a corner. "Just that one focused at the cash register. But it doesn't have a wide enough view to capture the entrance. So no help there."

"Camera footage has spoiled us, for sure. Helps cops find bad guys and solve crimes all the time," Carlson said.

"Speaking of which, deputies and officers are out there checking for any videos at area homes. We'll see what Sergeant Matsen gets from Holiday's camera footage," Smoke said.

My phone jingled at 10:35. Amanda Zubinski.

"Corky, Vince's heart stopped again—"

"*What?*"

"—in the ambulance. EMT Lisa gave him an epinephrine shot and used paddles to get it going again. When we got here they whisked him away . . ." She sucked in a sob. "They wouldn't let me go with him so I've sat here for almost an hour without another word. I'm petrified. I knew you'd be with the witnesses and didn't want to interrupt you but couldn't wait any longer."

"It's okay, we've finished the interviews and released the witnesses. Hang in there, Mandy. I'll be there pronto."

A flush crept up Smoke's neck when I relayed what Mandy had said. "We can't track down that monster soon enough. That hood we recovered has got to give up his identity."

I touched his hand. "Mandy needs me."

"Go. Keep me posted."

3

The Crime Scene Mobile Unit pulled in as I stepped outside. I waved at Deputies Holman and Ortiz then raced to my car, glad Oak Lea Memorial Hospital was just over a mile away. Weber's heart had stopped a second time. My own banged against my vest as I sent up a prayer. I drove to the back of the sprawling, single-story brick hospital building, pulled into the emergency parking lot, asked Communications to notify me by phone if they needed me, and hurried inside to find Mandy.

She was in the emergency area waiting room. Blotchy red patches dotted her face. Mascara was smeared under her eyes and on her cheeks. Some dried blood clung to the backs of her hands and soiled the front of her uniform shirt and long sleeves. We caught each other's eyes, teared up, and embraced for a moment.

"Nothing more yet?" I asked.

"No. They made a copy of his driver's license and insurance card, and I signed the admission form a while ago. They said they'd secure his possessions in a locker."

"Good. You know it takes time to do X-rays, scans, figure out how to proceed. He'll need surgery of some sort to repair his wound."

"Yeah."

The EMT had likely given her a wipe for her hands in the ambulance, but she hadn't removed it all. "Mandy, let's find a bathroom, clean up."

She followed me down the hall. I held the restroom door open for her, then checked the stalls for occupants. Nada. We had the room to ourselves.

Mandy looked in the mirror and gasped. "Oh, Lord."

I pulled paper towels from the dispenser and handed them over. Her hands shook as she grasped them then laid them on the counter. She stared at the sink. It was apparent her brain was not processing well.

"Mandy, wash your hands and face."

She bent over slowly, pumped soap from the dispenser and lathered her hands, over and over, until I stopped her. "That's good. Now your face."

Mandy added more soap to her hands and scrubbed her face. After she rinsed and dried, the mascara smudges were gone and the red blotches had lightened to a tone less noticeable on her fair complexion. "Feeling a little better?" I asked.

She shrugged and her bottom lip quivered.

"Let's check on Vince's status, see what's happening. If he's getting prepped for surgery, or what." Mandy let me guide her out the door. My insides were wound up in knots but I put up a brave front or we'd both go down. A small part of me was thankful her fragile state gave me something—someone—to concentrate on besides myself and my own anxiety.

In the emergency waiting area I remembered the brown sweater with the sheriff's patch I kept in my car. "Mandy, I'll be right back." I retrieved the sweater then held it up for her. "Here, slip this on." She didn't argue—I don't think she had the energy to—and slid her arms into the sleeves. It covered most of the blood stains. "How about you zip it up?" I asked. When she didn't react, I did it for her. Again, without any protest.

I guided Mandy to a chair. She sank down and stared straight ahead. In all our years working together, except for the time she'd been drugged against her will by a cult member in a prior case, I had never seen her in a near-catatonic state before. It alarmed me, big time. We'd been through how many critical incidents together and she had never acted so removed. Mandy was in emotional shock, and if she needed medical intervention, at least we were in the right place for help.

A woman in scrubs waved me over to the counter and glanced at my name badge. "Sergeant Aleckson, I'm a surgical nurse. We wanted you to know we'll be taking the deputy, Vincent Weber, in for emergency surgery. Do you have the names of his next of kin? His fiancée was so distraught she wasn't able to tell us."

"His fiancée?"

She waved her hand in Mandy's direction. "Amanda Zubinski."

They weren't engaged so it took me a second. "Oh. Um, you need Weber's next of kin?"

"Yes."

His deceased wife's parents, a normal sister-in-law, and a crazy sister-in-law, incarcerated for trying to kill Vince and me. "Well, no blood relatives that I know of. He was an only child and never knew his father. His mother died young. Vince does have in-laws he isn't very close to. I don't have their contact info, but we can get that for you."

"Okay, good. As I said, Vincent is being prepped for surgery and will go in momentarily. The bullet went through his left lung and that collapsed it. We had to resuscitate him and put him on a ventilator."

Resuscitate him. Again? And a ventilator? No. This cannot be happening. I glanced back at Mandy, and she looked like a statue propped in the chair. Two dear friends were in trouble and my brain had turned to mush. "How long will the surgery take?" I asked her.

"Likely around three hours."

Three hours? "That long, really? Vince *has* to be okay," I said.

The nurse gave a slight nod. "The surgeon and other personnel are doing all they can to ensure he will be."

Will be. I stumbled back to Mandy, sat down, and laid my hand on her arm. "Mandy, look at me." I was relieved when she did. Her big green eyes were red-rimmed and tears clung to her lashes. "Did you hear what the nurse said?"

Her head did a slow move to the left, right, and back to center. "No."

"The bullet went through Vince's lung, and they're taking him into surgery to repair it."

She grabbed my hands. "Oh, God."

"Mandy. Question. Do you know what Vince's current status is with his in-laws? Are they still cordial?"

"Pretty much, after the whole thing with Darcie. They told Vince they should've been kinder to him over the years, before and after his wife Stacie died. They knew how torn apart he was when she was killed in that crash. But it's not like they keep in close touch. Probably because of the whole thing with Darcie," she said.

I nodded. "I get that. But they're the closest thing he has to next of kin, except for Darcie and her sister, the one that Vince never talks about."

"No, he doesn't know a lot about her. She moved east after college, works out there somewhere, and rarely comes back for a visit. She had already moved away before Vince joined the family. I take it there was some sort of family drama going on. Maybe it was with Darcie. Who knows?"

"Yeah, who knows, but we need to contact the Wilsons," I said.

"Their contact info's in Vince's phone."

Of course. "Right. I'll see if they'll let me take a look at it."

Her eyebrows lifted. "I can ask. I told them I'm his significant other." And they had interpreted that to mean *fiancée.*

Vince and Mandy had been closed-mouthed about their relationship status for months. My eyebrows narrowed as I studied her face. "You are?"

Her shoulders lifted. "Not in the way you might think, but yes."

I didn't know what to think. "Okay."

Mandy walked over to the reception desk. She needed a task, something to keep her occupied, and I hung back to let her handle it. The medical tech returned to the desk a moment later. They spoke in quiet tones then the tech left and returned with the phone. Mandy swiped and scrolled—she obviously had his passcode—pulled a memo pad from her back pocket, scribbled on it, and handed back the phone.

She returned and offered the pad to me. "I told the tech we'd notify them, but I've never talked to them myself. They weren't in court, at least not when I testified," she said.

"Let me check with Smoke, see who in the office should call them." I sent him a text, *Call when you can.* My phone dinged a second later and I walked down the corridor, away from Mandy and the handful of people in the waiting room.

"How's Weber?" he said.

"There've been complications. The bullet went through his lung, collapsed it. He's going into emergency surgery, on a ventilator."

"*No.*"

"We're really scared, Smoke. How long will you be at the café?" I asked.

"Our crime scene team, Holman and Ortiz, are close to wrapping up, so I'll be clearing in a few."

I glanced at a clock on the wall. "It only took like forty-five minutes?"

"Wasn't a whole lot to collect from the small area here. They recovered a nine-millimeter bullet from the back of the booth, and its casing on the floor several feet from the door, but didn't find fingerprints on either one of 'em," Smoke said.

"Man."

"The team searched for possible black fibers from the robe in the atrium, the entry, and area around the outside entrance. They lifted one, but we'd need the suspect's garment to compare it with. They collected other fibers and particles that are likely from vehicle carpets or other rugs. They found different sets of fingerprints, and lifted some, but the shooter wore gloves when he was there, so we don't believe he left any fingerprint evidence. He was careful and prepared," Smoke said.

"Frustrating."

"You got that right. One positive is the recovered bullet. That, and the black hood you found could provide a possible DNA match."

"That's two positives," I said.

Smoke made a "mmm" sound. "Oh, and the owner Pete's here. Trying to come to grips with what happened."

"It'll be tough, poor guy."

"Hang tight, I'll be there shortly," he said.

"Good." I released a long, slow breath to calm myself and joined Mandy in the waiting area. She stood and started pacing. "Let's walk and talk," I offered.

We headed down the corridor. A nurse darted out from a room and we fell in behind her, but her pace was faster than ours and she left us in the dust. If any dust was allowed in that nearly sterile environment, that is. "The crime scene team wrapped up so Dawes will be on his way soon. I'll ask him about calling the Wilsons when he gets here," I said.

Mandy stopped and turned to face me. "Wow, they cleared the scene already?"

"I guess there wasn't a ton of evidence to collect. They recovered the bullet from the booth. And we have a black hood the shooter may have left behind. It was on the ground outside the café."

She touched my shoulder. "Really?"

"Yeah, I should've told you about it before. I happened to spot it after the ambulance cleared the scene." I found the hood photos in my phone and showed them to her.

"Wow, let's hope." She stopped, leaned against the wall, and looked down as she balled her fists. "It didn't register at first that Vince was shot. It was only like seconds before I was out of the booth onto the floor, but the shooter was already gone. Why didn't I go after him?"

"Mandy, like you said, it happened in a flash. Your first priority was attending to Vince, the right thing to do. If you'd gone after the shooter, your own life would've been in jeopardy. Maybe others' lives."

"What if Vince doesn't make it?" Her voice rose with each word.

I elbow bumped her. "We cannot go down that road right now. But we can hold on to positive thoughts and pray."

"Non-stop." Her eyes were wet with unshed tears. "Let's wait for the detective in the chapel."

"I'll let the front desk know where to find us." I gave the tech our phone numbers so they could contact us. She jotted them on a note pad. Then I sent Smoke a message and joined Mandy in the small chapel, grateful we were the only ones there.

The room was painted a grayish shade of blue. Eight silver sconces on the walls provided a subdued lavender glow. A flameless candle sat on a table beneath a gothic, muti-colored stained-glass window, and soft meditative music played at low volume. I took a cleansing breath and it lessened my stress a tad.

Mandy collapsed onto a soft chair, rested her folded hands on her knees, and bent her head. One by one tears dropped on her thighs. She'd said she was Weber's significant other, but not in the way I'd think. Then how? I knew they were close, and each one had at least one toxic relationship in the past. Was that the pull that had drawn them together?

We'd get the skinny on it sometime down the line.

"Mandy, should we get you some help here, like a professional to talk to?"

She shrugged. "This whole thing still seems unreal. I know I'll need help to deal with it, get through this. And I will. Like before, like the other times."

"Yes, you will. We have a long list of resources to tap into and we'll make sure you get what you need. We're all here for you."

It warmed my heart when she nodded.

Other critical incidents we'd experienced and survived flashed through my mind. They came with the job. Debriefings, therapy, and healthy relationships helped us cope and assured us those incidents didn't define us as people, or hinder how we performed our duties. When we got the help we needed.

The worst part about this case was the victim was our dear friend and trusted colleague. I didn't know exactly how Mandy felt, but I'd had an eerily similar traumatic event. The difference was, my boyfriend had taken a fatal bullet seconds before I killed his killer. Mandy didn't get that chance. I'd spent months in therapy and worked in the sheriff's office on warrants and other duties as assigned until a mysterious case had drawn me back into the field. I wondered if Mandy would request a reassignment to warrants or the bailiff's division to get off patrol for a while. Or forever.

4

Smoke entered the chapel at 11:40, and it snapped me back to the present. When our eyes met, my insides warmed. Even in the midst of tragedy—or especially then—he was my rock on earth. Mandy lifted her tear-stained face. Smoke went to her, sat beside her, and drew her in for a bear hug.

"I don't want Vince to die," she said.

"No. And we're in the right place to ask for help," he said.

Mandy sniffled, and new tears fell.

Smoke squeezed her shoulder. "We interviewed all the people in the café. Those who saw the shooter described him as very tall, wearing a black robe with a hood that covered his face, with holes for his eyes and mouth. Folks saw similar variations of the incident. Some saw his black gloves and the gun, others didn't. Nobody could describe him, or the incident more than that, given how fast it all went down."

"Corky told me, and I heard the man tell Communications about the same thing you just said when he called it in."

"Corky tell you she found the hood on the ground outside the café? We figured he dropped it," Smoke said.

Her eyebrows lifted. "Yeah, and all I could think was *wow*."

"Sergeant Matsen stopped by the café just before I left. He and Todd Mason got some video footage from the Holiday Station in case the suspect took that route. There was a lot of vehicle traffic in that time frame, and a fair amount of foot traffic. It'll take a while to examine the tapes," Smoke said.

"What about the homes around the café, other businesses?" I asked.

"They'll be checking north, south, east, and west. The businesses north are closer to the café than the downtown businesses south of it are. We're not having a whole lotta luck at homes around there so far. But I have to believe we'll capture the suspect on video from one source or another," Smoke said.

"Concentrating on a tall guy with a backpack?" I said.

"Backpack?" Mandy said.

"Seems to make the most sense. *No one* saw a guy in a long black robe, so we believe he did a quick change in the café's atrium. The suspect had to stash his garb somewhere. Unless he lives close by," Smoke said.

Mandy nodded, then frowned at the thought. "Lives close by? What are the chances of that?"

"Wouldn't hazard a guess. Just threw it out there as a possibility. At this point, the suspect seems to have disappeared into thin air. And nobody can do that, especially in the era of security almost everywhere. Deputies and Oak Lea PD were on the scene in minutes, and no one spotted him. If he was running away, robe or not, a cop would've gone after him."

"Yeah," Mandy said.

Smoke stood and moved next to me in front of the stained-glass window. He slid his arm around my back and gripped my bicep. I leaned against his chest and we were silent a moment, until I remembered. "Smoke, Mandy's got Vince's in-laws' phone numbers from his contacts. The hospital wanted us to notify them since we don't know of any next of kin. You should make the call, tell them what happened," I said.

"I can do that. What're their names again?" He pulled his phone from its holder.

"Art and Joan Wilson," Mandy said.

"Art's number?" Smoke hit numbers as Mandy recited them. When it stopped ringing, Smoke hit the speaker feature on his phone. "Art Wilson?"

"Yes?" He sounded wary.

"Detective Dawes, Winnebago County Sheriff's Office."

"Oh?"

"I regret to have to tell you this, but your son-in-law, Vincent, was seriously injured this morning."

"Vincent was? How?"

"He sustained a gunshot wound to the chest. He's in surgery now," Smoke said.

Wilson coughed then said, "*What?* Who shot him?"

"We don't know yet. He was on break at an Oak Lea café when an unknown person entered and fired a hand gun at him. There was a deputy with him who wasn't injured."

Mandy let out a small whimper, then coughed herself.

"Unknown? Does that mean the shooter's on the loose?" Wilson asked.

"Unfortunately, yes. But we'll track him down."

"You think it was random, or was it someone who knew Vince?"

"We know next to nothing at this point," Smoke said.

"What an awful thing. Vince will be okay, won't he?"

"We're counting on that."

"What hospital's he at?" Wilson asked.

"Oak Lea Memorial."

"Oh." He paused then added, "We'll head down there as soon as the missus gets back from her dentist appointment. She hasn't been gone long so it might be a couple hours before we get there. You'll call if anything changes?" They lived about an hour away.

"Of course."

"Thank you, Detective. Another nightmare for our family." Their daughter Stacie—Weber's wife—had died in a vehicle crash some years back, and their daughter Darcie had been taken to Oak Lea hospital after she crashed her car the year before.

"All of us at the sheriff's office are with you on this one," Smoke said. He looked at us as he disconnected. "His concern seemed genuine."

I nodded. "I know they didn't have a great relationship, but I don't think they hated Vince, not like he thought."

"Who wouldn't love that 'ugly mug' he called himself?" Mandy said.

That coaxed smiles from all of us.

Smoke took a chair next to Mandy's. "Amanda, you gave us some details of what happened at the café, but I didn't write it down and need your official account for the record." He pulled out his memo pad. "No question how tough this has been for everyone, and for you in particular."

She gripped the chair's arms. "It's okay. It keeps playing over and over in my mind, and I can't stop it. Like a horror film I didn't want to see in the first place, much less a thousand times since." She squinted and blinked. It took her a minute to go on, "Vince and I were both free to take a coffee break at nine twenty and met at Brookings, a central location between our call areas."

"As you often do," Smoke added.

"Yes."

"We talked about the fact that anyone tuned in to the sheriff's radio could've heard you go ten-ten at Brookings." Smoke again.

"That's how we keep track of each other's locations," Mandy said.

"But since airwaves are considered public property, anyone else can listen on their scanners. To most channels anyhow. Could be a potential problem in this case, if that's what the shooter did," I said.

Smoke nodded. "And something to take into serious consideration. We know there are sick people out there who kill cops. Mandy, this'll sound harsh, but from what we've gathered, the suspect knew Vince Weber was at Brookings. And he also knew you were in the café. At least he did when he entered the café. He shot Vince, but not you. It makes us wonder why he targeted Weber."

She swiped away tears as they rolled down her cheeks. "That question has burned through my mind a gazillion times."

"Weber must've been his intended victim," Smoke said.

Her shoulders lifted then dropped. "I know, but why?"

"Did he ever complain about anyone harassing him, mention feeling threatened by anyone?" Smoke asked.

"No. Not since Darcie. Or even before her," she said.

Smoke's eyebrows lifted at Darcie's name. "We'll go through Weber's history of arrests, ones that landed offenders in prison, or a long stint in jail. We'll start with them, see where it leads."

Mandy looked at me. "Darcie's still incarcerated at Shakopee Prison, right?" The Minnesota Correctional Facility Shakopee was the state prison for women.

"She is. Since Vince and I were her victims, they'll have to notify us when she's released. She's got over eight months left on her sentence," I said. Her release date was fixed in my mind.

"The other thing is, Darcie is of average height and build, not the description the witnesses gave us. So that pretty much would rule her out anyway." Smoke rubbed his fingers back and forth across his chin. "We got a little sidetracked there. Go on, Mandy. Give us every detail you remember."

"Okay. Vince got to Brookings ahead of me and was sitting in the booth when I walked in. I'd rather sit at a table where we both can see the entrance, keep an eye out for the occasional character that shows up."

Smoke and I both nodded.

Her eyebrows drew together. "But I slid into the booth anyway. Vince was facing the door. The server brought me water then went to deliver an order. We talked about nothing special for a couple minutes, then Vince glanced up and got this weird look on his face. Like a combination of surprised and disturbed.

"He went for his gun but wasn't able to withdraw it before the blast. He jerked back, so I figured the bullet must've hit him but didn't see any blood on his shirt—not till later—and it really didn't register.

"By the time I rolled out of the booth, the shooter was gone. A guy helped me catch Vince as he fell to the side. I was about to radio for help but my helper had called nine-one-one by then. I said tell them Seven fourteen is down and Seven twenty-eight is with him."

Mandy looked at her hands as she spread her fingers. "I checked Vince for a pulse and found it. But he wasn't breathing, so I started mouth-to-mouth." Her eyes met Smoke's. "You got there fast and helped stop the bleeding. Then I heard Carlson. Then you were there, Corky, asking to spell me."

She finished her account and we took a minute to reflect. I tried to imagine how I'd feel if our roles were reversed. What if I had been the one on a break with my friend and colleague and witnessed a brutal attack like that?

Smoke touched Mandy's arm. "Our crime scene team measured the trajectory of the bullet from where the shooter stood to where it entered the booth. So we know where Weber was positioned in the booth. Were you directly across from him?" Smoke asked.

Mandy closed her eyes. "No, Vince was closer to the edge and I was more in the middle."

"Witnesses said there was no one in the booth behind, or in front of you," Smoke said.

"That's correct."

"So the shooter had a fairly clear shot."

"I guess." She turned her face toward the stained-glass window. "Who in this world would want him dead? Besides Darcie, that is."

"Seems to me Darcie's motivations and actions differed from this shooter's. Darcie was irrational, delusional, thought Vince and Corky were involved and wanted to keep him for herself. When she saw the opportunity to run them both over at the same time, she acted on impulse. Two birds with one stone," Smoke said.

An involuntary cough escaped from my throat.

"Sorry, Corinne. That was crass," Smoke said.

I shook my head. "No, yeah. You're right on."

"Contrast that with the attack on Weber this morning. It was planned. The suspect disguised himself. He entered, took his shot, then exited in what witnesses estimated was less than a minute. More like twenty to thirty seconds. As I said before, he knew Weber was there, where he was sitting before he opened the door," Smoke said.

"He must've either seen him from the windows by the parking lot or looked through the window on the atrium door. Maybe both," I said.

"Maybe. Then in the chaos after he shot, he stepped back into the atrium, disrobed, threw his garments in a bag, or backpack, and walked, or drove away," Smoke said.

"But dropped his hood in the process." Me again.

Smoke blinked. "He was in a hurry. In his mad dash he may've been stowing his garb as he left, and the hood got separated from the robe. If his robe was made of the same light, silky material, I can see how it could happen."

Mandy's eyebrows drew together. "It still could've been any deputy the shooter was after. Not Vince in particular."

Smoke bopped his fist into the other palm. "That's what we intend to find out."

"Sounds like a lot of off-duty deputies showed up to help," she said.

"They have, along with Oak Lea PD officers. The BCA is sending agents to assist, also. We don't plan to turn the investigation over to them, at this point anyway, but their help is greatly appreciated." Smoke checked his watch. "It's less than three hours since the incident. We've covered a lot of ground with all the responders and I hope it leads us to the suspect a-sap. I'm counting on video coverage. If we can narrow it down to a likely suspect, we'll make copies of the tapes and get them to every law enforcement agency in the state. I'd also like the people who witnessed the incident to view it, see if the one we believe is the suspect triggers a memory in one of them."

"Like how, since he was covered from head to toe?" Mandy asked.

"His stature, his movements. I know it's a remote possibility, but people can pick up on nuances, even in a few seconds. I recognize most people I know some distance away by the way they walk and move," he said.

"Yeah," she agreed.

"The owner was still at the café when you left. How's he doing?" I asked.

"In shock, understandably. He's having signs made that say they'll be closed until further notice."

"Poor Pete. I wonder if they'll ever open again," Mandy said.

Smoke's shoulders lifted. "Brookings has been a mainstay in the community a whole lotta years, but similar incidents have caused long-term businesses to close up shop for good."

"Sadly," I added.

"Mandy, so you know, your deputy friends and other staff want to be here, show their support for Vince, and for you. But per the sheriff, anyone who isn't authorized to be here is asked to not visit him, at least today. Unless you want someone with you. Besides Corky, that is."

Mandy shook her head. "I'll call my sister, see if she can leave work early to hang out with me."

"That'd be good," Smoke said.

"Yeah."

Smoke's phone alerted that he had a text. He glanced at it then put it back in its holder. "I need to head back to the office."

"Detective, before you go, do you have the name of the guy who called nine-one-one, the one who helped me with Vince?" Mandy said.

"Sure." Smoke pulled out his memo book and flipped over a few pages. "Tony Edwards. Lives here in Oak Lea."

Mandy's lips curled up a tad. "I'll need to thank him sometime."

"He'd appreciate that, I'm sure. Everyone at the café was pretty traumatized—" Smoke's phone buzzed and cut him off.

He frowned as he pushed the accept button. "Sheriff? . . . Weber's in surgery to repair a collapsed lung as we speak. The shooter's still out there somewhere—no real leads yet—but we recovered a nine-millimeter bullet and the cloth hood he wore over his face. . . . Sure, I'll prepare an updated statement, get it out a-sap. . . . I understand, and I'd likely feel the same way, but there's no reason for you and April to cut your vacation short. You barely got there and you're a phone call away if we need you. . . . Focus on your wife. We're covered here. . . . Good. Later, boss."

Smoke pushed the end button and pulled in a breath through his nostrils as he dropped the phone into its case. "Kenner's having a heck of a time. Feels torn and guilty because one of his own is down. There he is in Hawaii with April celebrating their anniversary, and he thinks he should be here. Doesn't help knowing his chief deputy's at home sick."

"No. And Chief needs to stay home 'cause none of us want the norovirus crud he's got," I said.

"Like I told Kenner, he's but a phone call away, as we all are." He squeezed my arm and glanced at his watch. "I'd like to stay with you two but gotta get to the office. The media folks have been chomping at the bit for a statement for a couple hours now. On the flip side, their broadcasts could bring in some leads and help us track down the shooter. Oh, and we need to pull a meeting together a-sap, bring all the responders in, see what we've got so far. Lots of moving pieces."

5

Smoke lifted his hand in a goodbye wave. When he left, the room felt lonelier. While we waited, Mandy and I monitored radio calls, listened to voice messages, and answered text messages from fellow cops who checked in to see how Weber was, how we were. And from family and other friends.

Smoke phoned twenty minutes later. "Well, I gave the media an official statement."

"You go on camera?" I asked.

"No. With Weber's precarious condition and the suspect out there somewhere, Sheriff thought it was best to hold off on that for now. And stick with a written statement."

"I agree. So what'd you tell them?"

"Time of the incident, that a law enforcement officer was shot, gave the description of the shooter. Said the victim's name and condition will be released after notifications are made. That the suspect is considered armed and dangerous. If anyone has info to call our office a-sap," he said.

"You flooded with calls yet?"

"A fair share, per usual. And a bunch came in before that, not long after the shooting. Communications is assigning the calls to deputies so we'll see if they lead anywhere. And to let you know, we're sending deputies to take posts at the hospital, guard the entrances, and the surgical and ICU units.

"Anyone who enters, or tries to, will be checked. I gave them Art and Joan Wilson's names, so they shouldn't have a problem getting in. The shooter likely suspects his target survived the bullet. Especially if he was watching when the ambulance picked Weber up," Smoke said.

"Eew." Even though a similar thought about the shooter checking to see if Vincent Weber had survived flitted through my mind multiple times since the shooting, when Smoke verbalized it, it made goosebumps pop up over my entire body.

"I need to take a call. Bye." He disconnected.

I told Mandy that deputies would be standing guard at key entrances. She visibly shuddered. "To protect Vince?"

"Yes." I touched her shoulder. "Mandy, Vince will be in surgery at least another hour, according to what the surgical nurse told us. I think I'll sit in my car for a while, make some calls. It'll be more private, especially if someone comes into the chapel here to meditate."

Mandy stood. "I'll do the same."

But when we stepped through the emergency exit, Mandy's eyes danced around the parking lot. "Geez, I forgot my car's still at the café."

I'd blanked that out myself. "Oh, sure. I'll have a deputy drive it here, or we can have someone drop it off at your house later."

"No, let's go get it so I'll have it." She studied my face then added, "Corky, I'm fine to drive if you're worried about that."

She'd read my thoughts. "All right. Let's go." We opened the car doors and climbed in.

On the way we met two news vans from the Minneapolis metro area. They must've gotten wind Deputy Vincent Weber was at Oak Lea Hospital. "News hounds," I said.

Mandy made a humph sound. "If they think they can get a story about Vince, they won't get it at the hospital."

"I know they have protocols and don't let media bring their cameras inside in the first place. Plus our deputies will be there soon to ensure none of them get in," I said.

"Yeah."

As we approached the café Mandy said, "I'll never be able to go into Brookings again." The same sentiment witnesses and staff had voiced.

Crime scene tape spanned the front entrance, and two barricades blocked the driveway. Another Oak Lea PD officer had replaced Casey Dey and moved a barricade aside when she spotted my vehicle. I lowered my window and called out, "Thanks."

"Sergeant, you missed Paul Moore from the local newspaper and a couple of metro television crews. They left a few minutes before you got here," the young female officer said.

"We met their vehicles on the way from the hospital."

"Yeah, camera guys were filming reporters who pointed at the café. They said a deputy had been shot inside. Not named yet. And the shooter is at large and considered armed and dangerous. It was unknown whether he's threat to the public," she said.

Mandy sucked in a loud breath.

"Detective Dawes issued an official statement about a half hour ago," I said.

"Chief Becker told me about it and said to expect visitors. With dozens of cops in the area, and the café taped off, they've been waiting hours for the scoop. Reporters asked me some questions but all I could say was 'no comment,' per Chief Becker," the officer said.

"The sheriff appoints someone to give official statements for a reason. So the rest of us don't say the wrong thing that messes with the investigation and eventual court case," I said.

The officer nodded. "That's for sure. Owner Pete's inside if you want to talk to him."

I shrugged. "Maybe later." I had taken on emotional responses from many people in the last hours, and the day was still young. I'd save time with Pete for another day.

"Everyone at the PD is pulling for Weber. Let him know that, will you?" she said.

I gave her a thumbs up, drove in, and parked by Mandy's squad car. I stopped myself from asking if she still felt able to drive. "See you in a bit," I said instead.

"Yeah, thanks." Mandy sat for a moment before she reached for the door handle and got out. She slowly climbed behind the wheel of her vehicle, and I counted to fifty-eight before she started it, then waited until she pulled away before I shifted into gear and followed her.

As I passed the hospital's main entrance I saw the local radio station's van, along with two metro television station vehicles, parked in the front lot. Several people milled by the TV vehicles. Their cameras were set up, and pointed at the entrance. They had braved the elements whatever the weather, at the crime scene, and at the hospital where they were not privy to the victim's condition. Namely, that he was in surgery, on life support.

I drove to the emergency lot. Deputy Leo Roth had taken up guard duty by the entrance in the short time we'd been gone. Mandy had parked in the next row. I sat with my car running and listened to the sheriff's radio chatter on both channel one and channel three. Inside the hospital, we'd kept our radio volumes low, a step above silent, to monitor calls. It was easier to listen and concentrate in my car.

After some minutes, I phoned Smoke.

"Weber?" he said.

"No new updates. No, we picked up Mandy's squad car, and I thought you should know metro camera crews and our local radio station are camped in front of the hospital. They'd been by the café too. Trying to get info from Oak Lea PD."

"Johnnys-on-the spot, aren't they? I did get word about that, and it doesn't surprise me. They monitor the sheriff's radio channels they have access to. Not to mention how word spreads like wildfire from witnesses, neighbors, and people who pass by and see a bunch of emergency vehicles at a scene. Sergeant Roth at the hospital emergency entrance?" Smoke said.

"He is."

"Good. Later, Sergeant."

I pushed the end button and gripped my phone, trying to muster the courage to call my mother. She maintained a state of near panic when I was on duty, fearful something bad or fatal would happen to me. And she had valid reasons for concern at times.

Mother answered before the second ring. "Corinne, I thought you'd never call!"

"Smoke issued a statement about the incident. Did you hear him on the radio?"

"No. I turned it down when I was on the phone earlier and guess I forgot to turn it back up again," she said.

I blurted out, "Smoke didn't announce this but Vince was the injured deputy. He was shot by an unknown assailant."

"*No!* How'd that happen? He'll be all right, won't he? He's not *dead*?"

"Vince is alive, but in critical condition. He's in surgery to repair his lung. He and Mandy were at Brookings Café when someone came in and shot him."

"But he didn't shoot Mandy?"

"No, thank God. The shooter fled and is on the loose."

"That is so terrifying. Now it all makes sense. An Oak Lea police officer came in about an hour ago and asked if I noticed a tall man in the area and asked if I have an outside camera. I said 'no' to both," Mother said.

"Officers are canvassing the town, homes, and businesses in the search."

"This whole thing is awful. I can't imagine how Mandy feels."

"She's in tough shape, of course. Mother, Weber's name was not released, so don't tell anyone until it's made public," I said.

"I won't, dear. I know the drill."

Her choice of words made me smile. "We got a hold of Vince's in-laws, and they're coming to the hospital."

"Really? Well, that's good I guess," she said.

"Mom, I need to go. Let our family know, okay? John Carl, Gramps, Grandma and Grandpa. Not who was shot, but what happened."

"I will, dear. And I'll keep all of you in my thoughts and prayers. Especially Vincent."

"Thank you," I said.

Mandy sat in her car, staring straight ahead. She jumped when I gently rapped on her window and opened the door. "Hi," she said.

"Ready to go back inside?"

"Yes. No. I want to fast forward to when Vince wakes up and is okay. When I called my sister and told her what happened, she freaked," she said.

I nodded. "Same with my mother."

Mandy climbed out, and we headed to the emergency entrance. Sergeant Roth eyed us with a grim expression, knitted brows, pursed lips.

"Hey," I said.

He shook his head. "This stinks worse than anything I've been through since I started with the sheriff's office. One of our own shot. What in the world? I think of Weber as in*vinc*ible. Invincible Vincent. Always wanted to tell him that but figured he'd laugh, make a joke out of it."

Mandy smiled. "Yeah, he would've, but would've felt secretly pumped and proud you thought that. Invincible. I like that, and it's what we need Vince to be right now. Thanks, Leo."

I nodded at Roth, and noticed when I followed Mandy inside, she stood a little straighter, walked a little faster. Roth had said the right thing at the right time.

"Mandy, it's past lunch time. Let's go to the cafeteria, get something to eat."

"I'm not hungry."

"Neither am I, but we need nourishment. It's after one and we've already burned though about two days' worth of emotional calories," I said.

"I guess."

"And there shouldn't be many people there; they have breaks at different times. If there are, we can get our meals to go. Find a quiet place to eat so we don't have to answer questions, or have people staring at us, wanting to ask them."

"Okay. It's one way to pass the waiting time," she said.

Only six people—four in scrubs and two others, perhaps a patient's family members—sat at tables in the cafeteria. Two uniformed deputies got their attention. Some may have known why we were there. Others likely wondered. A few called out greetings. We nodded and smiled. Mandy and I shared a chicken salad croissant in silence.

We returned to the chapel, and a middle-aged couple joined us a short time later. Both were trim, close to the same height, with grim expressions: Vince Weber's in-laws. Their daughter, Darcie, was her mother's spitting image: pretty face, brown hair, and bright blue eyes.

I was face to face with an older version of the woman who'd tried to kill Vince and me. It caught me off guard, took me aback. Thankfully, the prosecution had other reliable eyewitnesses, including Mandy, so neither Vince nor I had to testify at Darcie's trial. It saved us from facing her in court. Or ever again, was the hope we shared.

After a moment of awkward silence, Mr. Wilson said, "We had to show our identity to get in, and the front desk said we'd find you two deputies in here."

I nodded. "Hello, Mister and Missus Wilson. Thanks for coming." I lifted my arm toward Mandy. "This is Amanda Zubinski, and I'm Corinne Aleckson."

Mrs. Wilson's eyebrows shot up halfway to her hairline, her eyes intent on me. "Oh."

Her husband cast his eyes downward then looked up and caught mine with a softened expression on his face. "Sergeant, to let you know, we deeply regret our daughter's actions, how she tried to hurt you and Vince," he said.

Mrs. Wilson threw her arms heavenward. "It's so awful, we can't begin to imagine how it came to that. We knew she had problems, of course, but didn't know she was that ill. We were beyond relieved Darcie didn't injure you. Or worse. And now here Vince is in the hospital because another crazy person *shot* him."

Another crazy person. I nodded. More uneasy moments ticked by. Mandy finally said, "Vince is still in surgery. Maybe another half hour." She waved her hand at the seats. "Should we sit down?"

Instead, the Wilsons moved so the four of us formed a circle near the front table and stained-glass window. "What happened, exactly, how did Vince get shot?" Mr. Wilson asked.

Mandy blinked her eyes a couple of times. A signal she struggled to answer him, so I stepped in and relayed what others had told me, minus the details, like that Mandy was with him. She was not in a good place to answer the pointed questions they were bound to ask.

"Wasn't Vince wearing his protective vest?" Mrs. Wilson said.

I nodded. "He was. The bullet entered his chest under his arm, just outside of it."

Mr. Wilson shook his head. "The guy who shot him must've either been damn lucky or damn accurate."

My gut told me it was the latter. He'd known what he was doing.

The Wilsons settled onto chairs, then Mr. Wilson reached for his wife's hand, and they clung to each other while we waited.

After some minutes I said, "You'll have to excuse us. Amanda and I need to make some calls. We'll check back in a bit, or as soon as we hear anything."

Mandy followed me into the corridor and rolled her eyes at the chapel door. "Thanks. It was kinda tense in there."

"Sure." We continued on to the emergency waiting room.

"They seem like decent people, like they care," she said.

"I think so too. Misunderstandings can drive wedges into relationships. They might have reasons they thought were good ones to be against Stacie marrying Vince."

"True. Plus a lot of parents don't want their kids to be cops or be married to one."

I nodded. "That's for sure. Like my helicopter mother."

"Yeah. My sister hates what I do. She wants me to see her kids grow up, be there when they get into sports and other activities. I asked her to let our parents know about Vince.

Mom has tried to call me, but I keep putting off calling her back. It's like if I do, it'll finally sink in that it's true, that it really happened, and I'll have to accept it. I mean I know it is, but don't know it, at the same time."

"I get that. How many times have we wished we could start the day over and do something differently, something that would change the outcome?" I said.

"Too many times."

"But that's not the way it works."

"Nope," she said.

6

By 2:03 p.m. Mandy and I had paced up and down the corridor ad nauseum until a middle-aged woman with sparkling brown eyes dressed in turquoise scrubs approached us, not far from the chapel door. "I'm Doctor Cynthia Yancey. You're the two deputies awaiting word on your friend."

"Yes," I said, and we introduced ourselves.

Dr. Yancey got straight to the point. "We needed to perform a thoracotomy on Vincent."

"A what?" Mandy said.

"A procedure where we surgically enter the chest, spread the ribs apart, then perform a lung resection, and remove the damaged section of his lung. In Vincent's case it was in the lingula."

It was my turn to ask, "The lingula?"

"The right lung has three lobes and the left has two. No middle lobe, but there is a lingula, a projection of the upper lobe. Lingula means 'little tongue' in Latin," the doctor explained.

I must have missed that detail in anatomy class.

Dr. Yancey continued, "We inserted tubes in Vincent's chest to drain excess fluid and release extra air to relieve any pressure inside his chest. We did need to stimulate his heart twice during the procedure." She paused a moment. "He's in the recovery room and will move to the intensive care unit within the hour. Vincent will need to remain on a ventilator for the time being and we will monitor him twenty-four-seven."

Mandy swayed toward me. I put my arm around her waist to steady her.

"He can't *die*," Mandy moaned.

"We will do everything possible to prevent that. To be frank, Vincent is in critical condition. The upside is the affected tissue has been removed so the healthy tissue will be able to function normally," Yancey said.

I cringed at the images that came to mind when I worked through the details Dr. Yancey had provided about Vince's surgery. What he had gone through, continued to go through. And that *his heart had stopped two more times.*

I cleared my throat to check my voice. "Doctor, how long will Vince have the tubes in, be on a ventilator?"

"For most people, the tubes stay in for forty-eight to seventy-two hours. Longer, in some cases. The ventilator is necessary until Vincent is able to breathe well on his own. It's giving him the needed oxygen for his body and brain."

"That part is good. So when can we see him?" Mandy asked.

"After he's out of recovery, most likely in about an hour. But it will be from the other side of the glass in the ICU. After he's stable, he can have bedside visitors." The doctor managed a small smile. "That could be as soon as tomorrow. Vincent is young, strong, and fit. Appears to be otherwise quite healthy. He has that in his favor, which is a huge plus. He just needs time to heal," she said.

But would he be able to run again, have the strength to hold his own in a physical confrontation? In the overall scheme of things, it didn't matter. What did was that Vincent Weber survived.

We joined the Wilsons in the chapel, and I shared what Dr. Yancey had told us. It struck me they could have heard the words from her mouth if we'd thought of that.

Mrs. Wilson teared up, and Mr. Wilson maintained a grim expression and shook his head through my entire message. I placed a hand on each of their shoulders. "Since it'll be an hour or so before Vince is moved, you might want to get a bite to eat somewhere. The cafeteria here has good food."

They looked at each other and nodded.

"Should we meet you back here?" Mr. Wilson asked.

I said, "Sure."

The Wilsons walked slowly out, and it seemed like they had aged ten years in the short time they'd been at the hospital.

Mandy released a loud sigh and rubbed her arms with vigor. "I can hardly stand all these hours and hours of waiting, not being able to see Vince."

"Mandy, why don't you go home for a while, lie down, shower, change clothes?"

"I can't leave," she said.

"At least think about it." I pulled out my phone. "I need to update Dawes." When we connected, I repeated Dr. Yancey's account.

"As if Weber hadn't been through enough trauma, that surgery sounds wicked," he said.

"I had a visceral reaction when the doctor described the procedure," I said.

"No doubt. Where's Mandy?"

"Right here."

"She'll need a lot of support through this," Smoke said.

"As we all will, Detective."

"Yes. Later, Sergeant."

The chapel was a private and consoling environment to spend our wait time. When my favorite classical piece, Chopin's Nocturne in e-flat major, resonated through the pipes, I closed my eyes and a recurring thought I had not shared with a soul—and probably never would because it would upset my loved ones if I did—came to mind. If I was on my deathbed, I'd want Nocturne to be one of the pieces played as I waited for eternity. Some considered the piece sad and somber. For me, it touched a place deep inside that felt like God was near. I was soothed, comforted, and pacified.

The Wilsons returned and broke my reverie. They hadn't been gone long and must have scarfed down their food. We chatted about nothing for a minute then sat with our heads bent, checking things on our phones like people did when they didn't want to talk.

Mrs. Wilson broke the standoff. "We were mistaken. Vincent Weber captured our daughter's heart like no one before him had. And there was no one after him, of course. We got off on the wrong foot with him, and worried he might not treat Stacie right. He had this kind of tough exterior, but Stacie said he had a kind and gentle heart. That he was a teddy bear."

Both were right. The Vincent Weber we loved, the wise cracker with a sensitive side he liked to keep on the downlow.

Mr. Wilson took over. "We weren't able to bridge that gap between us. We hadn't meant to be on opposite sides, but it turns out that's what we were. Stacie always sided with Vince on whatever the issue, as she should have. After she died, there didn't seem to be a reason to try to mend our relationship. We've known for quite a while now how mistaken we were. We were the only family he'd had for some time, and he probably needed us."

"We finally reached out a few times. And then when we found out Darcie was obsessed with him, had been for years, that added another strange, and as it turned out, very scary element," Mrs. Wilson said.

"I'm sure he'll appreciate that you're here now to show your concern and support," I said.

"And love. He gave our Stacie her happiest years. The best of her life. Maybe we were a little jealous," Mrs. Wilson added. The way she said it made me think there was more to the story. Something undisclosed from the past.

I sensed Mandy's discomfort with the Wilsons' confessions. Almost an hour had passed since Weber's surgery so I said, "Mandy, let's go see if they have any updates on Vince."

She nodded, and we made our way to the emergency room desk. "Wondering if we can get some information on a surgical patient who's supposed to be moved to the ICU soon," I said.

The tech pointed her thumb over her shoulder. "The best place to check would be the surgical center."

"Oh, sure, thanks," I said.

We stopped at the chapel room on the way. "We're headed to the surgery center to check on Vince. If you'd rather stay in the chapel, we'll let you know as soon as we get an update," I said.

The Wilsons both stood. "No, we'll go with you," Mrs. Wilson said. "And it's Art and Joanie."

We trooped down the corridor and hung a left into the surgical unit's waiting room. Deputy Levasseur stood by the door, feet spread, thumbs in his belt. He straightened when he saw us and raised his eyebrows at the Wilsons. I nodded, and he blinked a few times. Levasseur pulled open the door for us. The Wilsons went in first. Levasseur squeezed Mandy's and my arm as we passed through and uttered, "This whole thing is unreal."

A younger couple sat with their heads together, hands touching. They spoke in tones too low to decipher. A teen's eyes were glued to his phone. A middle-aged woman gazed at the vending machine like it was a puzzle she was required to put together, but had no idea where to start. Or maybe that was the way I felt, wondering how the sheriff's office or the BCA would solve the crime against Vincent Weber.

A nurse entered the room, and her eyes landed first on Mandy then darted to me. "You're waiting to see Vincent Weber? You two can come with me."

I nodded then waved at the Wilsons as we left them and followed our leader. She led us down an inside corridor to the intensive care unit, stopped in front of a glass window, and lifted her hand toward the glass. "Vincent seems to be resting comfortably but hasn't regained consciousness yet. Of course we'll continue to monitor him very closely."

Mandy and I put our faces close to the glass without touching it. I strained to find Vincent Weber among the array of tubes and under the ventilator mask, and it was difficult. Even his shaved head was covered with a blue cap.

Mandy reached for my hand and squeezed. "This is as terrifying as when he stopped breathing before. He's still not breathing on his own."

I tried to remember what I'd heard about the mortality rate of people who were weaned off a ventilator, and decided that a lot of factors were involved in those statistics. Some people were given a slim chance to live and had survived. As the doctor said, Weber was otherwise healthy and had that going for him. Big time. Add to that, I believed from the bottom of my heart Vincent Weber was too stubborn to die.

"I wish he'd wake up and make some stupid wisenheimer crack," Mandy said.

"That'd be a relief. He could be the biggest pain in the butt, but he knew how to pick me up when I was down without getting sappy about it," I added.

"One of the main reasons I started hanging out with him. Corky, you helped me a lot when I almost died. To cope and move on, and so did Vince. Neither one of us was interested in romance back then but we liked hanging out with the opposite sex, so it worked. Plus it gave us both an excuse if someone asked us out. We could say we were seeing someone."

"Yeah, and you were."

"We love and trust each other and we've managed this status quo the last couple years. It should seem like a long time, but it doesn't. We can be each other's date at things, go out, talk about anything, and it's comfortable. We both need to get over our 'what if' fears if we want to move forward, take it to the next level," Mandy said.

"Like Smoke." I hadn't meant to share that, but after she confided in me, it slipped out.

Mandy's eyebrows lifted. "Oh? Well, we all have reasons, right?"

"Right." Elton Dawes and I had gotten engaged the year before, and I considered us married in the eyes of God. I had no reservations about tying the legal knot. Not one. Should I have? My phone dinged. Speak of the devil, a text message from the man himself. *Update?*

We're in the ICU, on the other side of the glass from Weber. Still not conscious.

Ah, okay, he wrote.

Then I sent, *Lavasseur is standing guard outside surgery and should move to outside the ICU now.*

I'll take care of that, thanks, he replied.

I nudged Mandy. "We should let Vince's in-laws take a turn."

"I s'pose."

I gently pulled her arm, and when Weber was out of sight, she turned her head and stared at the floor as I guided her along. I told the ICU nurse Weber's in-laws would go in next and returned to the surgical waiting area to tell them.

Joanie put her hand on her heart. "How is he?" Neither Mandy nor I answered, but my eyebrows and shoulders lifted a tad. The Wilsons shared what seemed like an, "are we sure we want to do this?" look, then he led her into the ICU.

I wanted to run up and down the corridors screaming at the top of my lungs but could not do so. Deputy Levasseur stepped inside the waiting area, nodded, and twitched like he wanted to say something but didn't. I mouthed, "I'll text you." We held each other's stare a moment, then his eyes met Mandy's. He raised his brows and patted his heart.

At 3:02 Smoke sent me a message, *Briefing in 30. Can you be there?* I passed Mandy the phone. She read it, nodded, and whispered, "Go help catch that monster."

Yes, I wrote back.

When I got in my car, I phoned my brother. "Hey, John Carl."

"Corky. Mother told me about the shooting and I'm really sorry."

"Thanks. The deputy is out of surgery and we're just waiting for him to wake up."

"Sara wants to call but knows how occupied you must be." Sara was my best girlfriend and John Carl's fiancée.

"Yeah, Sara sent me a text earlier and I sent her a sad face back. We'll catch up later, but no idea when." I took a breath. "The reason I'm calling is to see if you could check on Queenie and Rex. They should be fine in the kennel, but sometimes Rex tips over the water dish."

"No problem."

"Might be hours before I go off duty."

"Do what you need to do. I'll make sure the dogs are good," John Carl said.

"Appreciate it. Later."

"Yeah, later."

On my drive back to the sheriff's office, I counted five squad cars parked on streets within a mile of Brookings Café. It was four blocks from the downtown business district. Homes, an apartment building, and post office filled in the area between. Brookings and Holiday were the only businesses one block south of Highway 55, in the mostly residential area.

A number of businesses and services sat on the blocks north of 55, along Highway 25: a realty company, dentist's office, chiropractor, attorney, bank, hairdresser, health club. Plus a bar, bowling alley, and two fast food restaurants. Some had outdoor security cameras, most did not. Indoor monitoring was a bigger concern for them.

The Winnebago County Government Center Complex was located in downtown Oak Lea, a block west of Highway 25, and fifty feet north of Bison Lake. It housed all the county departments except Highway and Parks. After I'd parked in the sheriff's lot, and radioed Communications my location, I sat for a moment and attempted to process the events from the past five-plus hours. When I'd entered the café the scene was surreal, yet all too real. A nightmare in broad daylight.

I looked at the sky and watched dark ominous clouds move slowly by, surprised none had opened up and released a downpour before then. The sky was gray, the lake was gray-blue, and I was just plain blue, the bluest I'd felt in a long time.

I trudged inside and passed office staff on my way to Smoke's cubicle. All wore somber expressions, and when my eyes met theirs, not one said a word. Must've been the grim look on my face that pleaded, "Please don't ask me how Weber is."

Smoke was on the phone. He closed with, "Greatly appreciate it, thank you," and disconnected. I sat down on his guest chair.

Smoke laid his readers on the desk and pinched the bridge of his nose. "That was Dean Gentry, the Deputy Superintendent of Investigations at the Minnesota Bureau of Criminal Apprehension. I'm keeping him in the loop with the steps we're taking and will brief him on any progress we make in the investigation. Per the Chief Deputy's request, the BCA sent four agents to lend a hand, and they've been a big help. We'll likely need to tap into more of their resources as we move along, what with that unidentified shooter who fled in an unknown direction."

I bent my head and stared at my folded hands.

Smoke reached across the desk and laid his hand on mine. "We'll get him, Corinne. The text I sent about the meeting went out department wide. Communications phoned Oak Lea PD and BCA agents to let them know, also. Randolph asked me to get an updated press release out to the television and radio stations. It went out statewide."

"What did you say?"

He picked up the paper and handed it over. It took me a moment to bring the words into focus.

At 9:26 this morning an unknown subject entered Brookings Café in Oak Lea and shot Winnebago County Sheriff's Office Deputy Vincent Weber with a hand gun. Deputy Weber underwent surgery for his injuries and is in recovery. The suspect was described as tall and covered from head to toe in a black garment. He is considered armed and dangerous, but not a known threat to the public. It is believed he is driving a white 2008-2011 Ford Focus sedan. If you have any information please contact our Sheriff's Office. Tips will remain anonymous. Thank you, Detective Elton Dawes.

I nodded. "Wow, you found out what he drove?"

"We think so. We'll view the tapes, get updates, find out what people have told officers." He glanced at his watch. "Meeting is in seven minutes, so I better get over there."

"You also want the café witnesses to view those tapes?" I said.

"I do, in case it brings something to mind for them, a detail about the shooter. Maybe they saw him walk by the café. Maybe they've seen him on walks prior to today. Carlson was able to get a hold of all of 'em, and they want to do what they can to help. I'll have our IT department make more copies of the tapes so we can visit each one before the end of the day."

7

Meeting Room 120 was a sea of brown and blue uniforms; and three men and one woman in suits with sidearms and badges, the Minnesota Bureau of Criminal Apprehension agents; plus fifteen deputies in brown, counting me. The six police officers in blue included Chief Becker and Casey Dey. Smoke's detective attire was a pair of navy pants, gray sports jacket, light gray shirt, and a tie with gray and navy diagonal lines. He kept a spare outfit in his locker and had changed from the clothes soiled at the scene.

The usual relaxed jabber was absent among the troops. Male and female, young and middle aged, didn't matter, every face displayed varied degrees of stress. Clenched jaws, tight skin, frowns, lips pressed together. No deputy or police officer had been shot in Winnebago County in over three decades.

The last was a tragic accident when a rookie chased a felon down a dark alley and mistook another deputy for the bad guy. When the deputy stepped into the alley with his gun drawn, the rookie believed he was the suspect. The deputy survived, but his injuries ended his law enforcement career, and the rookie left the field with less than a year under his belt. All new Winnebago County recruits were told that story and cautioned to remain alert and be certain a threat was genuine, not perceived, before using deadly force.

Detective Elton Dawes, Sergeant Doug Matsen, and Deputy Todd Mason stood by a long table in the front of the room. A whiteboard hung on the wall behind them. Mason inserted a flash drive into a laptop, connected it to the audio-visual system, and nodded at Smoke. "All set when you're ready to view it."

It seemed like Smoke made eye contact with each one of us before he spoke. "One horrific day, all right. One of our finest is fighting for his life. And his damn shooter has seemingly vanished. We'll do a recap of the investigation, what we've turned up so far.

"Six of you located homeowners south of the café, and that includes the east and west streets, who had motion detection cameras. An older woman, and a younger woman pushing a stroller, were the only ones captured on videos in the hour before, and the hour after the shooting. So it stands to reason he did not travel on foot to or from Brookings from those directions.

"That leaves us with north. So why didn't anyone see a tall man in a black robe outside Brookings before or after the shooting? Because he'd figured out a way to change in the café's atrium."

Smoke told them our theory and that in all likelihood the shooter had accidentally dropped the hood outside the café. He concluded with, "He would've had to hide the robe somewhere. Officers searched garbage cans and dumpsters and didn't find anything. We think he stashed his robe and weapon in a backpack and walked away in a manner that did not raise suspicion."

"How do you know he didn't drive there?" someone asked.

"I'll get to that," Smoke said and pointed a hitchhiker thumb at the whiteboard. "Go ahead, Todd."

Mason started the video and Smoke narrated as it played. "We got camera footage of a Caucasian male in a camouflage jacket exit a Ford Focus with a smaller size black duffel bag in Harry's Tavern parking lot at nine seventeen, nine minutes before the shooting. He managed to keep his face away from the cameras. Then he walked by Oak Lea National Bank at nine eighteen and Holiday at nine twenty-three, three minutes before he stepped inside the café's front door and shot Vincent Weber at nine twenty-six.

"There's no footage of him entering Brookings Café because they don't have outside security cameras, and no doubt the shooter knew that. But we do have his return trip past Holiday captured at nine twenty-nine, past the bank at nine thirty-four, and at Harry's where their camera shows his return to the white Ford Focus at the back of their lot at nine thirty-six, and then driving away at nine thirty-seven. Eleven minutes after the shooting. The suspect appeared in the videos over a time span of twelve minutes in his round-trip trek. And that doesn't count the six minutes from Holiday to Brookings and back past Holiday," Smoke said.

"The footage proves that he walked south from the bar to Brookings then took the same route back to his vehicle parked at Harry's," Mason said.

Smoke nodded. "Deputies interviewed folks at Harry's to find out if anyone saw a man get out off, or back into, the vehicle we've identified as an older model, two thousand eight to two thousand eleven white Ford Focus sedan. And if they noticed his license plate number. The bartender, server, and kitchen crew were there during that time frame. None of them even noticed the Focus, much less the plate. Customers had come and gone, and we're working to try and track them down."

"Problem is most people don't notice plates unless they're different than the standard Minnesota plate," Officer Dey said.

"You got that right. Cops notice more than the average guy." Smoke turned to Mason. "Can you zoom in on the parked Focus in the lot and freeze the shot?"

Mason played with the controller for a moment, and when the video was stilled, Smoke said, "The downside, as you can see, is he was parked on the other side of a truck, so we can't see the license plate. There were eight other vehicles in their lot; at least those were the ones visible within their camera range. Six were full size trucks, the others were a sedan and an SUV. A fair number given the time of day. The suspect might've chosen it for that reason, maybe thought he'd be less noticeable than in another lot. Certainly less so than at the bank."

"He could've spotted where the camera was and that's why he parked where he did," Carlson offered.

"Yes, he could have. Frankly, we were surprised he didn't park in an inconspicuous spot, but that might've garnered more attention from say, a home or business owner. 'Why is that guy parked in my alley?' Something like that," Smoke said.

People made quiet comments.

Smoke continued, "Now for the upside. As he pulled out from his spot and took a left to exit the parking lot, we noticed something on the right front wing, just behind the headlight." Smoke pointed at the board. "Todd, can you zoom in on that and freeze the image?"

"Sure." Mason selected and enlarged the vehicle's right side. It looked like the driver had either scraped against something, or someone had keyed his car.

"We estimate the scrape to be three inches long. Wouldn't be very noticeable on a dirty car, but it's a great identifier for this investigation. We'll make copies of the photo for everyone engaged in the vehicle search here in the county," Smoke said.

Chief Becker lifted his finger to ask for the floor. "That scrape is definitely a great identifier. Question, did you find footage that shows where the suspect came from in the first place, which route he took, how he got to the bar?"

"We checked to see if the Focus passed Holiday then went north to the bar, but we didn't see it on any footage in the thirty minutes prior," Matsen said.

Smoke cleared his throat. "We've had some conversations, come up with a scenario. It seems reasonable to conclude the shooter was sitting in his car near the café where he had eyes on the parking lot.

"When he saw Weber arrive, he put his plan into action and drove east up Fifth Street—what we'd call the back way—to the next Highway Fifty-five crossing at First Avenue. He crossed the highway, took the first left, drove to the bar, and then hightailed it on foot back to Brookings, figuring Weber would be on a fifteen minute—and up to a thirty minute—break."

"A half mile in seven or eight minutes is very doable," Carlson said.

"How do you figure the shooter knew Deputy Weber would be at Brookings?" a BCA agent asked.

"One of the burning questions. Did he target Weber specifically, or was he after any deputy? We lean toward the first supposition. Vincent Weber often took his breaks at Brookings. And if not today, then maybe tomorrow. If that was the case, the shooter did his homework, had to have kept tabs on Weber somehow," Smoke said.

"A sound theory," the BCA agent agreed.

Matsen nodded. "Now we come to the glitch. The man in the videos is seven or so inches shorter than the man witnesses saw in Brookings. He's more like five-eight, five-nine from what we estimated when we compared his height to a light pole he walked by. The BCA has a software program and can give us a more accurate height measurement for him."

"Yes, and we'll be happy to help with that," another agent said.

"All the people in the café who saw the robed suspect said he was over six feet. One person said he was *way* over six feet, like six seven she estimated," I said.

Smoke nodded. "That's what they said all right. Two of the witnesses said he was around six five. When our crime scene guys measured the trajectory of the bullet, from where the shooter stood to where the bullet entered the back of the booth, after it passed through Weber, they estimated the shooter was about that height."

"Only one man on the videos who walked by Holiday looked to be over six feet. He was older, a bit hunched over, moved pretty slowly. No backpack or bag. And he did not appear on the bank's or bar's videos. We believe we can rule him out as a suspect," Matsen said.

Smoke continued, "We know the shooter would've had to move along at a good clip, not shuffle at a slow pace, to escape like he did. The shorter guy captured on the videos made the half a mile trek to Harry's and was driving away fourteen minutes after Weber was shot. We figured he could disrobe in thirty seconds, and it was about a ninety second walk from Brookings to Holiday."

"Unless the taller guy deliberately walked like that at first to appear like he had nothing to hide, like he wasn't racing away from the scene of his crime. I know I didn't notice either him or the shorter guy when I responded," Officer Dey said.

Others made similar comments.

"But the taller one wasn't on the bank or the bar's videos," Matsen said.

"That's right. Sorry," Dey said.

"The guy on the video, the one we're interested in, kept his face looking straight ahead the whole way on both trips. Had on a ball cap, hoodie, glasses, and sported a bushy beard," Smoke said.

"The beard's a good identifier, and it would've been covered by the hood so the folks in the café didn't see it," Becker said.

"Right on, Chief. Todd, zoom in on a good shot of his face and pause it," Smoke said.

Mason ran the video until he found one he liked and froze the image. My stomach muscles tightened as I focused on the possible suspect. Was there anything about him, his stature, or the way he walked that I recognized? No. His shoulders were slightly hunched, but not as much as the taller guy's. More like most peoples' shoulders when they walked, especially at a brisk pace. I studied the man's profile. His stocking cap was pulled down around his ear and covered part of his cheekbone.

Smoke used a pen to point at the screen. "Our person of interest concealed his face well, and his nose was the one facial feature his cap and beard didn't cover. We got a fairly good shot of that."

His nose was on the fleshy side and neither long nor short. An average nose, like many present in the room had.

"This guy look familiar to any of you?" Smoke asked.

"No," was the collective answer.

"What about guesstimates on his age?"

"Studying what little we can see of his face, he doesn't appear to have deep wrinkles. Could be age thirty to forty," a male BCA agent offered.

"About what I figured," Smoke said.

No one offered another age range guess.

Becker lifted his hand. "Does the BCA have a facial recognition program? I've never had a reason to look into that before today."

The female BCA agent spoke up, "I can answer that. Currently, Hennepin County is the only law enforcement agency in Minnesota that has that program and they've assisted agencies around the state. Minneapolis PD stopped using the technology they had."

"Why's that?" Becker asked.

"A company who developed an artificial intelligence program was sued for selling what were deemed as private images and faceprints, without peoples' consent. They've been banned from selling to private companies. A civil liberties group wants the technology banned. Period," she said.

"Hah. So we could ask Hennepin if we need to? Or the FBI?" Becker wondered.

Smoke nodded. "The FBI has a facial recognition program for cases they use in their authorized investigations. If we bring them in on this investigation, it'll be one of their cases too. Aside from facial recognition where we may have a slim chance of identifying the guy, given what little we can see of his face, we're counting on DNA from the hood."

More mutters.

"Now the question is, after the suspect left Harry's parking lot, where did he go, what was his direction of travel? Since he didn't drive by the bank on either trip, he must have left via First Avenue, likely got onto Highway Fifty-five, and headed either west or east to parts unknown. He could have taken any county or township road north or south from there. There are businesses on the highway that have cameras, but with limited range so they don't pick up every vehicle on the highway," Smoke said.

"As far as I know, the ones who have cameras set the distance to pick up motion pretty close to their building. So they don't get constant highway traffic. Out maybe twenty, thirty feet," Becker said.

Smoke lifted his hands. "That's what we learned when officers canvassed the businesses. The shooter had everything planned to the smallest detail, no doubt about that. And when we catch him he'll be charged with premeditated attempted murder of a peace officer. We can be assured of that."

I caught Todd Mason's eyes and we exchanged looks that expressed both angst over Weber's condition and fury at the man who had caused it.

Smoke continued, "No idea how many older white Focuses are on the road these days, and we put in an agency assist request with the state. They'll get us a data report of every registered owner, hopefully sooner rather than later."

"What about photos of the vehicle and the suspect?" Becker said.

"Yes. After we obtained the tapes we sent photos of the possible suspect and his vehicle to every law enforcement agency statewide, along with various media sources. Asked them to post them," Smoke said.

"TV too?" Becker said.

"Yes. Along with our social media avenues. We were generic, told them to say, 'Do you know this man? He may have information on a crime. Please contact the Winnebago County Sheriff's Office,'" Smoke replied.

"And be prepared to hear from the hundred people who saw him this morning, or thought they did," a deputy said.

Smoke's shoulders lifted. "No doubt. We called in four communications officers to field the extra calls. People call and say they don't know who he is but they think they saw him walking by X,Y, Z. Human nature."

"Detective?" I said.

"Go ahead, Sergeant."

"Something just struck me. The height discrepancy between the man witnesses described and what we have on the videos?"

"Yes?"

"I thought of sheet rockers, how they use stilts when they're taping drywall. Guys in parades wear them in Uncle Sam costumes too," I added.

"And?"

I lifted my palms. "It'd be a good disguise. Instead of five eight or nine, you can appear to be over six feet tall."

Murmurs sounded among the troops.

Brian Carlson held up his phone. "Corky's got a point. I did a quick search and found some drywall stilts that are adjustable, from fifteen inches to thirty inches, others go up to sixty-four inches. Wait, here's a pair that's one foot tall."

Others pulled out their phones to search.

I watched Smoke's face as he glanced down, his brows knitted together, a sign his mind was running through calculations and considering possibilities. He raised his head. "One-foot-tall stilts would put him at six eight, six nine. Up where people might describe him as close to seven feet. I think someone would notice if he had to duck to get through the café's doorway, even in the chaos."

Officers agreed with Smoke and made various comments.

Chief Becker raised his hand. "And it's very rare to be that tall in the first place. Many decimal points less than one percent of people in the world are seven or more feet tall."

For some reason it surprised me Becker would know that. Maybe because I'd never thought about it myself. People chatted for a minute before Smoke gave a hand clap. "Getting back to stilts. I would think a person could make a pair pretty easily for whatever height they wanted," he offered.

"Yeah, right," an officer said.

"Maybe *you* could," another one chuckled.

"Stilts ten or twelve inches high would easily fit in a small duffle bag," I said.

Carlson scrolled through his phone. "If not stilts, then he could've worn elevator or platform shoes. They can give a guy up to twelve more inches in height."

Really?

Smoke jotted notes on his memo pad. "Aleckson, Carlson, thanks for thinking outside the box. Your ideas provide reasonable explanations for the height discrepancy."

Quiet applause sounded throughout the group.

"A lot of you deputies and police officers reported for duty on your day off—we're grateful for that. Also, hats off to the BCA agents. We got a lion's share of investigative work done in record time. Important when time is of the essence. With the person of interest's photo and vehicle out there, we'll see what shakes down. Next step: as soon as the registered owners report on Ford Focuses comes back from the state, we'll start tracking them down, checking them out."

"Any guesstimate of how many owners we're talking about?" Chief Becker said.

"That Focus style was made for four years, and I'd have no idea how many are still on the road. I do know there are about seven and a half million vehicles registered in Minnesota overall."

"So maybe a thousand?" Becker again.

"Could be. Could be more. Let's hope for less."

Becker shook his head. "That's a helluva lot of people to track down."

Smoke nodded. "No doubt. We'll concentrate on owners in Winnebago County first and ask other counties to check on theirs. We'll start with the owners who are in the suspected shooter's height and age range. But we can't rule out the little old lady or gent owners. Lord knows how many times I've investigated an incident or crime that involved a vehicle and found out the owner loaned it to a friend or family member."

"Seems to happen quite a lot," Becker said.

"It does at that. With all our available deputies on duty, I had Cindy from admin take the suspect's hood to the Midwest Crime Lab for the DNA test this morning. It's their highest priority case and, depending on how long it takes to extract the DNA from the cloth, we should have the results in twenty-four to forty-eight hours. We're praying he's in the system so we can track him down a-sap."

Smoke visually scanned the room and rubbed his hands together like he had lotion on them. "Meantime, while we're waiting for the Focus printouts, any of you deputies who weren't on the schedule today are free to take off. Otherwise, take a break. Oak Lea PD and BCA Agents, check in with your bosses. Thanks again, every one of you," Smoke said.

8

By 4:03 p.m. Room 120 had cleared, save Smoke, Matsen, Mason, Carlson, and me.

"The relative calm before the storm. This hurry up and wait time is downright onerous when Weber's shooter is on the loose," Smoke said.

Mason's clear hazel eyes teared up. "We're all caught up in the same nightmare. The worst in our careers. Mine for sure."

Carlson nodded. "The reality of it hasn't really sunk into my thick skull yet."

"Zubinski would've let us know if anything changed with Weber, but I'm going to see how she's doing." I pulled out my phone and selected her number. "Hey, Mandy."

"Corky. I can hardly stand it. Vince just lays there, hooked up to tubes and the breathing machine. Why can't he just wake up and be okay?"

I walked a few yards away for more privacy. "Hold on to the belief that will happen soon, but his body suffered great trauma. Remember what the doctor said, he needs time to heal."

"My brain knows that, but my heart is struggling big time," she said.

Mine too. "Are the Wilsons still there?"

"No, they left after you did, maybe a half hour ago. I overheard them talking. They said something about Darcie being here after her car crash, how hard it was. I didn't hear the whole conversation but got the impression the dredged-up memories of Darcie and her crime against you and Vince made it tough for them to stay here any longer. They told me they had to go and asked me to call if anything changed with Vince," Mandy said.

"Between what Darcie did, and their estranged relationship with Vince, they have regrets and probably carry some guilt. Let's hope this brings them closer to Vince, and vice versa," I said.

"Yeah, I think the Wilsons want that."

"So you know, we just wrapped up a meeting with responders and investigators. Deputies, Oak Lea PD, the BCA. They canvassed the area neighbors and businesses and got videos of the main person of interest and his vehicle, an older white Focus. Todd showed us the videos, but the guy didn't look familiar to any of us. And he's a lot shorter than witnesses said. I'll have him forward me the tapes so you can see 'em when I get there," I said.

"Can he send them directly to me?" Mandy said.

Of course, duh. "Sure. Sorry, my brain is a little slow right now."

"I get that."

"Oh, and the black hood is at the crime lab for testing," I said.

"Crossing my fingers."

"Smoke put in an agency assist request with the state for all registered owners for the years that Ford Focus model was made. We're waiting for the report so we can start checking them out."

"Wow. I'm impressed you got that much done already," she said.

"It's been all-hands-on-deck. A big team of officers showed up to help. Everyone is beyond driven to track down the guy who shot one of their own."

I heard Mandy suck in a sniffle and gave her a moment before I asked, "Can I bring you anything, do anything?"

"Thanks, no. Just send Mason's video. My sister left Saint Paul close to an hour ago and should be here any minute. She's going to stop at my apartment, get me a change of clothes," Mandy said.

"Good. I'll hang around here, see what comes back from the state, and do what I can to help before I head back there."

"That's fine. They told me it might be a long time before Vince wakes up. I know I have to accept that and quit freaking out every five minutes. See ya later then."

"Take care." We disconnected.

Dear God, please let Vincent Weber wake up soon and restore his health and strength. Thank you.

"Any changes with Vince?" Mason said.

"No. His in-laws, the Wilsons, left. Mandy didn't say so, but I gathered that was a relief for her. Plus her sister's on the way. Oh, and would you send her the videos? She'd like to see them."

"Sure thing. Along with the eighty-six other county sheriffs' offices and three hundred and sixty police departments and law enforcement agencies who have eyes on it already." Mason raised his eyebrows.

"But who's counting?" Carlson said.

Smoke back-slapped his hand into his palm. "We need to get organized. The state will have the registered owners report any time now. Then we can start contacting the jurisdictions where they live."

"Maybe you shouldn't have sent any of the troops home," Mason said.

Smoke glanced at the wall clock. 4:08 p.m. "Maybe, but our administrative assistants will help us sort through the list, contact folks if need be. They all offered to work a double shift. Plus the three PDs in our county will check any registered owners in their cities. Our office will work on the rest of the county," Smoke said.

Fourteen minutes later a large group gathered in the administration area outside Sheriff Mike Kenner's and other command staff offices. Chief Becker, Oak Lea PD officers, deputies, along with communications and corrections officers had volunteered to come in before, or stay past, their scheduled shifts. Sworn officers and civilians ready to do their part.

Smoke clapped his hands for everyone's attention. "Sheriff would be proud to see all of you lined up ready to tackle this assignment. Turns out there are eight hundred and fifty-seven Focuses in the four years we're looking at still licensed in Minnesota."

"Whoa," an administration assistant said.

"It's not many when you consider that we have eighty-seven counties in the state. So that's only ten per county, if that's the way it happened to shake down. The state was able to organize the list of registered owners by jurisdiction, a huge time saver for us. That said, the majority of registered owners—around two hundred of them—are in the Minneapolis/St. Paul area. No clue how many will fit in the height and age ranges."

"Whatever the number, we'll get 'er done," Becker said.

"It'd be less of a daunting task if we didn't need to locate the shooter a-sap. We'll assemble lists of possible suspects to check on, start the elimination process. Thankfully, it's a priority for about every law enforcement agency in the state." Smoke held up a still shot of the possible suspect. "Many of you have seen this, but for those who haven't, who is our person of interest? We're looking for a white male, and we're giving him a broader age range of twenty-five to forty-five, height between five foot six and six feet. We'll gather the list of males in those ranges to start with."

"Detective, the man in the video had a dark beard. Is that something we should consider?" a deputy asked.

"He may or may not have a beard on his driver's license, but it's something to look at, sure." Smoke handed the photo to Dina, the sheriff's administrative assistant, and she passed it on.

"I mentioned at the last meeting that we can't rule out owners who've loaned their cars to someone else. Maybe older folks to a grandson, a guy to a friend, a spouse whose husband drives the vehicle. If we don't locate the person in question on the first round, we'll move to the next. But let's hope we won't have to," Smoke said.

He pointed to stacks of papers on Dina's desk. "We printed out the eighty plus pages of registered owners, so you will each get four or five sheets. Chief Becker, you can supervise and work with your two officers. Go through and highlight or underline the owners that fit the suspect's general description to start with. We'll email copies to the other two PDs and the appropriate jurisdictions outside our county."

Smoke touched Dina's shoulder. "Dina is the lead on this assignment. When you've finished your lists, turn them in to her. Her team will handle the sheets that need to be emailed or faxed. Questions?"

I saw some heads shake as people formed ragged lines behind Dina's desk. She handed each person pages that had been paper clipped together. I was last in line. "You get the five-page stack, Sergeant," Dina said.

I gave her a smile and a nod then headed to the small sergeants' office, settled down at the desk, and started a search on the fifty-six listed names. I had a portion of the Minneapolis residents and found nineteen white males who fit in the age and height ranges. It turned out most men on the lists were over fifty. Could've been worse.

Officers and other staff were milling near Dina's desk waiting for their next assignment when I returned with my pages.

"Thanks," Dina told me. "We're getting down there. We don't have many Focus owners in our three PD cities, so far. When the last few people finish up, our staff will send the names to the three PDs and the other jurisdictions outside of Winnebago County. Detective Dawes will assign deputies to check out owners in the county's other cities and townships."

"Like the detective said, it's the hurry up and wait time," I said.

A deputy delivered the last list a short time later. Smoke appeared as if by extrasensory perception. "What have we got, Dina?"

"Only thirteen total within the city limits of the three PDs. Of course, people in the townships have Oak Lea or Allendale or

Harold Lake addresses. We haven't totaled the owners in the other fourteen cities and eighteen townships. But looking at the lists, there aren't too many. The greatest numbers are in the Minneapolis Saint Paul metro area, like you'd said. But there are plenty in some of the rural out state counties," Dina said.

Smoke picked up the stack. "All right. Let's divvy them up. We're concerned about criminal histories and prior offenses. Where the person in question was this morning. You know what to do. When our office staff sends the counties their lists, they can add that the counties should let us know if they need any assistance. Metro counties have a number of large cities with their own PDs, and will determine how to handle the assignments. That includes Minneapolis and Saint Paul, of course."

We each had our assignments in minutes.

"I want you to work in teams when you knock on doors. All right?" Smoke said.

No one objected.

My list of owners lived in cities and townships in the east central part of the county. Thirteen names. One I knew from past encounters. Pierre Dawson, a frequent flyer that most staff in the sheriff's office, probation, and the courts knew by name. I even had his date of birth memorized, along with a few others I'd dealt with multiple times.

Dawson fit the shooter's general description, minus the beard. That said, he could have grown one, or glued one on to disguise himself. But why? The shooter was covered from head to toe and that included his bearded area. I needed to maintain an open mind, but did not figure Dawson for the shooter. He wasn't mean-spirited or cunning enough. At all.

Pierre Dawson had gotten into trouble when he drank too much. It often led to poor judgement, and the bad habit of fleeing in a motor vehicle when an officer tried to pull him over for a driving offense. Or because he had an active warrant out for his arrest. Dawson would stop his vehicle somewhere along the way, then take off, and sprint until he needed to stop and catch his breath. Or the officer was faster, caught up with him, and took him into custody. Dawson had never resisted arrest.

He also had a habit of not paying his fines, so more often than not, that was the reason warrants were issued for his arrest.

I ran the remaining owners' driver's licenses and checked for outstanding warrants. Three had speeding tickets but no other driving offenses. I ran their criminal histories, and all except Pierre Dawson had clean records. Or if they had been involved in criminal activity, they hadn't gotten caught.

I found Smoke in his cubicle jotting something on a registered owners list. He looked up, pushed his readers to the top of his head, and ran his fingers back and forth across his forehead a few times. "Corinne." He didn't need to say more. His sky-blue eyes looked duller, the lines in his face deeper.

"Pierre Dawson is on my list," I said.

"Pierre, huh? Didn't remember he drove a Focus."

"Since last July according to the records. You told us to work in teams when we contact the owners on our lists whether we know them or not. I'll start with Dawson, the only one I know. It'll be like old home week, a mini reunion. It's been a while since he was in trouble. A good thing for him, huh?"

"Sure is. You got a partner?" Smoke asked.

"Not yet. I'll check with Mason or Carlson." I thought for a moment. "Smoke, we arrest a lot of people from outside the county who commit crimes here."

Smoke nodded. "Even if it turns out the suspect is a Winnebago County resident, he could be halfway to Chicago by now. Or on a plane to Mexico for all we know."

A shiver ran down my arms. "For sure. How many times in the heat of the moment have arrestees threatened to sue us, or worse? I keep wondering if Weber had an encounter like that where the bad guy harbored a grudge and carried out his threat?

"Until we find the shooter, I still question whether he was after Vincent Weber in particular, or if Vince was in the wrong place at the wrong time. The shooter may've seen squad cars at the café in the past. He decided today was the day so he watched for a deputy to show up, and then carried out his attack."

"I can't count the number of times those questions and scenarios have gone through my mind in the last hours. Between that, and the abject fear I have Weber won't make it," Smoke said.

I was too overcome with emotion to respond and nodded instead. When Smoke's office phone rang, I lifted my finger as a goodbye wave and left. Mason and Carlson were in the squad room bent over reports when I joined them.

"Hey," I said.

They both looked up.

"Hey," Mason said.

"You look as worn out as I feel," Carlson said.

I nodded. "Aren't we all?"

"I know I am," Mason said.

"You got through your lists?" I asked.

"Yeah, I got four to contact," Carlson said.

"Seven here," Mason said.

I held up my report. "Eight for me. Only one with a criminal history. Pierre Dawson."

"Pierre? Haven't heard that name in a while," Mason said.

"No. Musta quit drinking. I have to say he's one of the most likeable crooks we ever had to deal with," Carlson said.

"To answer your question, neither of us have anyone with a criminal history on our lists," Mason said.

"Good," I said. "You two have partners to do your checks?"

Mason shook his head. "Yeah, I'm going with Holman."

"I got nobody so far," Carlson said.

"We'll go together then," I said.

"Sure. In our separate squad cars?" he asked.

"Yes, in case one of us gets a call we have to take. Let's meet at Dawson's place," I said.

"He still live in the mobile park?"

"According to the report he does."

9

Pierre Dawson had a double-wide in Crossings Mobile Home Park just outside Oak Lea city limits, in Oak Lea Township. The sun had set about thirty minutes before, and with the cloud cover, it was darker than dark after we left the lights of the city. I turned into the park. Trees loomed overhead on both sides. A bright street lamp illuminated them and caused eerie shadows. Another chill of many that day ran through me and I was relieved to have a partner on the call. Carlson pulled in beside me in the guest parking area, a short distance from Dawson's home. We walked to his door, and Carlson held back when I stepped to the side of the door and knocked.

Dawson opened the door. He was a wiry guy in his late thirties with thin blondish hair and soft brown eyes. His brows lifted, and it deepened the multiple creases that ran across his brow. "Whoa, Sergeant, what the hell? I didn't do it, whatever it is." He looked around me. "And you even brought back up with you? What the hell?"

"Mind if we come in? I think it's about to rain again," I said.

"Okay, but you're not gonna arrest me, are you?" Before I answered, Dawson stepped back to let Carlson and me in. We filled the small entry area. His mismatched furniture indicated he'd likely picked up pieces here and there. Aside from a pile of clothes on the couch, the place was otherwise tidy.

"No plans to arrest you, Pierre. I'll cut to the chase. An older white Ford Focus was linked to a crime today, and we're checking with people who own that model."

"What the hell? You're talking about the deputy who got shot? It's all over the news," he said.

"I can't get into specifics, but I need to ask where you were this morning."

"Like all morning? Um, well I worked the evening shift at the factory yesterday and got home at twelve thirty this morning. Watched a little TV, got to bed about two, and slept until close to nine-thirty. Got cleaned up and decided to get breakfast at Mac and Don's in town." Slang for McDonald's. He paused and frowned. "Wait a minute. I was waiting at the stop light at Twentieth Street when I saw a Focus like mine—same year I think—going east on Highway Fifty-five. I noticed because there aren't a whole lot of 'em around here."

"What time was that?" I asked.

Dawson bobbed his head back and forth. "Close to ten o'clock, thereabouts."

"Did you see the driver, what he looked like?"

"Not a good look at him, although he kinda glanced my way as he drove by. I figured it was because we have the same kind of car. Had a stocking cap on and I thought to myself, 'it's not that cold out', but then again some people wear them fall to spring, so go figure. Anyhoo, I did notice he had a beard, but that's about it. I saw him for like two seconds," he said.

My heart rate picked up. "Did he appear tall, or short?"

"More on the average side."

"Did you notice if anyone was with him?" I asked.

"Nope. Didn't see anyone else."

"What about his license plate, did you see any of the letters or numbers?"

"Nah, just that it wasn't a Minnesota plate," he said.

"Not a Minnesota plate? Where was it from?"

He shook his head. "Couldn't tell you."

"What about the colors on the plate?"

"It had blue on it with dark, maybe black, lettering. Not sure. Just saw it was different than Minnesota's."

"And not a specialty plate, like a critical habitat or support our troops?" I said.

"No. Don't see too many of them on cars, but I recognize them. And those vanity plates with some clever or goofy name on them. They can be good for a laugh."

He was right about that. "Okay. Deputy Carlson, will you bring up the license plates from the other states on your phone?"

Carlson pulled the phone from his belt, found the list, and held his phone so we could see the plates. Pierre said "no" from Alabama to Colorado. "It's possible that's it," he said of Connecticut's. "Keep going." Iowa, Illinois, Kansas, Kentucky, Missouri, North Dakota, and Rhode Island were other possibilities.

"Sorry, I just got a glimpse before another car pulled up and blocked my view of the plate. I couldn't read the state," he said.

"It's all right, Pierre, that helps. But when you feel more relaxed, if you remember any other details about the car or the license, let us know. Okay?" I handed him my card. "We appreciate your help."

"I can say the same about the sheriff's office. If it wasn't for Detective Dawes, I'd probably still be trying, and failing, to navigate the legal system," he said.

Smoke had never mentioned he'd helped Pierre Dawson. "Oh? How's that?"

"He gave me a loan to pay off my court fees and fines and helped me get the job at the factory. A lotta places won't hire guys with records. The detective said I was too good a guy to keep screwing up. He said he had faith in me to get on a better track. First person I ever remember saying they had faith in me," Pierre said.

That made me smile. "Detective Dawes is a good judge of character, and it's good to know he has your back."

"That's for sure. We talk from time to time, but it's been a while. When you see the detective, tell him I said 'hi' and that I'm staying clean."

"Will do."

Carlson and I made our way down the mesh metal steps, then I told him, "Hop in my car. We'll need to regroup."

Once inside, Carlson said, "Detective Dawes has a big fan, huh?"

I made a fakey sighing sound. "Another one. It's a growing list. I hadn't heard how he'd helped Pierre, but he keeps his good deeds to himself most of the time. I'll let him know what Dawson told us, rub it in a little bit."

I selected Smoke's number and he answered on the third ring. "Corinne."

"Just left Pierre Dawson, and it turns out he probably saw the suspected shooter in a Focus going east on Fifty-five at around ten this morning, when he was on his way to McDonald's. He said the driver was a male with a beard and a stocking cap," I said.

"Sounds like he could be our suspect. The timing is close. It's possible the suspect hung around somewhere for ten, fifteen minutes before he headed out of town."

"Dawson thought the Focus was the same year as his, so that could narrow our search if we were to continue it. But here's the kicker, according to him, it didn't have Minnesota plates."

"Where were they from?" Smoke asked.

"He didn't know, didn't get a good look before another vehicle blocked his view. He saw it was blue with dark letters, and assured us it wasn't a specialty or vanity plate. Carlson showed him license plates from each state." I pulled out my memo book and recited the ones Dawson had named.

"Eight of 'em? That's a lot of states. Iowa and North Dakota are neighbors, but it could be any of the others. The suspect might've bought the car in another state and hadn't gotten new Minnesota plates yet. Maybe on purpose," he said.

"Who knows?"

"It seems downright serendipitous you stopped at Pierre's first. I gotta say for all the trouble he used to get into, I can't recall a time he lied to me. If he's convinced the plate was from out-of-state, there's likely no reason to continue the owner search in Minnesota. That'll save us hundreds of hours trying to run down all those Focus owners.

"On the other hand, we need to be thorough. Even though Pierre was convinced, and I trust him as a reliable witness, there's still a chance he was mistaken. I need to run this by the chief deputy before I call it one way or the other," Smoke said.

"Sure. Should Carlson and I take a pause then?"

"Yeah, hang tight."

Smoke phoned a couple minutes later. "We're on hold with the checks unless new information arises."

"All right," I said.

"I know you're worried about Vince and Mandy if you want to go check on them."

Carlson heard Smoke, looked at me, and huffed out a breath.

I nodded at him and told Smoke, "Brian should take a turn. He helped save Vince's life."

"Of course, you're right. You'll tell him?" Smoke said.

"I will." We disconnected.

"Thanks," Carlson said.

We fist bumped, then he climbed out of the car.

As I left the mobile home park, a message from Smoke popped up on the squad car's laptop: *Due to new information, everyone on the Focus owner detail can cease that operation. Per Chief Deputy Randolph, we've halted the search. Report back to the office for further instructions.* That would raise eyebrows and questions among the searchers.

As I drove to the sheriff's office, dark rain clouds opened and released heavy dime-size droplets that bounced on my windshield and darkened my mood. My dear friend was fighting for his life, and the man who'd shot him had disappeared in a car with a license plate from one of eight possible states. A needle in eight different hay stacks.

At 5:46 p.m. Smoke stood about dead center between the rows of desks in the sheriff's administration area. Dina, Cindy, and six other assistants were at their computers. Four deputies were seated on chairs they'd grabbed from somewhere, one was perched on the edge of an empty table, and two leaned against the wall. A sense of both determination and frustration reverberated among the troops. As I looked around, a few nodded at me while others appeared lost in thought.

Until about seven years before, deputies had dictated their reports and administration staff typed them up. Since then deputies typed their own reports that were reviewed by two command staff before they were sent to the county attorney's office. It freed admin staff to attend to their many other duties.

Smoke gave his single clap signal. "All right. We're eight hours into this ordeal, and Sheriff Kenner asked me to tell you he thinks every responder in the department has gone well beyond the call of duty. He's proud, and is bound to be even more so when he gets the full report. Some of you have been on duty for eleven hours already, and I won't keep you past twelve. I sent those on the power shift home after they'd put in their twelve."

Some shrugs and half smiles among the group.

"As you all know, the attempt to locate that Ford Focus fizzled out, unless new information is brought to light." Smoke went on to tell them what Pierre Dawson had witnessed, and the out-of-state plates on the vehicle. "His report is viable. It fits the general time frame from when the suspect left Harry's parking lot to when Dawson spotted him going east on Highway Fifty-five at the Twentieth Street intersection around ten. With one glitch. If Dawson's time checks out with the tapes at McDonald's, that he was at the drive-thru shortly after ten, that leaves about fifteen minutes from the time the suspect left Harry's to when Dawson saw him. So what did the suspect do during that time?

"We'll look at McDonald's tapes tomorrow. An important note: since the suspect drove a vehicle with out-of-state plates into Minnesota where he committed the crime, it can be considered an interstate crime with a possible federal offense attached to it. So I contacted the FBI's Office in Minneapolis and asked for their help locating the vehicle, and if other things arise beyond our resources and expertise," Smoke said.

"Good to have them on board," a deputy said.

Smoke held up a sheet of paper. "Ironically, before I connected with their Field Office here, I spoke with Special Agent Kent Erley from the FBI's Behavioral Analysis Unit in Washington D.C. We've consulted with him on cases in the past, and he's been a great help."

I could attest to that and nodded along with others.

"Special Agent Erley told me he's worked similar cases—too many—and that in this year alone over two hundred and seventy law enforcement officers were killed in the line of duty. Over eighty of them in ambush attacks. That's a high number. No matter how vigilant we are, it still happens," Smoke said.

Rumblings and mumblings sounded throughout the room.

"There's a long list of reasons why people target a cop, or cops. Erley said one problem is they're profiled *after* the shootings. That said, the FBI has interviewed hundreds of cop killers and assembled a list of average attributes. These may not be specifically applied to this suspect, but it gives us a general idea."

Smoke glanced at the paper. "Male. Late twenties. Single, but may have been married. No real family ties. A higher percentage of cop killers were brought up in middle class homes, some in upper middle class, others in lower class.

"Many suffered physical and/or psychological abuse. Families may have been involved in criminal activity. Odds are they have committed violent crimes, but some stuck with lower-level crimes, until they shot a cop and it took them to a new level. Most have an unstable work history. The majority have a personality disorder, likely antisocial. They may have served in the military and trained in weapons and tactics."

The list of characteristics fit many people I knew who'd been convicted of felony, gross misdemeanor, or even misdemeanor crimes. Or committed petty misdemeanor offenses.

"Sounds like a lotta guys in jail," Mason said.

"About right." Smoke laid the sheet on a desk. "Erley added there are other complex psychological and social issues that lead a person to kill, or try to kill, a law enforcement officer."

More quiet comments.

We all have a background, things that shape us. Some people rise above bad things they've lived through. Others can't, or won't. And commit evil deeds they feel are justified, I thought.

"So getting back to the average age factor, does it mean he could be eighteen, or forty? Or older?" an admin assistant asked.

"Likely not as young as eighteen or twenty. From the videos we got of the suspect, the BCA agent estimated his age between thirty and forty. A fairly broad range."

"Not too bad," a deputy said.

"This morning I asked our admin assistants to pull Vince Weber's arrest reports. As it turns out, Weber made a DUI arrest at seven twenty this morning. Guy was on his way to work."

"What a way to start the day. Drunk and then get arrested because of it," Mason said.

People thought if they consumed alcohol before bed, no matter how much, they could sleep it off by morning. Alcohol burned off at a rate of .015 per hour, on average. I did a quick calculation and figured if the person had a .22 blood alcohol count, or BAC, at midnight, it would take over fourteen hours for the alcohol to leave his system. At seven in the morning he would be at .08, the illegal level for intoxication in Minnesota.

"The man was still in custody when the shooting occurred, and his wife picked him up a while after that. He was not a viable suspect in the first place and easy to rule out," Smoke said.

"I would've rather stayed in jail then have my wife pick me up. She'd hang that over my head the rest of my life," a deputy said.

"Yeah," another agreed.

"As you all know, we're notified when offenders who were arrested and convicted in Winnebago County are released from prison. Chief Deputy Randolph is good at keeping track of them besides. A lot of 'em are on probation when they get out, so court services always have that list" Smoke paused then lifted his hands. "My point in all this is we're looking at two main groups of folks that Weber had encounters with.

"First, people he arrested who were recently released from prison, ones that had been incarcerated a while, likely with a history of assaultive behavior. The others are people who threatened him, including the people who spewed out a threat in the heat of the moment. I've had some who later felt stupid about what they said when they sobered up and apologized. If they remembered, that is."

Several verbal "yeahs" and nods.

Smoke continued, "Others may have walked around with a grudge for some time, weeks, months, years. We include those behaviors and incidents in our reports for a reason, whether we take them seriously at the time, or not."

I got a text message from Calson and tuned Smoke out for a moment: *Vince doesn't even look like himself. I keep hoping he'll wake up and make some wise crack remark so I'd know it was him. Mandy and her sister went to the cafeteria. I'll stay with Vince till they get back.*

I wrote back, *Okay. We're in the meeting with Dawes now.*

Carlson responded, *I checked when I got here to see if they needed me. Dawes said no, tomorrow's another day so I'm gonna head home.*

I sent him a thumbs up emoji. Then another wave of Vincent Weber panic rolled through me. I drew in a slow breath through my nose and shifted my attention back to the meeting.

10

"We've started a list of possibles from Weber's arrest reports and got through about two years so far, right Dina?" Smoke asked.

She nodded. "Yes, just over. Twenty-five months."

Smoke's phone buzzed, and when he looked at the message said, "Before we dive into more reports, there's a guy with a stack of pizzas at the back door if someone will help me get them."

Deputies started to follow Smoke. He turned, and said, "Three of you will suffice." The four returned in short order with armloads of pizzas, a bag of plates, flatware, napkins, and a case of bottled water. They set them on a long table admin used for projects. A couple deputies opened the boxes and the room filled with delicious smells from a pizza restaurant. And made my stomach growl. The options were meat lovers with Italian sausage, pepperoni, and beef; veggie with olives, peppers, tomatoes, and artichokes; chicken and wild rice; and a gluten free beef and broccoli.

Smoke invited the admin staff to be first in line. Before long, plates were filled and people were eating with gusto. I wasn't a pepperoni fan and helped myself to a slice of veggie, and a slice of chicken wild rice.

Smoke's gesture seemed to have lightened everyone's mood and made it easier to take on the next assignment.

"Dina and staff brought up the records of Weber's reports and put them in files by the year. Since they're all digitized, you'll be given a range of dates to check. Make notes of the offender's name, and date and time on the incidents you think we need to take a deeper look into. Questions?" Smoke said.

"What if we don't get through the range before we need to leave?" a deputy asked.

"Good question. Note that also. List the dates and times of the first report you look at and the last report. That way, the next person can pick up where you left off. You can use computers in here, or in the squad room. Dina will provide the access codes. Any other questions?"

None.

As deputies and admin assistants got their assignments, I joined Smoke by the table. "What would you like me to do?"

"I'll start going through Weber's phone, if you want to help me with that. We'll check through the list of calls, see if Vince had suspicious voicemails or text messages that we need to look into."

"All right."

"Let's go to my cubicle, and use my office phone if we decide to make any calls," he said.

We took seats on opposite sides of his desk. The deputies had the same passcode since the phones belonged to the sheriff's office, and after Smoke opened it, he looked through Weber's phone for a while. "He has a ton of text messages, some missed calls, but I'll check his contacts first."

He scrolled through the list. "Mostly sheriff's office and other county personnel, towing companies, businesses in his service area. Doesn't have any personal contacts here. That I recognize as such, anyway."

"He was listening when Sheriff said we shouldn't use our work cell for personal calls," I said.

"Yep. Best to keep 'em separate." He selected the text message icon. "Starting with the present and working back, all the messages today after nine thirty this morning are from Winnebago County deputies, and personnel in other county departments. That's about it. I'm not going to open them, but from what I see on the first lines, they're all well wishes. Technically, work related."

"Technically. Because it's the number his coworkers have, unless they hang out with him and have his personal number," I said.

"Going down the list, there aren't a lot of text messages from people outside our office. When we make official calls to people and get their voicemail, we ask for a return call," Smoke noted.

"And if they don't call back, we'll call again."

He smiled. "Going back through the last month, nothing looks amiss. Not that I'd expect anyone to threaten him in a written message but we have to check. All right, so phone calls. One from Zubinski at nine fifteen, probably to check if he was able to go on break, or confirm that she could." He scrolled some more. "Going back to last week, I see calls from the sheriff, the chief, other deputies, and businesses who are in his contacts. A few calls don't have names attached, and we'll follow up with them, if you want to jot them down."

"Sure."

Smoke recited the dates, times, and phone numbers for seven incoming calls from unknown entities in the past month, and I recorded them on my memo pad.

Smoke glanced at his watch. "Time to send our people home."

We returned to the administration office area and Smoke called out, "Folks, it's nineteen hundred, so we need to wrap this up for tonight. Some of you have been on duty for twelve hours, and that's long enough.

"I don't know about you, but my eyes are blurry and my brain has slowed down. Sergeant Aleckson and I looked through Weber's work cell and have a list of seven numbers to check out tomorrow.

"We've gotten through scores of Weber's arrests, and we'll finish up that task tomorrow. Dina, where do you want folks to leave the lists they have, what they've gotten done so far?" Smoke asked.

Dina rose from the chair and pointed at her desk. "Right here, in the basket."

"I'll let the deputies in the squad room know," I said.

"Thanks," Smoke said.

When I told them it was quitting time, Matsen, Mason, Holman, and Ortiz exercised various movements as they stood. Matsen stretched his arms toward the ceiling, Mason rubbed his closed eyes with the backs of his hands, Holman bent his upper body right then left, and Ortiz ran in place for some seconds. Then they delivered their reports to Dina's desk.

Smoke said, "There's pizza left, so grab some on your way out."

When all the reports were in and the last of the crew was gone, some with a piece or two of pizza in hand, I gave Dina a bear hug. Smoke followed suit.

"Thanks for helping us this long day with what seemed like organized chaos at times," he said.

Dina managed a chuckle. "Detective, I'd like to thank you for taking the helm on this operation. You too, Sergeant. It's been full steam ahead all day." Dina and her husband loved to boat and she often used nautical expressions.

When she started to clear the empty pizza boxes from the table, Smoke said, "We'll take care of that. Go home, get some rest."

"I'll try, and you too. Good night." We nodded and she picked up her jacket and headed to the door.

"The pizzas were a hit, and the good news is every last piece is gone," I said.

"They needed a little pick me up, and all of 'em seemed to enjoy it."

I lifted the stacked boxes. "We can leave these by the trash bin in the breakroom. The custodians will collect them sometime tonight."

"Sure. I'll put the extra water bottles in the fridge." He gathered them up, followed me to the breakroom, and put them in the refrigerator. I set the boxes by the bin.

After we'd finished, Smoke turned to face me and rested his hands on my shoulders. "Should we head to the hospital?"

"That was my plan."

"Drive separately?"

"Yeah, in case one of us decides to stay longer," I said.

"I'm dog tired, but maybe will get a second wind on the way."

I gave him a peck on the cheek. We shut off the office lights, and the doors automatically locked behind us as we stepped outside, then we headed to our vehicles. The rain had stopped, but the wind had picked up, and the chill in the air was a cold reminder that winter was around the corner.

"Beat you there," I called out.

"You're funny. I know a short cut."

"So do I."

Smoke let me win the pretend race and pulled into the emergency parking lot a few stalls from mine.

Sergeant Roth still guarded the entrance but had moved into the sally port area, between the outside and inside doors. When one door closed, the other one opened. "You're still here, huh?" I said.

"Yeah, for a couple more hours. Had no idea how many people came here for emergency services. It's been almost a steady stream."

"Here comes one now." I pointed at Smoke, and Roth smiled.

"Levasseur and I switched places a couple times. Zubinski's still in ICU with Weber. On the other side of the glass from him, that is. Her sister left a while ago, needed to get home to help put her kids to bed."

"Ah. You need anything, Leo? Food or beverage or to use the restroom?" Smoke asked when he was inside.

"I'm good. Carlson gave me a break before he left, and the chief deputy has a rover he sent in to give us breaks. The staff here brought me coffee."

When a couple with a small child approached, Roth pulled out his memo pad, then asked for their names and recorded them. "Are either of you carrying a weapon?"

The man's eyebrows raised, and the woman frowned. They both answered, "No."

Roth lifted his hand for them to pass. "The not fun part of this assignment," he said.

Smoke and I headed down the corridor to the Intensive Care Unit. Levasseur nodded and sort of smiled. "I feel almost as bad for Mandy as I do for Vince. She just sits and stares at him."

I nodded. "You doing okay?"

"Fair to middlin'," Levasseur said.

Smoke gave his shoulder a squeeze, and I pushed the door open. Weber was in the same position, and looked like he had hours before. Mandy turned her head slightly but kept her eyes on Vince. I slid my hand under her arm. "Come on, let's take a break, go for a walk. The detective will keep watch."

She wore a blank expression when she studied us a moment. "Okay."

The way Smoke lifted his eyebrows silently expressed his apprehension, his concern for Mandy's wellbeing. He shifted his attention to Weber and slowly lowered himself onto the chair in front of the glass that separated Vincent Weber from the rest of us.

Mandy and I navigated our way back to the chapel, a safe haven in the hospital, away from personnel that scurried by on their way to assist other staff or someone in need. Or the people who paced the corridor floors with worried looks on their faces. It added to the unease we already felt.

We sat in front of the stained-glass window, quiet in our own thoughts for a time until Mandy said, "What updates have you got on the investigation?"

I shared details of the meeting where we viewed the videos. "Did you get the tapes Todd sent?"

"Yeah, and I watched them a bunch of times, studied the man, his profile, the way he walked. But from what I could see, I have no idea who he is," she said.

"Same here." I went on to tell her about the vehicle owner's search. "We hit a dead end after Carlson and I knocked on our first door."

"Brian told me. And about your visit with Pierre Dawson and his account."

"Randolph and Dawes determined Dawson was reliable, believed what he said. So did I. But the time he said he saw the Focus doesn't quite line up with when the alleged shooter drove away from the bar," I said.

"How's that?"

"The shooter left Harry's at nine thirty-six and Dawson saw him just before ten o'clock. It's only a couple minutes from McDonald's to Twentieth Street."

"You're right," she said.

"To check Dawson's story, we'll look at the McDonald's videos. To verify he was there, and the time. If he was at the drive-thru when he'd thought, then the shooter either drove around, or stopped somewhere in between."

"Like where?" she said.

"I don't know. There was a lot of activity at Brookings. Maybe this guy is like people who set fires and then watch the responders work to put them out."

Mandy's upper body did a shimmy move. "That's a creepy thought. But given his cold-blooded crime, he could've stuck around a while to watch the aftermath. One thing some psychos do."

"Yeah, and it's creepy all right."

"What a bummer the plates weren't Minnesota's since you got records of all the owners here. Brian told me a lot of hours went into the effort, considering the number of people involved."

I nodded. "Like our favorite detective said, it's good we found out as early as we did, or we'd still be chasing our tails. But since the shooter likely crossed state lines, at some point anyway, Dawes will ask the FBI to help with the investigation."

"With the FBI and all their resources, it's gotta help."

"For sure. We also got a jump on Weber's arrest reports, looking for potential suspects. And we'll check his work cell phone calls and messages. See if anything turns up there."

My own work cell rang and I answered, "Sergeant Aleckson."

"Oh, hello Sergeant. This is Opal Reynolds. I met you at the café today. I hope it's okay to call this late, after work hours." Her voice sounded strained.

"Of course it is. Are you okay?"

"Not the best, but that's not why I'm calling," she said.

"What is it?"

"You said to let you know if I thought of anything else. You know, about the man who shot the deputy."

That brought me to my feet. "Yes?"

"Well, I was sitting here with my eyes closed listening to music, meditating, trying to clear my thoughts. Just put the whole thing out of my mind when I remembered a bracelet I saw on the man's arm," Opal said.

A possible identifier. "Tell me about it, how you happened to see it. What it looked like." My heart pounded while I waited.

"Right before he lifted his arm, I saw a gold chain on his wrist. I guess what happened after that put it out of my mind till now."

"Would you recognize it if you saw it again?" I said.

"I can't say for sure, but I think I so, now I've got it in my mind."

"Opal, this could be helpful information. Would it be all right if I came over tonight so we can look at different types of bracelets, see if one looks familiar to you?"

"That'd be fine. I'll be up a few more hours, maybe longer," she said.

"I'll call you when I get there. It'll be within the half hour."

"That works well for me, Sergeant."

When we disconnected, Mandy lifted her hands. "What?"

I told her the details then said, "It might lead nowhere, but if the shooter had it on when he committed the assault, it stands to reason he wears it all the time."

"But we won't know that until we find him," she said.

"True." I took a moment. "Mandy, I know you feel like you need to be here with Vince, but he'll be isolated in ICU until tomorrow, at least. He's being monitored around the clock. As much as we wish we had a way to speed up his recovery, we don't. Go home, take a hot bath, have a glass of wine, rest. You need to stay healthy so you can help take care of Vince when he gets home."

Her eyes narrowed. "You believe he will get better?"

"I do."

Mandy nodded. "You're right. I should go home, try to sleep."

"You want some company?" I offered.

"Thanks, but no."

Smoke was reading messages on his phone when we got back to the ICU. He stood, clipped the phone in its holder, and lifted his hand toward Weber. "As tough as this is, I keep thinking as long as he's sleeping his body is healing."

Before we left, I sent up another prayer request that Vince would return to good health soon. On the way to our vehicles we stopped to chat. First with Levasseur then with Roth. While Smoke and I waited in the lot for Mandy to drive away, I told him about Opal's phone call. "I'm stopping at her house before I head home."

"Want me to go with you?" he said.

"Nah, I'd rather you check on the dogs, let them run around the yard a while. John Carl stopped by earlier, but they're probably wondering why we're so late."

"No doubt," he said.

Smoke and I each owned a house, but he and his dog Rex were at my home more than Queenie and I were at his.

When I got to Opal's, I phoned Communications to let them know my location. I was no longer officially on duty, but it was protocol. Opal opened the door as I walked up her driveway. She'd changed into a jogging suit and attempted a smile when I stepped inside. I was still in the same uniform over ten hours later and hoped I passed the literal smell test.

"I hope this isn't too much trouble for you," she said.

"Not at all. I'm glad you called me."

"Can I get you anything to drink?"

"Thanks, but I'm good. Would it be all right to sit at your kitchen table so you can take a look at men's bracelets?" When Opal looked at my empty hands, I said, "Online."

"Yes, that's fine. Right this way." I followed her through the living room to the kitchen. Her home was a clean and comfortable rambler. The warm shades of brown, beige, and rust were dated, but blended well with the autumn bouquet and mini pumpkins and gourds on her table.

Opal sat at one end of the small rectangular table. I took a seat on her right and opened the search feature on my phone. "Maybe to narrow down what we're looking for, can you describe the bracelet?"

Opal stood. "I'll be right back." She left the room and returned with a photo album. She laid it on the table as she sat down then slid it in close to her. Opal glanced at each page as she flipped through them. "When I remembered the bracelet, I wondered why it had a familiar look to it. Then realized it was because my late husband had a watch with the same link pattern. I gave it to my son after he passed, but I have a picture of my husband wearing it."

The photo showed the two of them in what looked like a church photo. They were standing with their bodies at an angle to the camera. Opal's arms were at her side, and her husband's left arm was bent and rested against her arm, his hand on her shoulder. A gold watch was visible on his wrist. The band was a classic and timeless style called Cuban link. One of the features men loved was that interlocked links laid flat and didn't twist.

"What a nice photo," I said.

"Yes, it's good to have the album to look through. My husband wasn't a saint, but he was a kind man, and I treasure the memories we made together."

"That's a good thing." I touched her hand. "I do know your husband's watch style is a popular design. It's called Cuban link. I bought a similar one for my brother on his birthday a few years ago. The jeweler who sold it to me said men like them because they're durable and never go out of style."

"That's what my son says too. He loves it and knowing it was his father's makes it extra special," she said.

"Yes. I know you just got a quick glance, but you think the chain you saw this morning is like the one on your husband's watch?"

"I do. Not with really small links, but not with really big ones either. About medium size, like my husband's."

"Mind if I take a picture of the watch?"

"You go right ahead, Sergeant."

I snapped the photo, and thanked Opal again. "And if you think of anything else, please call, day or night. Okay?"

Opal nodded. "I will."

I drove away from Opal's and wondered where in the world we'd find the unknown suspect who drove an older Ford Focus and wore a gold Cuban link bracelet. Little did I know that as the investigation progressed, and events unfolded, more complex issues than the vehicle he drove and the bracelet he wore would be brought to light.

11

Relief washed over me as I pulled into my driveway and parked in front of the two-car garage. My old, classic GTO occupied one stall inside, with the other reserved for Smoke's vehicles, either his detective squad car or personal SUV. Not that we tried to hide our relationship and his comings and goings, but we didn't want to make a public announcement about it either.

When I climbed out of the car, I heard Queen and Rex barking from inside the house. Before I punched in the code on the opener, the overhead door lifted and Smoke stood in the kitchen entrance in flannel pajama bottoms and a T-shirt. The dogs' tails wagged, and Queenie appeared to smile at me, as she did when I returned after a long day away. Or when I asked her to go on a run. And a lot of other times.

When I stepped into the garage, Smoke pushed the door close button. I gave Queenie and Rex some head scratches, then stepped into Smoke's warm embrace. He'd showered, and a hint of eucalyptus scent clung to his skin. He held me like he'd never let go until I said, "I need to shower. I'm probably contaminating you."

"I doubt it. Your face smells like soap of some kind."

"I washed up a couple times, as much to refresh my mind as to freshen myself," I said.

"So what'd you find out at Opal's?"

"Her husband had a watch with the same link style as the shooter's bracelet. I got a photo of it."

"Huh. We mentioned false memories earlier, how people can get things planted in their brains that aren't completely true. Could be partly true. My point is that it seems more than coincidental the bracelet she saw, or allegedly saw, looked like her husband's," he said.

I pulled out my phone and found the photo. "Opal was convinced, and it convinced me. Ninety percent, anyway. Hey, you're the one who doesn't believe in coincidences, per se. You're convinced things happen for a reason," I countered.

"You got me on that one. And you feel pretty much the same way. Your antennae are always picking up something out there."

"We all have different gifts, and you know I often feel in tune with others. It might be a perception, or a whisper from above—"

My phone buzzed and cut me off. It was Mandy. "Hey."

"Corky, something strange is going on." She spoke in a lowered and strained voice.

I thought I'd run out of adrenaline for the day until she'd said that. My heart rate picked up. "Like what?"

"When I left the hospital, I thought I'd better check on Vince's house, in case he forgot to lock his door, which he sometimes does. I let myself in through the garage because the front and back doors were locked."

"That's good," I said.

"You told me your witness had seen a bracelet on the shooter. And it made me think about the one Vince wears when he's not on duty. His wife gave it to him for their first anniversary."

"Sure, I know the bracelet, but he never mentioned that Stacie gave it to him."

"It means the world to him, so I thought I'd pick it up so he'd have it when he wakes up. Maybe it'd help him heal," she said.

"That was thoughtful of you."

"But it's not here. The bracelet, I mean. Vince keeps it on his dresser in a jewelry holder. He'd wear his watch the days he worked and his bracelet on his days off. I checked his drawers. His bathroom, kitchen, living room. In case he took it off somewhere and forgot to put it away. Because it's *always* in the box. And now it's nowhere to be found." I had a similar habit. I didn't wear my engagement ring at work, so people I arrested or questioned wouldn't home in on it, and ask me about my personal life.

"Mandy, tell Smoke." I passed him the phone and watched his face screw up like he was in pain as he listened.

"All right, all right. No sign of a break in?. . . He had it on yesterday? . . . It's possible when Vince went on duty this morning, after three days off, he saw he had it on and maybe put it in his squad car glove box.

"Or maybe he brought it with him because he planned to drop it off at the jeweler's for cleaning or repair. . . . Ortiz drove Vince's vehicle to the sheriff's lot, so it's parked there. . . . No, I'll go have a look. Mandy, you head home, and I'll let you know if I find it. We need to take this one step at a time. . . . Take care."

Smoke disconnected and passed my phone to me. "For some reason, this missing bracelet is giving me a gut ache," he said.

"Me too. A bad feeling. We're creatures of habit, and from what Mandy told us, Vince surely was when it came to his bracelet. I'm surprised he never mentioned it was from Stacie."

"Yeah. Watch on work days, bracelet on personal days. Knowing Vince, it makes sense. A lot of us are protective of our personal lives, but he is especially so."

"He is. I worked with him for what, five years before I found out he'd been married and then widowed."

"My point. I'll throw on some clothes and go search through Weber's squad car."

Smoke headed up the stairs, and I went into the laundry room next to the kitchen. It had an adjoining bathroom. I hung my duty belt on a hook then stripped off my clothes, hung my Kevlar vest on another hook, threw my uniform in the washer, released my shoulder length hair from the bun on top of my head, turned on the shower, and stepped under the running water. I shampooed, lathered, and steamed until I felt cleansed inside and out.

As I stepped from the shower, I heard the overhead garage door close. Smoke was headed to the sheriff's parking lot. I towel dried and found a tank top, flannel pajama bottoms, and zippered hooded sweatshirt, in the pile of clean clothes on top of the dryer. I dressed then pulled on a pair of thick wool socks to warm my feet.

My mind worked on Weber's bracelet mystery. *Where was it?* I phoned Mandy. "Hey, are you home?"

"Yeah. Any word from Dawes?"

"He left a few minutes ago. Mandy, do you have a photo of Vince with the bracelet on, where it's visible?" I asked.

"Probably. I must. Can I check after my shower?"

"Of course. Don't rush, take a nice long one, let the water loosen your muscles."

Fifteen minutes later Mandy sent me the photo with the message, *You can't see it but I know the inscription on the backside says, V, my one and only, S.*

I responded with, *Thanks,* and added a heart emoji. I knew hers was hurting big time. Not because Vince treasured the bracelet his wife had given him, but because he was injured and unconscious and his special gift's whereabouts was a mystery.

I enlarged the photo and studied the bracelet although I'd seen it hundreds of times. I selected the photo of Opal's husband's watch. It had the same design as Vince's bracelet, with smaller links.

Smoke returned a half hour later. His facial skin was tight, his jaw clenched. "I did a thorough search, even used the large magnet I carry in my trunk to check between the seats, figuring the bracelet was not pure gold so it might pick it up. But no such luck."

"Have you told Mandy yet?"

"Yeah. And I asked her if Weber had cameras installed outside his house. After the incidents with Darcie, he mentioned getting some. Mandy said he wasn't worried after

Darcie was incarcerated and the craziness had stopped," he said.

"Darcie isn't the only cause of craziness in the world."

"No doubt about that. A couple other things. I contacted Communications, asked them to have an available deputy on the night shift get a nondescript vehicle from the impound lot and sit near Weber's house, keep an eye on it. If anyone sets foot on his property, he needs to call for back up and let me know a-sap."

"Good plan," I said.

"The other thing, I alerted Holman and Ortiz that they'll likely need to search Weber's house in the morning, as soon as we can get either a warrant, or permission."

"What a mess."

"You got that right. Change of subject, and it's a personal matter," he said,

My eyebrows lifted. "What is it?"

"On my drive back here, my stomach growled so loud it sounded like a critter was in the car with me."

I chuckled and gave him a gentle push. "Smoke. Even after the pizza a few hours ago?"

"I ate one slice and called it my late lunch. So if we have any of the goulash left over that your mother delivered a couple days ago I'll call it my late supper." My mother loved to cook, and one of the things that concerned her was my not always well-balanced diet.

I opened the refrigerator and pulled out the bowl. "Why don't you get back into your comfy clothes while I warm platefuls up for us?" A small one for me, a big one for him.

When Smoke returned, we sat at the kitchen counter to eat. The dogs laid at our feet, hopeful for any leftovers. Between bites, we looked at the photos of the watch and bracelet. "Opal only saw the bracelet for a second, but I'll show her the photo I got of Weber's, see if she thinks it looks like the one the shooter wore."

Smoke made a "mmm" sound when he looked at the photo. "We know the shooter was organized, planned out the details of his crime. Would he steal Weber's bracelet before he shot him? If he took it after the fact, our FBI profiler would say he took it as a trophy."

"Wouldn't the same thing apply if he took it before?" I asked.

"Sure. Stalkers like to collect things from people they're obsessed with. If and when they gain access to them."

"Smoke, you know when Mandy asked about Darcie, if she was still in Shakopee. They're supposed to notify us, but what if she got an early release, and there was a snafu with the victim notification?"

"One way to find out." He pulled out his phone, did a search, selected a number, then hit the call button. "Yes, this is Detective Elton Dawes, Winnebago County. I wanted to confirm that Darcie Rae Wilson is still in custody there. . . . Sure."

He hit the speaker button so I heard the woman reply, "Yes. Her release date is July of next year."

"Thank you." He disconnected. "A phone call's faster than a computer search. For me anyway." The records of incarcerated persons in Minnesota were public information and available on the Minnesota Department of Corrections website.

"Darcie is likely still in love with Vince. Or maybe she hates him by now. Either way, unless she's gotten some miracle therapy in prison, I bet she's still obsessed with him. I can see her trying to convince another inmate to help her find someone to hurt him. With the promise of a big payment when she gets out," I said.

"Happens more than you'd want to believe. What I can see is Darcie wanting Weber's bracelet for herself, especially if she knows her sister gave it to him. But to arrange an attack plan like this against him? I don't see her fingerprints on that one. That said, she has had lots of time to come up with a plan if she was intent on doing so."

"One more thing. I told Mandy about the time lapse between when the suspect left Harry's and when he was spotted by Pierre Dawson. If it turns out Pierre was right about the time, the suspect was somewhere in town for at least twenty minutes," I said.

"Yep."

"You think he found a spot to watch the café?"

"Or the hospital. That's what's been rolling around in my mind. None of us knew at the time that we should look for an older Ford Focus. There's a deranged shooter out there. And we don't know who he is, or where he is. One of the reasons we've got deputies at the hospital, to be on the lookout," he said.

I let out a loud sigh. "Will this day ever end?"

"Doesn't seem like it."

We finished our meal, lost in our own thoughts. I filled the sink with soapy water. We set our dishes in it and headed to the living room. As Smoke dropped down on the couch, I gathered the afghan my Gram Brandt made for me before she died. I sat down, and we covered our laps with it. We both stretched our legs, rested our feet on the coffee table, and leaned back into the cushions. Queenie and Rex settled on the rug near us. I interlocked my arm with Smoke's, and the sounds of the dogs' combined rhythmic breathing lulled us to sleep.

I awoke with a start, disoriented. Through the slats in the blinds, I saw it was still dark out, sometime before 8:00 a.m. when the sun rose. It took me a moment to realize I'd slept on the couch. No clue if Smoke had repositioned me, or if I had worked myself into a prone position in my sleep. Smoke and Rex weren't in the room. I patted my hoodie pocket, found my phone was still there, pulled it out to check the time: 5:53 a.m. I went on duty at 7:00 and felt relieved I hadn't overslept.

Where did Smoke and Rex go?

Queenie alerted when I sat up. We trekked to the kitchen and found them. Rex wagged his tail and let out a "woof." Smoke sat with a cup of coffee at the counter, his fingers tapping his phone. "Mornin', darlin'. Looks like the sleep refreshed you."

I couldn't say the same for him. His eyes brightened when he saw me, but he still looked haggard with dark circles under his eyes. I smiled and kissed him. "How'd you sleep?"

"I crashed hard for an hour or so till my body decided that was a long enough nap. I fell asleep again in the den about three o'clock and got a couple more hours."

"That makes me feel guilty. I slept like a rock."

"No guilt allowed. My brain would just not shut down. I'm heading to the office shortly. Lots of details to take care of. We need to set up two debriefing sessions, one for the civilian witnesses in the café, and another for the first responders, the officers at the scene," he said.

"You may want to open it up for anyone in the sheriff's office. Whether they were there or not, they're suffering with the rest of us."

"Sure. Should've thought of that. In fact, we should offer at least two sessions, so it gives more troops an opportunity to be there. Sergeant Matsen's completed the leader's training, so he can conduct at least one of the debriefs."

"That'll help. After Mike Kenner stepped into the role of sheriff and turned that detail over to you, you've done a great job. But you have more than enough going on right now, Detective Dawes."

"Too many balls in the air, at that." He squeezed the bridge of his nose. "You know how a lot of Minnesota law enforcement agencies offered their assistance? Well Chief Deputy Randolph reached out to our six neighbors last night: Carver, Hennepin, McLeod, Meeker, Sherburne, and Stearns. Requested help to beef up the security at the hospital. Chief sent me a message that four are sending one deputy and two will send two deputies. Eight total. They'll report to the hospital at eight o'clock this morning."

"Nice. That'll help stretch our resources," I said.

"No doubt. Also, the FBI has special agents in the eight states Pierre Dawson named as plate possibilities, checking on registered owners for white Ford Focuses. I'm not holding my breath, but it might help locate the shooter. Truth be told, the vehicle search could turn into a futile effort, twenty hours past the incident. If I was the shooter, I'd dump it somewhere. Say he stole it in Iowa. The problem is, law enforcement in other states wouldn't know it was stolen unless they ran the plate," Smoke said.

I shook my head. "We go down a lot of rabbit holes in our investigations."

"That we do."

12

Smoke was at his desk when I arrived at the sheriff's office. He pushed his readers to the top of his head. "Corinne, optimistic news. Weber made it through the night, but hasn't regained consciousness yet. Mandy talked to the surgical team and they're going to start lessening the dose amounts of the sedatives a little at a time. They believe he'll wake up gradually. Even better news is he's off the ventilator, breathing on his own. Still on oxygen, but he's making headway."

That brought tears to my eyes. "A weight just lifted off my heart. When you talked to Mandy, how did she sound? How's she doing?"

"Fair to partly cloudy. She requested personal time off, and Chief Deputy approved it, gave her six days for now and will take it from there," he said.

"Good. And how is Randolph doing?"

"Better. He's on day three of the virus and said he'd be back in the office if he knew he wouldn't infect anyone. I told him with our resources stretched thin as they are, he should work from home another day or two."

"Agreed. I'll stop by the hospital on break this morning, spend a little time with Mandy," I said.

"I'm meeting with deputies from the other counties at eight, and plan to pair them up with our deputies at the four locations. I'll also post one at every emergency exit, in the event the shooter lays in wait for a staff member to open the door so he could slip in as they went out."

"He'd be dressed in scrubs, I suppose."

"And have a fake badge on a lanyard," he said.

"What are you, a cop?"

Smoke smiled. "That's what my badge and ID say. Our deputies have been vigilant in their hospital duties, but the team effort gives me an extra measure of assurance."

"A whole lot more." I pointed at the stack of papers on Smoke's desk. "Are those the lists of possibles to check on from Weber's arrest reports?"

"Yeah, I'm reviewing them," he said.

"Any potential leads?"

He pinched the bridge of his nose and shook his head. "Not so far. Funny thing is, I arrested a lot of these same guys back when I was a road deputy. Seems like most of the frequent flyers are guys that got caught up in the system. Ones like Pierre Dawson. Not a mean bone in their bodies. But they gave into weaknesses and did something stupid, broke the law. Some over and over again."

"The man who shot Vincent Weber is not like those guys who drank too much and got into trouble. He had a definite purpose for doing what he did."

"That he did." Smoke was silent a moment, then said, "Change of subject. Circling back to Weber's bracelet. It's gnawed at me since Mandy told us it was missing. The shooter's attack was bold beyond belief given the way he shot Weber in broad daylight in a public café. He targeted Weber. He knew him. And if he knew about Weber's bracelet, that means he knew him well."

I rubbed my arms against the chill that ran down them. "There are different factors to consider. So if the shooter knew him well, does that mean he was a stalker who picked Vince for some sick reason? Someone who didn't know him personally. Could be someone he arrested or a stranger out there looking for a target with certain physical characteristics."

"A very sick someone," Smoke said.

I nodded. "Besides Vince's work life, how about someone from his personal life? Maybe back to his childhood even. Someone he picked on. Not that I can see Vince ever being a bully."

"No. Could be another reason. Could be someone who was jealous of him."

"We should ask the Wilsons if Stacie was dating someone else when she met Vince. Maybe he stole her from some other guy. Like Stacie stole Vince from her sister Darcie," I said.

"I'd forgotten that detail."

"Vince was dating Darcie, and when he met her younger sister, he said it was all about Stacie from then on. It would've been over fifteen years ago, but some people carry grudges for a long time before they snap."

"Yes, they do," he said.

"I'm going to throw out something that may sound bizarre. Say when Darcie got dumped, Darcie and Stacie's potential old boyfriend struck up a mutual pity party kind of relationship, and all these years later Darcie convinced him to kill Vince."

"Sergeant, I'd say the answer to that question is slim to none. But if that were the case, and this man—who in all probability is fictional—has a mental illness similar to Darcie's, then I'd say there might be a one percent chance," Smoke said.

"That high, huh? But I agree, it was way out there."

"Sometimes you gotta throw crap at the wall and see what sticks."

"Just brainstorming." I pointed at the list of phone numbers from Weber's work cell. "You need help checking them out?"

"Thanks, no. I went through most of them already. Two businesses, four spam calls, an attorney," he said.

I thought for a moment. "Smoke, back to Vince's bracelet. I'll zoom in on the picture of Vince's so he's not in it, snap a photo, and show it to Opal. See if it looks like the one she saw."

"That brings up another thing I've been tossing around in my mind. Opal remembered seeing the bracelet when she was meditating. It reminded me of people who have seen or experienced something but can't remember it, or they've blocked it from their minds for some reason. High school buddies have said to me, 'Remember when . . .' and I have no memory of it. I'd been part of something special to them, yet had zero recall.

"But would I remember it through hypnosis? Maybe. It's a controversial practice, I realize that. Some experts think it creates false memories. I'm no expert and don't have a strong opinion one way or the other, but it made me wonder: would it hurt if Pierre Dawson wanted to try it? Would he remember what the plate looked like?"

I studied Smoke's face to see if he was serious. He was. "Gosh, I don't know. It surprises me you came up with that. Especially since you thought the plate search might turn out to be futile."

He let out a short laugh. "I have to admit I surprised myself. Maybe you and all your 'out there' ideas are starting to rub off on me." He moved his eyebrows up and down in a classic Groucho Marx move.

I smiled at his expression then thought of a question I'd meant to ask. "Anything from the deputy who watched Weber's house last night?"

"No. We've had deputies take two-hour shifts to break up the monotony. No sign of any unwanted guest on Weber's property."

"That's good anyway," I said.

"I did write the warrant, waiting for a judge to sign it, so we can search Weber's house. But since it looks like he'll wake up soon, we can wait to get his permission before we search it."

"Given Vince's condition, do you think it's wise to tell him his valued treasure is missing when he wakes up? Maybe you should talk to his doctor about it first."

"You got a point, and we need to take that into consideration." He rested his elbows on his desk then moved his forearms and hands up and down like balances on a scale as he talked. "On the one hand, the missing bracelet might cause a setback in Weber's recovery. On the other hand, we've got a shooter on the loose. In my book that means Weber's life is still in danger. So a possible setback, or a possible attack?"

I sucked in a long breath in an attempt to slow my racing heart. "We'll have extra security at the hospital, but maybe we should consider moving Vince to another facility the shooter wouldn't know about, to give him greater protection."

"We can look into that if need be." He glanced at the list on his memo pad. "I did arrange that debriefing with Matsen for the civilian witnesses at the café. It's set for this afternoon and our admin assistants will contact them."

"It will be a good thing for them. Any idea when our office will have ours?" I asked.

"It needs to be soon, and another detail I need to attend to this morning." He looked at his watch. "After I meet with our guest deputies, get them situated."

"I'll let you get back to it. I have a detail to attend to myself that I didn't finish last night. Namely my report."

"Best take care of that a-sap, Sergeant."

I retreated to the small sergeants' office and stared at the computer in the early morning quiet. I'd submitted the witness statements in the crime against Vincent Weber the night before. As I worked through the account of my actions and observations from the time I arrived at the café to the time I left for the hospital, the same range of emotions I'd experienced returned.

The main difference was twenty-two hours before, I had no idea whether Vincent Weber would survive, or if he'd succumb to his critical injury. His progress was encouraging, but as I wrote the report, my heart pounded.

When I'd finished and checked it for errors, I sent the report to command staff for review. Then I sent Mandy a message, *Checking in, call when you can.* The phone was still in my hand when she did. "Hi, Mandy. Things are better, huh?"

"They are, but I'm waiting for the moment Vince opens his eyes or moves an arm or something. They plan to move him out of the isolation area this afternoon, and they're hoping he'll be awake by then," she said.

"Even if he needs to sleep longer, it's huge that he's breathing on his own. I'll be there in a bit."

"Thanks."

Squad cars from our neighboring counties were parked in the front, side, and back parking lots. Two squads drove in as I parked in the emergency lot next to Smoke's unmarked car. I waited until three deputies got out of the squad cars and waved for them to follow me. Two from Hennepin and one from Sherburne. We introduced ourselves. They shook their heads and said they couldn't believe what had happened.

"We greatly appreciate your assistance with this detail," I said.

"No problem," one said.

"Glad to help," said another.

"Detective Dawes said to meet him in the conference room on the lower level," the third one said.

I nodded. "I'll walk you to the elevator." We trekked down the corridor to the main entrance. I pointed at the stairs around the corner from the elevator. "If you'd rather walk."

They chose the stairs. A few people seated in the main waiting area were watching us with interest. "Good morning," I called to the group in general then headed to the ICU.

Aside from the fact she was in jeans and a sweatshirt, and not in uniform, Mandy looked like she hadn't moved. Her eyes were glued on Weber as they'd been for hours the day before. I put my hands on her shoulders and she leaned her head against my arm. "It is so awesome that Vince is off the ventilator. We can see his face."

"If you'd asked me before this if I could sit and stare at someone lying on a bed hour after hour, I would've said 'no,'" she said.

"We don't know what we'd do in a lot of situations unless something happens."

"I guess."

I sat down beside her. "Did Dawes tell you we got agency assistance from our six neighboring counties, and it'll more than double our security here? The deputies are getting briefed by him now."

"He did, and it makes me feel a lot better. We need to do all we can to keep Vince safe. I got my personal weapon in my ankle holster."

I elbow bumped her. "And you got through security with it?"

She elbow bumped me back and chuckled. "Go figure."

"Have they started lowering Vince's drug levels yet?" I asked.

"Not sure. They check his vital signs and fluids about every fifteen minutes, and might've started to."

I pulled my work phone from its holder, found the photo I took of the watch at Opal's, and showed it to Mandy. "The witness who noticed the bracelet on the shooter's wrist said it looked like her husband's watch, only with larger links."

She stared at it. "Yeah, it does." She turned to me, her eyebrows drawn together. "You think the shooter took Vince's bracelet?"

"We have to consider it as a possibility," I said.

"Why? How?"

My shoulders lifted. "The why? No clue yet. The how? He had to have gained access to Weber's house. Either walked through an open door, or lifted an unlocked window, or knew the garage door code."

Mandy stood and started walking down the short hallway. When she got to the end she turned around, returned to her chair, and grabbed onto the back of it. "The same dreadful thought keeps running through my mind. That it's someone Vince knows, someone who obviously hates him. If the shooter was in Vince's house, we need to search it, look for evidence he was there. And check Vince's phones."

"Dawes wrote a warrant to search his house, but thought if Vince was about to wake up, we should wait for his permission instead," I said.

"But that could be hours. They warned me it might even be days; God forbid. We shouldn't wait. I think Vince would say 'do it now' if it was one of us lying there, and someone had one of our personal items. If someone was in his house, I say search it, the sooner the better."

"You want to tell Dawes that, or you want me to?"

"I will," she said.

"We took Vince's work cell at the scene, didn't need a warrant to check that. We got a short list of callers to look into. A few more numbers to check, but nothing suspicious so far," I told her.

"I'll tell Dawes they need to check his personal cell. He doesn't have a landline."

Forty minutes later I met Smoke, Ortiz, and Holman at Weber's house. We had donned coveralls and vinyl gloves, put flashlights in our pockets, and brought a case of tools if needed. Smoke held the warrant with the judge's scribbled signature in his hand. He had the overhead garage door code committed to memory.

Smoke punched in the code, and as the door lifted, he said, "The warrant states we can search for fingerprints and DNA evidence on windows and entry doors with an emphasis on, and around, Weber's dresser where his jewelry box sits. Also his medicine cabinet, in the event the suspect was looking for drugs.

"No need to go through his drawers or search other personal items. The way I look at it, if the shooter was here before he committed the assault, he would've had to get in and out a-sap. Either he knew what he wanted, or was looking for a personal item and found the bracelet. Ortiz, will you dust the outside garage door remote and look for fingerprints on the trim? We know Zubinski's and Weber's will be present," Smoke said.

"Sure thing."

"Holman, check doors and windows. Zubinski said the doors were locked when she checked last night, but it was dark, and she didn't look for signs the locks had been tampered with," Smoke said.

"Okay."

"The suspect had a beard and could've lost a hair somewhere. Weber kept his face and head shaved. Zubinski's hair is long and auburn. Sergeant, you can check the bathroom and I'll start with the bedroom," Smoke said.

Vincent Weber was a neatnik. He kept things clean and organized. No piles of newspapers or debris in the living room, dining room, or kitchen. He must have spent some time cleaning on his days off.

I headed to Weber's bathroom. Two bath towels hung on a rod by the tub, and two hand towels were on a rod by the sink. I kept the overhead light off and shined the flashlight on the walls, woodwork, sink cabinet, medicine cabinet—on the inside door and outside mirror—and the faucets.

I spotted a number of partials on the side of the medicine cabinet door, the likely spot Weber used when he opened the door. I studied them and saw only one person's prints, a person with large fingers. Vincent Weber's. I opened the cabinet and there were a few over-the-counter medications, i.e., ibuprofen, allergy nasal spray, cough syrup, and stomach acid relief.

If anyone else had accessed the cabinet, it would've been before it was cleaned. Weber's personal hygiene items and shaving equipment were no doubt in the cabinet drawers. I opened each one, and didn't spot anything amiss.

The advantage of going through a clean house; it was easy to spot something out of place, or any fingerprints left behind by an intruder in personal spaces.

Vincent Weber had not been at his home since 7:00 a.m. the day before when he went on duty. Mandy had been there the past evening, and we had reason to believe the suspect had entered his home after Weber left for work and before the shooting. That would give him a timeframe close to two hours to commit the burglary before he moved on to the more deplorable crime.

It didn't take long to explore the house. If the shooter had taken anything besides the bracelet, we didn't spot anything like pictures missing from walls or memorabilia we knew that

Vince had. Aside from sets of fingerprints on the two outside entrance doors, the ones we found inside on the TV, laptop, and some furniture and appliances were consistent with Vincent Weber's and Amanda Zubinski's. The shooter had worn gloves in the café, and had he been in Vince Weber's house, he'd worn them in there too.

I pointed at Weber's laptop that sat on the dining table. "Not included in the warrant?"

"Nope. Since we have access to his work cell and work emails, we'll stick with those for now. If we get the warrant for his personal phone, we can look through that. If we deem it necessary to interrogate his personal laptop in the future, we'll ask the BCA to handle that," Smoke said.

13

On my way to Opal Reynold's house, an alert came across the squad car laptop. *Haven County Deputy ambushed, shot on County Road 12, Sweden Township. Responders en route. Condition of victim unknown, identity currently withheld. Be on the lookout for a Black Shadow Honda Motorcycle, no license plates. The driver is in black leather with a black helmet. Armed and dangerous. Believed to be headed northwest.*

My stomach tightened, and I pulled over to the curb on the city street. Haven County was about three hours southeast of Winnebago County, not far from Rochester, with a population smaller than ours. The shooter was headed northwest. Our direction?

My work cell on the dashboard lit up with the same message, followed by a text message from Smoke. *Report to the office.* I sent him a thumbs up, and arrived minutes later.

I walked into the sheriff's administration area, and there stood Sheriff Mike Kenner in uniform, surrounded by admin assistants and Smoke. It surprised me, yet didn't surprise me. I doubted he could stay away, twenty-fifth anniversary vacation with his wife in the warm sun, or not. He greeted me with a nod. My bottled-up emotions bubbled to the surface. I struggled with what to say and gave him a tight hug instead.

His brown eyes appeared darker when he was under stress. "We had no choice but to come home. After I got the call yesterday at zero four fifty Hawaii time, all I did was pace. I walked up and down the beach until April told me to pack, that she'd booked a flight home. The eight-and-a-half-hour flight and the hour drive home from the airport were among the longest in my life, when I needed to be here yesterday."

"We're sorry you had to cut your trip short, but it's a big relief you're here. That's an understatement. It's been a helluva an ordeal," Smoke said.

Kenner gave Smoke's shoulder a pat, then said, "Everything's upside down. I barely got to the office to check on Weber's investigation when we got notification Haven County's got a deputy down. Ambushed. Another cop shot, the day after ours. Haven sent a message to all the sheriffs in the state saying we'll get footage from the deputy's squad camera via email at some point today."

"Any word on the deputy's identity or condition?" Smoke said.

"No, they're keeping it under wraps for the time being. You know the process." Sheriff Kenner looked around the room at the assistants. "Dina, and all of you in admin, kudos for all you've done in the effort to help locate Weber's shooter."

Quiet "thanks" echoed around the room.

"Detective, Sergeant, let's go to my office. You can bring me up to speed on any details I might've missed on the investigation so far."

Smoke and I followed the sheriff to his office. As usual, my eyes were drawn to the collections of sheriffs' patches from the eighty-six other Minnesota counties framed behind glass on his walls.

When Kenner didn't sit down, neither did we. Smoke and I were tense, but the sheriff seemed even tenser with his clenched jaw and fists. He stretched out his fingers, scrubbed his face with his hands, then moved his jaw back and forth. When he'd finished his de-tensing exercises he said, "I've got the reports and videos to read and review. But I'd like you to walk me through every detail related to the event, starting from the time the call of the assault came in up to the present."

Smoke straightened his shoulders and clasped his hands behind his back, maybe to gain some confidence. "What started out as a regular day on the job imploded into anything but at nine twenty-six when Communications radioed that Seven fourteen was down." He released his hands, shook his head, and launched into a detailed account from the time he'd arrived on the scene to our search at Weber's house that morning. "We'd just wrapped that up, so no written reports on it yet."

Kenner turned and stared out his window, either at Bison Lake or at nothing in particular. "I can't think of a stone you've left unturned. But twenty-five hours later we still have no idea where the shooter disappeared to."

"That's a fact. And now Haven County will likely need to tap into the same resources we did to help track down their shooter. One thing in their favor, you said the deputy's squad camera filmed the incident," Smoke said.

Kenner's phone dinged, and he read the message. "That was fast. Haven County emailed the video. Let's take a look." He sat down behind his desk. Smoke and I pulled chairs in beside him. Kenner accessed his account, and the subject line on the email read, DISTURBING VIDEO NOT FOR PUBLIC VIEW. My shoulders twitched when he clicked on the link.

It appeared the deputy saw the motorcycle in his rearview mirror, maybe heard him approach, because he activated his lights and sirens seconds before a black motorcycle sped past him on the left side of his squad car. The deputy followed it for a short distance until the motorcycle slowed, and pulled onto the shoulder. The deputy gave the county dispatch his name and location and reasons for the stop: speeding and no plates.

Then a bulked-up male deputy exited his vehicle and approached the motorcycle, his gun drawn and in the ready position. When the deputy was a few feet away, the motorcyclist made a quick upper body turn toward him, extended both arms halfway, gun in his hands, and fired once. The way the deputy jerked, it looked like the bullet hit him below his vest, in the lower abdomen or upper thigh. The deputy bent over and fell to the ground. His weapon dropped beside him. The motorcycle sped away, and the deputy shouted into his radio, "I'm shot; send rescue. Shooter on a black Honda motorcycle, no plates." The video ended.

My insides shook, and we were speechless, trying to process, to comprehend what we'd seen and heard, the horror of it. The deputy went from taking command of a situation to taking a bullet seconds later.

Kenner coughed. "I'm praying he makes it."

"Looks like the shooter went for the deputy's carotid, below his vest," Smoke said.

The carotid was the major artery that supplied blood to the brain.

"The Mayo Clinic isn't far from there, and they have a Level One Trauma Center. Once they get a helicopter in the air, they could be there in a few minutes, land close to him on the road," I said.

The sheriff's phone alerted him again. He read the message out loud, "'Haven County's shooter seems to have disappeared. Not yet seen on any roads. Likely drove off the roadway. The county has ten thousand sink holes and four hundred caves, including one of the longest in Minnesota. Many ways to disappear.'"

Smoke shook his head. "Disappeared in plain sight, like our suspect did. Well disguised, like ours was. Turned his head enough to see the deputy, but not enough so the camera captured his face. And with that big helmet on, it would've been tough to see his features in the first place."

"The deputy was targeted, like Weber was. Maybe not that particular deputy, like Weber was, but a deputy," I said.

"Yes. He got the deputy to stop him, maybe had positioned himself a ways back behind some cover, laid in wait for one to pass by, and then set his plan in motion. His goal was to kill a cop. You gotta wonder if it was rolling around in his mind for a while, then he heard about our deputy and decided today was his day to do the same," Kenner said.

"What goes through a mind like that? Winnebago County certainly can sympathize and empathize with Haven County," Smoke said.

"I'll touch base with Sheriff Joe Heller later. They've got their hands full, what with notifications and press releases. I don't know Heller well, but I've talked to him at sheriffs' meetings. Good guy and a great sheriff, from what I hear. They'll handle this horrific event in the best way possible."

Smoke nodded. "Meantime, Sheriff, forgot to mention that we talked about getting a warrant to access Weber's personal phone, check his calls and messages, look for anything out of the ordinary."

"Maybe you should wait until he wakes up and he can tell you if he's gotten any unusual calls, messages, possible threats," Kenner said.

"That's what I'd hoped to do, but it's been over twenty-four hours since the incident, and the shooter's been out there unidentified this whole time," Smoke said.

"We hope he'll wake up soon, like any minute, as they reduce the amount of sedatives he's on. But the surgical staff told Mandy it might be days. Mandy told me this morning we *need* to look at Weber's phone," I said.

"Sheriff, It's more of a look for people outside his known friends and connections. No reason to read messages or listen to voicemails from his close friends and coworkers, unless it's a quick scan. At least at first pass. Zubinski likely knows connections that I don't. Or we can ask a BCA agent to interrogate the phone for us," Smoke said.

Kenner shook his head. "I don't think that's necessary, Dawes. Get the warrant written and signed." He looked at his watch. "If Weber isn't conscious by sixteen hundred, go ahead with it. You can work with Zubinski on the search. It's possible something in his calls or messages will give us a lead."

"Thanks, Boss. We'll do all we can to protect his privacy," Smoke added.

"And let's hope Weber understands why we did it," I said.

Smoke raised his eyebrows. "Wouldn't you?"

"Yes. But if someone threatened me, even if it was veiled, I'd tell you about it. I'd hope Vince would do the same. Tell Mandy, or one of us," I said.

"Yep." Smoke clasped his hands. "Chief Deputy put in a data request with our IT guys to access Weber's work emails, asked them to go back six months, and pull them up for us. They used their computers, so we can view them in there. We'll assign deputies to work with admin assistants for two-hour shifts, with your stamp of approval, Sheriff."

"Sure. Randolph's feeling better and would be happy to schedule staff for that detail. In fact, if I'd been thinking, I would have put us on speaker phone, included him in our meeting here," Kenner said.

Smoke nodded. "Will you ask Chief to send me the schedule a-sap? I'm available if they have questions, or if they come across anything suspicious," Smoke said.

"Will do. I plan to check on things at the hospital this morning, sit with Zubinski for a while," Kenner said.

Smoke nodded. "Sheriff, one more thing, I asked Sergeant Matsen to do a debriefing session with the café witnesses this afternoon, at fourteen hundred." Two o'clock.

"Good. What about our guys, others involved, staff?" Kenner asked.

"Haven't had time to arrange it yet. We thought we should have two sessions. One at sixteen hundred, and one at eighteen hundred, if we can pull them together," Smoke said.

Kenner gave a slight nod. "Sure. I'll take one, you can have the other. That work?"

"Sounds like a plan. I'll ask Dina to get the word out," Smoke said.

We stopped by Dina's desk on the way by, and she said she'd be happy to take care of that detail.

Smoke and I were in the corridor that led to the squad room when he leaned in closer, and said, "Now that Sheriff's back, I feel like a hundred pounds got lifted off my shoulders. Problem is, they got loaded onto his."

"I know. But we'll help. Vince is on the mend, and I pray the Haven County deputy will be okay too. We've seen videos of other cops getting attacked or shot or hit by a car, and it's the worst. Maybe because of Weber, this one feels more personal."

"That it does. Because it is," he said.

Cindy, an admin assistant called out, "Detective Dawes?" We both turned around. "There's a man at the front counter who wants to talk to you."

"Who is it? Did he say what it's about?" Smoke asked.

"That it's personal, about Vincent Weber," Cindy said.

"Be right there, thanks." Smoke touched my arm. "Personal, about Weber. You should join me, Sergeant."

I spotted a restless man who looked familiar moving back and forth from leg to leg and thought, *personal is right.* He was in his fifties, a taller, leaner version of Vincent Weber, with a neatly trimmed brown beard and thinning hair, both peppered with gray. And blue eyes. He wore an unbuttoned dark gray coat with a light gray shirt and black pants.

I heard Smoke suck in some air as he pushed open the door from the sheriff's office to the entry area. I hung back, but heard them through the opening in the bullet-proof glass.

Smoke offered his hand and the man shook it. "Detective Elton Dawes."

"Thank you for meeting with me. You're the detective who gave the statement, the one who's working on Vincent Weber's case. I'm Jonathan Bauer, his father."

Suspicion confirmed. *Oh my gosh, oh my gosh, oh my gosh.*

Smoke managed to not twitch or even blink. "I'm one of many working the case."

Bauer glanced from the entry area to the pool of administrative assistants on the other side of the glass, then to me. I smiled a little.

He gave me a nod back then turned to Smoke. "Is there somewhere more private we can go to talk?"

"Sure, we have interview rooms. Anything in your coat pockets?" Smoke asked him.

"No."

"Go ahead and hang it up there." Smoke pointed at the hooks on the side wall.

Bauer slipped off his coat and hung it up.

"You have your ID with you?" Smoke asked.

Bauer pulled his wallet from a back pocket and withdrew his license. Smoke read it, nodded, and handed it back. "You can lay your wallet on the counter, along with anything else in your pockets. You have a weapon of any kind, like a jackknife?" Smoke said.

"No."

Bauer withdrew his cell phone from his breast pocket and laid it next to the wallet. Smoke did a pat search, from Bauer's neck to his ankles. "Anything hidden in your shoes?"

"No."

"Okay, grab your phone and wallet and follow me." Smoke swiped his badge, and held the door for Bauer. "This is Sergeant Aleckson. She's part of the investigation and will join us," he said.

Bauer nodded. "Sergeant."

All the interview rooms were empty, and we filed into A. Smoke pulled out a chair for Bauer, moved to the other side of the table, and sat down. I took a seat by the table's corner edge.

Smoke folded his hands and rested them on the table. "Word has it Vince has never met his father; didn't know he had a father."

Bauer's shoulders lifted. "That was his mother's doing. We met in Minneapolis where we both worked at the time, and had a brief affair. My job took me to Chicago for a while. I tried to contact Linda, but she wouldn't take my phone calls. When I got transferred back to Minneapolis, I made more of a concerted effort to find her, hoping we could start over again. I found out from her friend she had moved back home, up north to Ely. So I got her address and headed up there one weekend thinking if she saw me, she'd want to reconnect.

"Well, I got two shocks that day. When she opened the door she said, 'I've moved on. I have a new life, a family.' Then a little boy about two years old moved in close beside her. He looked like me in childhood photos. I was blindsided, speechless.

"Then Linda said, 'You need to leave, go back to your other girlfriends, never contact us again, or I'll call the police.' The way she pulled her son tighter, I knew he was a major part of *us*. I didn't know if she had married someone else, or what was going on, but I sure didn't want to make a scene in front of the boy. The whole thing ate at me. I knew Vincent had to be my son. I felt it, but could also see how much his mother hated me, so I left."

"But you knew who he was, that his name was Vincent Weber, and he was a deputy here?" Smoke asked.

"Yes. I'd hired a private investigator to gather those details, and kept track the best I could, without him knowing it. It was tough. His mother hadn't married, never married. I didn't know what she'd told him about me, but I figured it wasn't good. Vincent could've easily found me if he knew my name." Bauer stopped for a moment. "You know, he was a star football player in high school and college. I went to a few of his games."

"Without getting recognized?" Smoke said.

"All those years later I'd changed, put on weight, grew a beard, wore glasses, stayed in the background. I didn't see Linda at the games. And didn't know it at the time, but she'd been battling cancer for years," Bauer said.

Smoke's eyes narrowed. "You knew when she died?"

"I did. I wanted to reach out to Vincent then, but couldn't. Didn't know how. Out of respect for his mother. I was able to help by making anonymous donations for her medical and funeral expenses, and with Vince's college expenses. He had a football scholarship and was told benefactors helped pay for miscellaneous costs."

"But you're here now?" Smoke said.

"I couldn't stay away any longer. Someone shot my son, and I don't want either one of us to die before we've had a chance to meet, to talk, to get to know each other. I don't know if he'll want to meet me, but I *have* to meet him, tell him how proud I am of him in what he's accomplished, how brave he is."

When tears formed in my eyes, I looked down and blinked them away.

Bauer pulled a business card from his pocket and slid it across the table. "Can you help me, arrange it so I can see my son?"

Smoke picked up the card then stood. "I don't see how that'd be our call. The sergeant and I will run it by the sheriff. Hold tight, we'll be back in a few."

We stepped into the hallway, and Smoke rubbed his temples. "This was an unexpected twist."

"Knock me over with a feather. But you were right when you questioned our role in this. It's between him and Vince," I said.

"I agree. If Weber was conscious, in good health, it'd be a no brainer. They could hash it out."

"You saw his DL; where's he from?"

"Maplewood." A suburb of St. Paul. "I'll check with Kenner, if you'll hang out here," Smoke said.

"Sure."

I believed Jonathan Bauer was who he said he was. Or a very close blood relative. He said he'd been involved in Vince's life in an anonymous way. It'd be easy to verify if he'd helped pay for medical and funeral expenses, and had contributed to Vince's college funds.

I stepped into the interview room's observation area and studied Jonathan Bauer. When he turned his head to the side, I snapped a photo and returned to the corridor. I brought up the profile of the shooter's face on my phone and compared it to Bauer's. Aside from them both sporting a beard, from the little I could see, the shooter had a narrower face, different nose shape, and cheekbone curve.

Smoke returned and raised his eyebrows when he said, "Sheriff said Bauer can go with him to the hospital. He asked if you wanted to join them."

"He wants me as an escort?" I said.

"Could be."

14

After a quick meet-and-greet between the sheriff and Bauer at the office, we were off. Ten minutes later I pulled into the hospital's emergency lot behind Jonathan Bauer, who was behind Sheriff Kenner. It was among the more unusual assignments I'd had in my career.

Leo Roth was back for another shift after twelve hours off. A Sherburne County deputy stood on the opposite side of the entrance. Roth blinked a couple times when he saw Bauer. And a couple more when he saw Kenner. "Sheriff, good to see you."

Kenner nodded. "Thanks for being here, Sergeant." He turned to the other deputy. "And you too. We surely appreciate the help from your county."

"Yes, sir. It's for a good cause, glad to be here."

Kenner dipped his head toward Bauer. "He's with us," he told Roth.

After they were inside, Roth whispered, "Who is he?"

"We'll talk later," I said and followed the sheriff and the alleged father.

Seasoned veteran Deputy Bob Edberg was outside the intensive care unit. His eyebrows lifted when he saw Kenner. "Sheriff." And narrowed when they fell on Bauer.

"Good to see you, Bob. Mister Bauer is with us," Kenner said.

I smiled and nodded as I passed Edberg, and he shook his head in return. Who was this mysterious, stylish man who closely resembled Vincent Weber?

As we approached Mandy, she jumped up and gasped out loud. Before she spoke, Sheriff Kenner said, "I needed to be with my troops." He waved his hand between Mandy and Bauer. "Jonathan Bauer, Amanda Zubinski." They locked eyes for what seemed like five minutes. Then the men stepped up to the glass. Mandy held back and gave my forearm a soft pinch. I gave her a sideways glance back. We stayed in the back row behind the men.

It was reassuring to see Vince sleeping with the small oxygen tubes in his nostrils and IV tubes in his arms, without the ventilator pumping away.

Bauer did a quiet throat clear. "Oh my. I guess if you look on the positive side, I'd say his color looks good. That's a positive sign, right?"

"It is to me. But strange to see Vincent Weber sleeping. Or being still at all," Kenner said.

"The times I saw him in action was at his football games. Given his stocky build, it surprised me how fast he could sprint," Bauer said.

Mandy bumped my arm but unless Bauer identified himself as Vince's father, she'd have to wait for my account.

Bauer went on, "I wasn't in Vincent's life, but his mother did very well by him. My other son's mother, not so much."

Mandy and I grabbed each other's hand at that big reveal, but I didn't dare look at her.

"How's that?" Kenner said.

"Vincent followed the law, chose enforcing it as his career. My other son has done his best to skirt or break it. That started in his teens. His mother and I divorced when he was two, and I only got to see him every other weekend. His mother never said no to him. He got about everything he wanted, did what he wanted. He's thirty and hasn't learned his lesson. I keep asking, how many times does he have to hit bottom before he changes his ways?"

"Serious trouble?" Kenner said.

"Serious enough to do prison time."

""That can happen to the best parents." One of Kenner's sons had served time. "Your son in prison now?"

"No. He's been out a few months. Met a special someone and is trying to start over in Iowa," Bauer said.

"Whereabouts?"

"Waukon. Got a job at the Walmart in Decorah stocking shelves. They pay pretty well, and as long as he's gainfully employed, that's fine by me. Not everyone will hire someone with a record."

"That's true," Kenner said.

"As much as I feel the need to get to know Vincent, let him know who I am, I'm reluctant to introduce him to Duke."

"Duke?"

Bauer turned to Kenner with a slight grin. "My younger son. His mother got her love of John Wayne movies from her mother. Named him John Wayne Bauer, nicknamed him Duke. I doubt most people in his life even know his given name."

Vince kept things close to the vest, unlike his father who let it all hang out. I sensed from Mandy's vibes we were both curious, yet reluctant, witnesses to what felt like a small group therapy session between two law abiding fathers with law breaking sons.

"Does Duke know about Vincent?" Kenner asked.

Bauer nodded. "I told him last year, and I've felt guilty about it ever since. I was frustrated, at the end of my rope with his criminal activities, so after I explained that he had an older half-brother, I said, 'why can't you be more like your brother? He loves the law.' You should've seen the look on his face. But there was no way to take back what I'd said. Know what his off-the-wall response was?"

"What?" Kenner asked.

"He hadn't even met Vincent, and said, 'If I have a brother like that, then I hate him as much as Cain hated Abel.' It made me sick to my stomach that he said such a thing," Bauer said.

What? Cain killed his brother Abel in the Bible.

Mandy's foot bumped my ankle.

The sheriff kept his voice even when he said, "I can see how that would've disturbed you. I have two sons myself. Did Duke ever get in fights? Sadly, one of my sons did."

"Duke? Some. But mostly it was burglaries and thefts that got him into trouble."

What?

It was my turn to bump Mandy's ankle.

Why wasn't Smoke here to hear all this?

"Mister Bauer—"

"Jonathan, please."

"Jonathan, we agreed that you could come here and see Vincent. But he'll need time to recover before you introduce yourself. It might be a couple more days before he wakes up. We don't want any setbacks when he does," Kenner said.

"I understand and of course I agreed to that. It helps me to see him, to know he's going to make it," Bauer said.

"That goes for all of us. I'll escort you out," Kenner said.

Mandy and I stepped aside as they turned to leave. Kenner looked over his shoulder and blinked a couple times.

Mandy turned to me and grabbed my shoulders. "Spill it."

I gave her every detail I knew.

Mandy sank down on a chair. "I didn't want to say anything to Mister Bauer, or Sheriff Kenner, but I'm not sure how Vince would feel if he found out the truth. He told me he asked his mother about his father, who he was. And she told him, if you can believe this, she had too much to drink at a party and was raped. She said she had no idea who his father was."

"Why would she do that, make his father seem like a monster?" I asked.

Mandy shrugged. "We can't ask her that. And neither can Vince. Sometimes people get caught up in their lies till they believe them."

"True. Aside from his father, he has a brother who's lived a life of crime. And supposedly never met Vince, but hates him anyway."

"We need to investegate John Wayne Bauer, find out what he drives, where he was yesterday," Mandy said.

"Kenner heard Bauer say the same things we did. That Duke was a burglar, a thief, got into fights, and hates Vince. I'm sure he'll set an investigation in motion as soon as he gets back to the office. I'm heading there myself and will keep you in the loop. Unless you want to join us?"

She shook her head. "I feel like I need to stay here."

When I walked into the sheriff's administration area, Dina pointed at Kenner's office. "They're in there."

Sheriff Kenner and Smoke stood behind his desk and glanced at me when I joined them. "Sergeant. Just telling Dawes about John Wayne Bauer," Kenner said.

"I'll look into his criminal history, his mug shots," Smoke said.

"We'd be especially interested in his facial profile shot," I added.

"Yes," Kenner said.

Sheriff Kenner got a text message and read it to us, "Our much-loved deputy did not survive his gunshot wound. We'll release his name and other details later today. Suspect is still at large. Keep his family and friends in your prayers. Sheriff Heller.'"

We were already on emotional overload, and that added still more weight. Smoke and Sheriff blinked away their tears, but mine escaped and rolled down my cheeks. After minutes of silence, we needed to refocus and get back to the investigation of the crimes against our own deputy, still unconscious in the ICU.

"Do you want me to finish checking calls and messages on Weber's work phone while you look into Bauer's history?" I asked Smoke.

"No, I finished that task and was able to clear the rest of them."

Kenner looked at his memo pad. "Dawes, did you get the warrant signed to access Weber's personal cell phone?"

"I did, so we're all set to start the search, if he doesn't wake up by four, per your orders."

"Good. This whole father and half-brother thing has added another wrinkle," Kenner said.

"More than one." I told them about the lie Weber's mother told him, that she didn't know who his father was.

"From another wrinkle to a tangled web," Smoke said.

"What a deal. And I have to say, Jonathan Bauer seems like a decent man." Kenner shook his head. "Next steps for us?"

"Sheriff, there's been no reports of unwanted persons on Weber's property. Is it necessary to keep someone posted there?" Smoke said.

"No. It seems like the suspect got what he was looking for. I think frequent drive bys will suffice," Kenner said.

"Randolph got deputies assigned to look at Weber's email records, and two of them should be in IT by now," Smoke said.

"I can check in with them while you get started on the John Wayne Bauer search," I said.

"Sounds like a plan. All right by you, Sheriff?" Smoke said.

"Sure. Fine." Kenner held up his cell phone. "This thing's blowing up with messages from other sheriffs. They're trying to figure out what we can do to help Haven County. One thing's for sure, we'll all want to show our respect and support in the best ways possible. And rest assured, with every law enforcement agency in the state, and beyond, looking for the cop shooters, we're bound to flush them out. But keep the deputy's death under wraps for now, until it goes public."

Smoke and I agreed and left Kenner's office.

When we were out of earshot, I told Smoke, "I was planning to stop by Opal Reynold's house, show her the photo of Weber's bracelet, but I'll see if she comes to Matsen's debriefing, and can talk to her then."

"With all that's going on, I kinda doubt Kenner will have time to do one of the other debriefs," Smoke said, and headed to his cubicle.

I left the sheriff's department and made my way down the main floor corridor in the Government Center to the Information Technology Department. Inside, I passed several employee cubicles where they sat tapping away on their keyboards. Holman and Ortiz were seated at desks at the far end, next to the department head's office.

"Hey, Sergeant," Ortiz said.

Holman nodded. "No overtly threatening emails, so far. We've copied and pasted two iffy ones onto a document to look into. One man asked how Weber could have the audacity to arrest his saintly son, but he used other choice words. Another said she was going to file a lawsuit against him for arresting her husband. Weber didn't respond to either one of them."

"It seems to backfire when you respond to angry people. They can get even more riled up, I've learned," I said.

"As tempting as it is, right?" Ortiz said.

I lifted my hand in a wave. "I'll let you get back to it."

Smoke had John Wayne Bauer's criminal history pulled up on his computer. "Find his mug shots?" I asked.

He minimized the tab and opened another with both a front and side view of Bauer's face. He had dark hair, brown eyes, sunken cheeks, a narrow nose, and pointed chin. "Doesn't look much like his father, or his supposed brother."

"Supposed, huh? But you're right, only his mother knew for sure." Smoke opened another tab with the image of Weber's suspected shooter. "There are similarities, but with so little of the shooter's face visible, I couldn't say one way or the other with any confidence."

"No, I know I couldn't."

"I'll check with both Hennepin County and the FBI, ask if they'll use their facial recognition software to compare the two, and let us know. Doesn't hurt to have two opinions," Smoke said.

"True. So what'd you find in his criminal history, what landed him in prison?"

"Bar fight. He broke a booze bottle over a guy's head and fractured his skull."

"So there is a violent incident in his past," I said.

"Yep. That was seven years ago. The other crimes were burglaries, thefts, check forgeries."

"Vince would not approve of Duke's behavior."

"Nope. But nothing new on his record since he got out of prison. That he got caught for, anyway." Smoke checked his watch. "It's twelve thirty, you have anything to eat today?"

"Yogurt. You?"

"A granola bar."

"Now that they've added more deli options in the vending machines I'll find us something good to eat," I said.

"Sure. Anything. We both have junk-food-proof stomachs that might catch up with us one day. Meantime, we need to get something into them." His phone rang. "Detective Dawes. . . . Yes. . . . Good to know, thanks." He disconnected, and said, "That was Doug Matsen. He checked the tapes from yesterday morning at McDonald's and reported Pierre Dawson did go through the drive-thru at ten oh three. I had no reason to doubt Pierre, but needed to confirm he was telling the truth, and verify the approximate time he spotted the alleged shooter on Fifty-five."

"Yes. You want to eat in the breakroom?"

"No, here is fine. I need to get Bauer's photos sent off to those agencies and be here in case they have questions."

15

Smoke's eyebrows lifted when I returned. "What have you got? It even smells good."

I handed him a paper plate with his lunch. "A chicken sandwich breaded with herbs that I warmed in the microwave for you, and a chicken salad croissant for me. They even have giant dill pickles so I got a couple." One on his plate, one on mine.

"I got the two images sent to both the FBI and Hennepin for comparison," Smoke said.

I swallowed a bite. "Good. We're working hard for Vince, but I can't stop thinking about the Haven County deputy who died. I wonder if I've met him at a training class at some point."

"When they release his name, we'll figure it out."

Smoke had a case of water on the floor behind his desk, picked up two, and passed one to me. We ate in silence, then I stacked his plate on mine and carried them to the larger trash bin by the entrance.

Sheriff Kenner phoned a minute later, and Smoke took the call. "What? . . . I'll be right there." He stood. "They found a Ford Focus abandoned in the city of Babbit in Vernon County, southwestern Wisconsin, and think it might be our shooter's."

At 1:03, I tailed Smoke to Kenner's office.

Kenner held his office phone in his hand. "I've got it on speaker. A deputy noticed its back end sticking out from a grove of trees not far off a county road. Iowa plates, and when he ran 'em, it came back as stolen. Long story short, the dispatchers there reached the owner who has a used car lot. Their sheriff wondered if it's the vehicle we're looking for, the one the shooter escaped in."

Iowa plates?

"Sheriff, who have you got on the line?" Smoke asked.

"Deputy Wilcox," Kenner said.

"Deputy Wilcox, Detective Elton Dawes here. There's a scratch on the right front wing of our suspect's vehicle. Can you take a photo and send it to my cell phone?" Smoke said.

"Sure Detective, go ahead with the number. I can tell you right now there is a scratch, about three inches long," Wilcox said.

Smoke gave Wilcox his number then opened the saved photo collection on his phone while we waited. He selected the photo from the suspect's vehicle and showed it to us. He got the photo from Wilcox a minute later. Smoke held it up for Kenner and me, then went back to the photo captured at the bar and showed us again.

I nodded and Kenner said, "Yep."

"Deputy, the three of us looked at the photo we have of the suspect's Focus and compared it with the one you sent. We all agree it's a match. It's gotta be ours," Kenner said.

"Oh. Well good then," Wilcox said.

"Very good. Do you see other tracks nearby? Shoe prints, indications of how he left the scene, which direction he traveled?" Smoke asked him.

"We're in a natural grasslands area. It's been dry and windy besides. Didn't spot any, even by the driver's door. Don't even see my own, except where I bent some blades of grass over. But I'll take a closer look," Wilcox said.

Kenner took over, "Before you do that, can you give me the vehicle owner's name and phone number? I'll contact him, tell him our office needs to impound his vehicle."

Wilcox relayed the name and number.

"Thanks, I'll give you a call after I've talked to him." Kenner hung up, dialed the used car lot's number, and identified himself. "I'm looking for Greg."

A baritone voice on the other end said, "Sheriff Kenner, I'm Greg. I bet you're calling about the Ford."

"That's correct. There's a high probability the suspect used it for criminal activity."

"I was worried about something like that, seeing how he stole it," Greg said.

"Do you know the details, how and when he did it?" Kenner said.

"Sure do. It was Monday, two days ago, early afternoon. A guy came in, wanted to take the Focus for a test drive. He was scruffy looking, long brownish hair, beard, and wore a stocking cap. He had dirty fingernails, like maybe he was a mechanic."

"He have a jacket on?" Kenner asked.

"Yeah, a camo hoodie," Greg replied.

Kenner and Smoke sucked in breaths. I released the one I'd been holding.

Greg continued, "I tried to be a little conversational with him, but he was one of those guys that gave one-word answers, if at all. Said his son needed a vehicle. I got that much out of him."

"Did you look at his driver's license, get his name?" Smoke asked.

"Sure, and I shoulda snapped a photo of it as it turns out, so there'd be evidence that it was a fake ID. His license said his name was Kaleb with a K, Vance, Wisconsin resident, from La Crosse. Anyways, the guy drove off and never came back. I reported it to the police, maybe half an hour later.

"When the police got back to me they said there was no one by that name in the state's system. Then lo and behold, two days later here we are. And come to find out the worst part is that whoever he was used it for criminal purposes. And a *bad* crime too," Greg said.

"Did the guy leave his vehicle at your lot?" Smoke asked.

"No, said he walked over from a friend's house in town," Greg said.

"Question. How'd you happen to have a vehicle with Iowa plates for sale in your lot?" Kenner asked.

"It belonged to a buddy of mine. Only lives six miles away, but we're in different states. He transferred the title, and I was waiting till I sold it so they could get new plates at that time," Greg explained.

Smoke rubbed his temples. "All right. We'll need to impound the vehicle, do a thorough search of it, see what we can uncover."

"That's fine," Greg said.

"Did you clean the car when your buddy brought it in?" Smoke asked.

"Yeah. It was pretty clean, but we detailed it anyway. I have a reputation to uphold here."

"Sure. I can't tell you how long it'll take to search the car, but we'll get it back to you as soon as we've finished," Smoke said.

"That's fine, no problem. Not sure if I ever want to see it again, anyways," he said.

"Thanks, Greg," Kenner said and hung up.

"Sheriff, do you want Matsen, and our crime team to go down and look at it first, or should we have them tow it here?" Smoke said.

"Let's have it towed," he said, and dialed Wilcox's number. "Deputy, it's Kenner."

"Oh, Sheriff, while I was waiting for your call, I searched some more around the front of the vehicle. I figured the suspect must've walked away, because I didn't see other vehicle tracks near the back of the car. Well, I found some. Single tire tracks that go further into the woods from the car. They're wider than a bicycle's so it's gotta be a motorcycle," Wilcox said.

A motorcycle?

"I figured he must've had the motorcycle parked here then went off and stole the car. When he came back with the Focus, he must've positioned the car so one set of wheels covered the motorcycle's tracks when he drove in. I found the spot where he turned the bike around. When he got on the back side of the Focus, he followed one set of the tire tracks out. Must've missed them cause the motorcycle's tires didn't make deep depressions. I had to kind of brush the grass aside. Looks like he rode a motorcycle in, and then back out again," he said.

Smoke, Kenner, and I all shook our heads.

"Deputy Wilcox. This just got a whole lot more complicated. You heard a deputy in Haven County, Minnesota was shot this morning?" Smoke said.

"I did, and started to connect those dots when I found the tracks," Wilcox said.

"How far a walk is it from that site to where the place the guy stole the Focus from?" Smoke asked.

"Gosh, maybe two miles."

Kenner cleared his throat. "I need to get on a three-way call with your sheriff and the Haven County sheriff. Alert the FBI. Now we have proof positive the shooter crossed state lines. Haven County will no doubt want to get photos, maybe take casts of the motorcycle tracks."

"Like I said, they're pretty faint, but they can get photos, I'll take some more myself."

"All right. I'll give Haven County Sheriff Heller your number so he can talk to you directly," Kenner said.

"Sure, I'll stand by. Our sheriff will probably report to the scene here, or get one of our detectives out here for sure," Wilcox said.

"Your sheriff will also want deputies to check with area businesses and residents, find out if anyone saw a scruffy guy, beard, long brown hair wearing a stocking cap in the vicinity Monday afternoon," Kenner said.

"I'm sure he will," Wilcox said.

They disconnected and Kenner said, "We got a serial killer out there?"

"Seems like a reasonable conclusion," Smoke said.

"Proves Pierre Dawson was right when he said the car had out-of-state plates. And he named Iowa as one of the possibilities," I said.

"What's stuck in my craw is Vincent Weber's father said Vince has a brother in Iowa who hates him. Like Cain hated Abel," Kenner said.

"That's been eating at me too," I said.

"Sheriff, I gotta admit when you relayed that to me, it raised the hairs on the back of my neck. But why would the suspect leave Iowa, go to Wisconsin, and steal a vehicle with Iowa plates?" Smoke asked.

"Maybe he went to Wisconsin to steal one with Wisconsin plates, seeing how he had a fake Wisconsin license, then found an older nondescript Ford Focus that just happened to have Iowa plates," I said.

"You got me on that one. Maybe he thought he was doing Greg, the used car guy, a favor when he returned the stolen vehicle to the vicinity from which it came," Smoke said, likely in jest.

"Maybe. But why would he care?" Kenner said.

"I'll look into John Wayne Bauer's whereabouts Monday, Tuesday, and today," Smoke said.

Sheriff Kenner checked his watch. "The debrief with the witnesses is in twenty minutes. I'd planned to be there for part of it at least, show them my support, but I need to make that call to the other sheriffs, and the FBI. And attend to whatever comes out of those conversations."

Smoke lifted his hand toward me. "The sergeant here wants to talk to Opal, the one who spotted a bracelet on the shooter's arm."

I nodded. "I'll head to the debrief, talk to Opal, see if Matsen needs a partner."

"Thanks. I'll stop by if I'm clear before you've finished," Kenner said.

"On my way," I said.

"Oh, and tell Matsen about the Focus." Kenner added.

Sergeant Doug Matsen was going over some materials when I entered the smaller Meeting Room 118. The larger Meeting Room 120 was reserved for the staff debriefings at 4:00 p.m. and 6:00 p.m.

Matsen was the age a lot of people claimed to be in jest: thirty-nine. He'd had a wild side he tamed as he grew older, and had never crossed legal lines during arrests or questionings. He was astute, had good instincts, worked his way up, and attained the position as head of the Winnebago County Crime Lab. I'd always liked him.

Before the witnesses arrived, I told Matsen the Ford Focus had been found, and relayed what Deputy Wilcox and the used car lot owner Greg had said. "Sheriff's going to arrange a phone meeting with the other sheriffs. Inform the FBI. The Focus will be towed here after they release it."

"Big relief they found it, stolen or not. We've got fibers from the café's atrium rug to compare to the carpet in the car, for starters. We'll need to check if the car was cleaned after it was brought in to the lot. Some clean 'em, some sell 'em as is," Matsen said.

"Dawes did ask the owner that, and he said it had been detailed."

"So in theory, aside from the detailer, and any car lot worker who'd touched it, the suspect's DNA and fingerprints should be the only other ones present. Unless he had gloves on the whole time, or wiped it clean, we'll get his prints. Plus we'll have the DNA results on the hood back from the Midwest Crime Lab either today or tomorrow."

"We're all waiting with bated breath for that. Doug, I need to talk to one of the witnesses, Opal Reynolds. You know the bracelet she saw, how it might be Weber's?" I asked.

"Sure."

"I want to show her the photo, see if it looks like the one she remembered on the shooter."

Matsen's eyes narrowed. "You're asking out of personal curiosity, or what?"

"More or less. We suspect, but are not certain, it's Weber's. At this point what some of us have is an ominous feeling about it. When he wakes up, Vince can tell us if he put the bracelet somewhere other than its usual spot. If he didn't, then when we have the shooter in custody, we'll find out what he did with it."

"Not a good situation," he said.

"No, and Vince would be devastated if his bracelet was gone for good. Don't repeat this, but from what I've gathered about how much the bracelet means to him, if given the choice, I think Vince would've rather taken a bullet than lose the bracelet his wife had given him before she died."

"The bad thing is he got both, so far anyway. A bullet and a lost treasure," he said.

"As long as the shooter didn't toss it in a ditch somewhere, there's hope."

"Yeah."

"Anything I can do to help you with the debriefing?" I offered.

Matsen lifted his hands and looked out at the empty room. "If you want to hang out, show moral support, that'd be great."

16

I waited in the corridor outside the room and greeted witnesses as they arrived. Opal smiled when she saw me.

I smiled back. "Glad you could make it today."

"Me too. I've never had call to do anything like this before."

"I've been through several of these sessions, and they've helped me a *lot*. Opal, I have a photo to show you. I planned to stop by your house earlier, but couldn't make it."

"That's understandable, Sergeant. What with all you sheriff's people have to do."

I opened the photo on my phone. Opal squinted as she studied it. "It sure does look like the bracelet the shooter had on, but he was gone in a flash. So all I can say is it looks like it."

"No worries, Opal. You helped us a great deal with that piece of information," I said.

She patted my shoulder. "It makes me feel good to hear that, Sergeant."

I greeted others as they arrived, and was happy to see Brookings' owner Pete there to participate. He hadn't witnessed the shooting, but there was no doubt he'd been traumatized by what happened in his café, and what his employees and customers had seen, heard, and experienced.

Sergeant Matsen was well-trained, an adept leader who guided the witnesses through the session with care and concern.

"I'd like you each to describe what you saw, heard, perceived. It's normal after a traumatic experience for the event to keep playing over and over in one's mind. And it's important to recognize not one of you had control over what had happened, had no power to stop it. It's important to talk about it, how you feel about it so you can move the event from the front of your thoughts to the back of them." Matsen touched his forehead.

All the participants were able to verbalize their feelings and fears. Matsen encouraged them to take care of their health: physical, emotional, and mental. To seek counseling, to eat well, exercise, spend time with people they cared about.

He also cautioned them not to drink to excess as a way to try to forget. He said it might seem to help for the moment but could cause more problems in the long run. I noticed server Cleo give Ed the cook a nudge. When he greeted me on his way in, I had detected a slight odor of alcohol on him.

Overall, the debriefing went well. Each person was willing to share his or her own account and the desire to move on. None could ever forget, but they would not let it rule their lives.

The session ended with an hour to spare before the first scheduled staff debrief.

Matsen got a text, shook his head, and typed a response. "Looks like I'll be doing the debrief for Sheriff Kenner at four."

"With the latest developments I'd wondered how he could facilitate that. He came home to a full plate, and more, then still more got added to it as the day went on," I said.

"And it doesn't look like it'll let up anytime soon," he said.

"Or for the rest of us either. Doug, I didn't speak up, share anything during the session since it was for the witnesses, but I was working through some of my own issues right along with them. And you did a standup job. Thank you."

"Appreciate you saying that. Well, we got two more sessions if you need 'em."

I smiled. "Thanks."

My phone buzzed on the way back to the sheriff's department. A text from Smoke. *Sheriff Heller had a press conference, shared the deputy's name, Damon Wilkins.*

I wrote back, *Where are you?*

My cubicle. I sent him a thumbs up.

Smoke was standing by his file cabinet. He dropped a folder inside and turned toward me. "What is it?" He pulled off his readers and laid them on the desk.

I was too keyed up to sit down. "Damon Wilkins. He's one of Weber's buddies."

"You're kidding?"

"I wish. I never met Damon, but I know he and Vince, and a couple others, have an annual guy's fishing trip. Every June. They went through skills and training together in Alexandria," I said.

"I know about Weber's annual fishing trip with his school buddies, but he never said much about it."

"He didn't say a lot to me either, and I can't come up with the names of the other guys. But if I heard them, I think I'd recognize them. This is beyond horrible for Damon's family, but it'll be terrible for his friends to deal with," I said.

"No doubt about that."

"How can we break it to Vince?"

"One step at a time, Corinne. First Weber has to wake up. He'll need to be told, and we'll see what the doctors say. If they advise us to wait a day or so, we will. It boils down to his condition, and not making it worse," Smoke said.

"I'm trying to think of the best way to tell Mandy. I don't know whether or not she's met him, but it's going to make her worry even more about Vince when he gets the news."

Smoke's office phone rang. "It's Kenner." He lifted the receiver to his ear, listened for a few seconds, said, "Okay," and hung up. "The sheriff beckons. Wanna tag along?"

Sheriff Mike Kenner was walking back and forth across the width of his ten-foot office. When he saw us he launched into a briefing. "Haven County got photos of the motorcycle tracks as evidence, and a Vernon County detective took photos of the scene also, the vehicle, tire tracks, etc. They'll email them to me pronto.

"There is no doubt among the three sheriffs and the FBI that the same villain is responsible for shooting both deputies. The question that came up is whether he's working alone or has a partner. He was the driver with no passenger spotted in the Ford Focus here. And he was the only person on the motorcycle in Haven County. So it leads us to believe he is acting alone.

"Haven has been searching their nooks and crannies since the incident. But given all their caves and sinkholes, it's an overwhelming task. Like they did with us, a lot of other counties and PDs have stepped in to help. Still, they can't be certain the shooter hid the motorcycle in their county at all. What makes them think it might be is because law enforcement was on the scene in minutes and were alerted about the black bike."

Before I could tell Kenner that Damon Wilkins was Weber's friend, his phone rang.

"Sheriff Mike Kenner." He nodded and hit the speaker button. "Sounds good. Deputy Wilcox, you got a reliable towing company to call?"

"Yes, sir."

"Give them a call if you will. Have 'em bring the Ford to our office. We have a garage that's marked Sheriff's Crime Lab on the south side of the complex. Give 'em my number so they can give us an ETA, ask any questions they have," Kenner said.

"I'll do that, Sheriff," Wilcox said.

"Appreciate it." Kenner hung up, and said, "Saves us a lot of time on this end." He checked his watch. "It'll be some hours by the time they get to the scene, load the vehicle, and drive up here."

I lifted a couple fingers. "Sheriff, I have some news about the Haven County deputy who was killed. He was Vince Weber's friend. They went through training and skills together."

When Kenner's face tightened, my stomach muscles followed suit. He looked from me to Smoke. "A coincidence?" he said.

"Doesn't seem like it," Smoke said.

Smoke's phone buzzed. "The Midwest Crime Lab." He hit the accept and speaker buttons.

"Elton Dawes."

"Detective, it's Ben at the crime lab. We were able to extract viable samples from the suspect's hood for the DNA tests. That's the good news. The bad news is that there is no match for it in CODIS." The Combined DNA Index System.

Kenner uttered choice words under his breath.

"Ben, that's not the news we were counting on, hoping for. All I can say is after we catch the SOB, his DNA *will* be in the system."

"Yes, for sure," Ben said.

"Thanks, Ben." Smoke disconnected. "My gut was telling me that'd be the case, but I didn't want to believe it."

"Sheriff and Detective, the shooter may not be in the DNA database, but his fingerprints must be on file, because he's been very careful not to leave them anywhere," I said.

"Good point, and it raises a question I have about John Wayne Bauer. Was he required to provide a DNA sample for any of the crimes he committed?" He pulled a business card from his breast pocket and fingered it. "Wonder if his father knows the answer to that."

"If John Bauer's DNA is in the database, it'd be a way to either clear him or put him at the scene of Weber's shooting," I said.

Kenner got another call, and after some seconds said, "This gives us a whole other can of worms to deal with. Thanks." He hung up and shook his head. "That was Bob Edberg. A group of folks are gathered at the hospital holding a vigil for Weber. Bob said there's about thirty of 'em. With signs and everything."

"I guess it's a thoughtful way to show their support," I said.

"Except there are people taking videos that will likely be posted all over social media before the day is done. Edberg said it's making the deputies on guard duty uneasy. Since the shooter is on the loose, the question they raised is what if he decides to join them, blend into the crowd, try to find a way into the hospital. Edberg wondered if we should do something about it."

"It also draws more attention to our deputy who's down, and we're trying to keep a low profile on his status," Smoke said.

Kenner's shoulders bobbed up and down. "We haven't shared any updates about Weber's condition with the media, and they are chomping at the bit. You're right, Dawes. It does draw more attention to the fact that Weber's at Oak Lea Hospital. We have tight security there, but we can't begin to know what the shooter will be up to next. He's managed to vanish after shooting two deputies, one in front of a number of witnesses. And the other in front of a squad car's camera. We should ask the doctors about moving Weber to an undisclosed location."

I had thought the same thing. Again.

Kenner stared out the window for a moment. "Sergeant, ready for your next assignment?"

Oh boy. "Sure."

"Report to the hospital, talk to the people at the vigil. Thank them for showing their support. Then find a kind way to ask them to cease and desist."

"All right."

"Sheriff, it's getting close to four o'clock, and there's no word on Weber, that he's woken up. In light of his buddy getting killed this morning, I think it's prudent we pick up his personal cell phone. I can send the warrant with Aleckson," Smoke said.

Kenner nodded a few times.

"Corinne, Mandy needs debriefing more than anyone, so after you get Weber's phone, ask her to bring it here when she comes in at eighteen hundred, or she might be tempted to skip the debrief. Tell her after it's done, I'll need her to go through Weber's phone with me. She can help look for anything out of the ordinary," Smoke said.

I suspected sending the group of supporters on their way would be an easier task than getting Amanda Zubinski to abandon her post. Especially when she learned that Deputy Damon Wilkins was the one gunned down in Haven County.

I arrived at the hospital and parked in the front lot. It warmed my heart to see the large group of people there to show their love and respect for the Winnebago Sheriff's Office in general, and Vincent Weber in particular. They held balloons and signs. One read, "Deputy Weber saved my life." Another was, "Our County Sheriff's Office Has Our Backs." The one that brought on my widest smile was, "Deputy Weber is a 10."

I pulled my phone from its holder and took a short video and snapped photos to show Vince when he woke up. And I'd ask him to explain why the thankful middle-aged woman thought he was a ten. As I approached the group, I thought of loud parties I'd helped break up over the years.

This was the first peaceful support rally I'd been asked to disband, and would've rather joined them instead. I recognized members of the community, many active in various service organizations, and they quietly cheered when they spotted me.

I raised my arms. "Hey everyone if I can have your attention. I'm here on behalf of Sheriff Kenner, the sheriff's office, and especially Deputy Weber. We want to thank you for the amazing outpouring of support you're showing here in this chilly weather. You're a peaceful group, yet it's raised some concerns among various powers that be."

I heard a few quiet remarks.

I went on, "And we have to consider staff, patients in the hospital, and their visitors. As much as we appreciate you being here, I need to ask you to leave. But when Deputy Weber is back at work, it'd be great if you'd be there with your signs and your smiles to greet him."

More quiet cheers.

"So if the person who got you all together could give me your contact information, we'll be sure you're all invited. All right? Get someplace warm, and have a good evening."

Some shrugged, some shook their heads, some frowned, some smiled at others as they gathered their things and headed to their vehicles. Candy, an upbeat woman who worked in my mother's dress and accessory shop, handed me a slip with her number. "I kinda helped get it going," she said.

"Did my mother put you up to this?"

"No, and I hope she won't be mad at me that I did," Candy said.

"Why would she? It was a sweet gesture."

"Thanks." She smiled and walked away.

My mother wouldn't be mad at Candy. But how would Sheriff Kenner feel when I told him I'd invited around forty people to the office for a welcome back to work party for Vincent Weber?

17

It was 4:04 p.m. when I handed the search warrant request for Vince Weber's personal phone to the emergency room medical tech.

She studied it. "Oh, I've never seen an actual warrant signed by a judge before. I'll get his phone for you." She returned a minute later and handed it to me.

"Thanks." I slipped it in my pocket and headed to the ICU. I greeted the deputy then found Mandy in her usual spot on the other side of the glass from Weber. She looked more relaxed, her long auburn hair loose around her shoulders. I sat on the chair next to hers.

"Corky, his lips moved into a slight smile a while ago. The nurse said he wouldn't do that in a deep coma, that it appears his coma is getting shallower. I didn't even know that was a thing. Vince hasn't responded when they've asked him questions or when they've touched him. But everyone seems hopeful he might wake up by tomorrow."

"That'd be a huge relief," I said.

"They're being extra cautious, but when he shows more signs of coming to, he can have bedside visitors. For shorter periods as long as he's in ICU, but even a half hour would be nice."

"Very nice." I laid my hand on hers. "Did you hear about the Haven County Deputy that got shot this morning at a traffic stop? Who he was?"

"Levasseur told me, but he didn't know who it was." If she hadn't checked the reports, it proved how much she had isolated and insulated herself from the outside world.

"Sheriff Heller announced it this afternoon. Mandy, I don't know a better way to tell you this. It was one of Vince's buddies. Damon Wilkins. Sadly, he died."

Mandy jumped from her seat so fast it startled me. "*No. No!* Vince will go berserk. Damon's one of the three guys Vince does that annual fishing trip with. They've been friends for over fifteen years, since their skills training. With their work schedules, they don't get together much more than that, but they keep in touch."

"Who are the other two guys?" I asked.

"It'll come to me." She thought a moment. "Um, Bart Johansen and Chase Loman."

"Are they serving as cops somewhere?"

"Yeah, they're both deputies. Loman's in Crow Wing and Johansen's in Itasca."

"Can you think of anyone who would have a grudge against both Vince and Damon? A big enough one to want them dead?" I asked.

She looked down, shook her head, and pulled on the ends of her hair. "No. I'm trying to remember the details of a comment Vince made one time. We were talking about our experiences in police training, how tough it was. There were a few in his class who didn't make it, didn't graduate. Not unusual. Vince mentioned something about two of the guys. He said it was a good thing they flunked out 'cause they wouldn't have made good cops."

"Did he say who they were, their names, why he thought that?"

"No. It was kind of a passing comment. I had a couple in my class who either dropped out or got canned too. Neither one surprised me," she said.

"Yeah, same here. One left after our first week. Mandy, you need to tell Dawes about Johansen and Loman." I phoned Smoke. "Mandy has some info for you," I said and handed my phone to her. She relayed what she'd told me then handed the phone to me. "I'm back," I told Smoke.

"I'll alert the FBI and contact those counties in case their deputies are in danger," Smoke said. "We know Weber and Wilkins were friends, classmates. Is that why they were targeted? We need to get their school roster, see who all was in that class, and where they are now," Smoke said.

"Yes. Also, I broke up the vigil and have Weber's personal phone."

"Good. Send the phone with Mandy when she comes here," he reminded me.

We disconnected, and I gave Mandy a brief summary of what had transpired in the last hours. That the Focus had been stolen from, and found in, Wisconsin and would be towed to our office. Sheriff Kenner was working with Sheriff Heller and the FBI to locate the shooter.

That the motorcycle used in Haven's crime hadn't been found. About the debriefing with Matsen and the witnesses. That the shooter's DNA was not in the database. That Dawes was taking a close look at John Wayne Bauer. That citizens had set up a support vigil outside the hospital, and I was sent to break it up over security concerns. And that I'd delivered the search warrant to obtain Weber's personal phone, and it was in my pocket.

She made comments here and there.

"I took some pictures and a short video of the vigil." When I showed her, we both got teary-eyed.

"Will you send those to me?" she asked.

"Sure." I selected the photos and video, found her name in messages, and hit send. "Mandy, before I left the sheriff's office, my last orders were to ask you to deliver Vince's phone to Dawes so the two of you can check who he's gotten calls and messages from in the last months, see if you spot any red flags."

She made a whimpering sound.

"And the second thing is they want you to be at the six o'clock debriefing. Dawes is facilitating that one," I said.

She shook her head.

"You really need to do that, Mandy. It's been over thirty hours since you witnessed what happened to Vince." I waved my hand toward Weber's bed.

"I don't know, Corky. How can I leave here?"

"I will stay, and I *promise* if Vince wakes up in the couple hours you're gone, I will call you. I'll also make the plea to Dawes and Kenner that if he does, even in the middle of the debrief, they'll let you return here ASAP. All right?"

She nodded. "I guess the sooner I go, the sooner I can come back."

I handed her Weber's phone, and she was out the door. I called Smoke. "Mandy's on her way to the office with the phone."

"Good. We'll have over thirty minutes to get started on the search before the debrief. To let you know, I called Alexandria for the school records, but it's after hours so they're closed. We may have to pull some strings, find a person who has access. Kenner contacted the FBI, and Randolph is getting a hold of both Crow Wing and Itasca."

"Things are in motion then. Smoke, I promised Mandy I'd keep watch till she gets back."

"All right."

"I hope all goes well with your debriefing session," I added.

"Thanks. IT set us up with a virtual option so Randolph can join us. And the sheriff said he hopes to pop in at some point, offer his support."

"Later." I pushed the end button, sat back down, and blew out a breath. We'd had two packed days searching for the man who'd shot Vincent Weber and then killed Damon Wilkins. They were deputies in different counties but shared commonality. They'd gone through police training and skills together and had remained friends. Along with two others who served in northern Minnesota counties.

Would that deranged person be after them too? We had their names and where they worked so they could be on the lookout, take extra precautions. With the FBI involved, they would be equipped to figure out ways to set traps for him if he tried to harm the other deputies.

Unless he was after others besides those two. Creepy crawlers made their way up my spine.

I watched medical staff check Weber's IV tubes and look at the monitors as he lay fast asleep. It was surreal to see my friend—a man normally active and somewhat twitchy when he got riled up about something, and that happened somewhat often—lying so still. I prayed he'd wake up soon and be okay. I longed to hear his one-liners; snarky ones included.

My thoughts turned to Jonathan Bauer and what Weber's reaction would be when Bauer introduced himself. "Yeah, well, I always wondered who you were." Or "Yeah, you kinda look like me." Or worst-case scenario, "You hurt my mother and no way do I want you in my life. Don't let the door hit you on your way out."

I shook my head to lose those thoughts.

The John Wayne Bauer issue was another problem. He was a felon who'd done prison time, and hated the brother he'd never met because he was a cop. Did that give him a motive to kill Vince, like Cain had killed his brother Abel? Plotted, cold-blooded murders were evil. Period. And the fact that those killers felt justified in what they'd done made them even worse.

The shooter had to be intelligent and cunning and skilled and organized. His attacks were well planned and executed in almost seamless ways. Were police trainees who'd flunked out of school, or John Wayne Bauer, who it seemed had led an aimless life, capable of the careful planning the shooter had demonstrated?

I pulled my phone from its holder and selected my search engine. I was curious about the distance between the places the shooter had traveled. Of course, I had no clue where he'd originated from. On the other hand, I knew he'd driven to and from Babbit, Wisconsin where he had a motorcycle waiting in the woods. From Babbit to Oak Lea, Minnesota was 230 miles, or 460 miles round trip. Around nine hours on the road. Did he live between here and there? Maybe somewhere in the south metro? Or had he stayed in an old motel along the way where they didn't care who you were if you handed the manager a hundred-dollar bill?

I jotted the numbers in my memo book. Then checked the distance from Babbit to Sweden Township in Haven County Minnesota. It was 108 miles. About two hours. From the way it sounded, the shooter did not drive the Ford Focus very far into the woods. But he had somehow driven from Oak Lea to Babbit without getting stopped. Maybe he thought he was home free when he drove off on the motorcycle to commit another heinous crime.

I had to wonder if he lived near either Sweden Township in Haven County or Babbit Wisconsin. Or both. I looked at a map of Iowa. John Wayne Bauer lived in Waukon, Iowa, about 50 miles from either place. Hmm.

Whenever we were deep in a complex investigation, I imagined the center of a wheel and how the spokes went out to different points. They were held in place by the inner and outer circles but didn't touch each other. That's the way it felt sometimes, chasing one lead after the next. How would our questions get answered? What would it take to draw the right conclusions and solve the crime?

I checked the time: 6:15 p.m. I'd sent my brother a text earlier and asked if he'd check on the dogs. He lived down the road from me and was a computer geek who worked from home. When I had long days at work, it was nice he was willing to help out. I phoned him, but his fiancée, and my best friend, Sara Speiss, answered instead.

"Hi Corky, John Carl's flipping burgers on the stove and asked me to answer. How is everyone holding up?" she said.

"Between Weber yesterday and the Haven County deputy today, it's been like one hour at a time, one step at a time."

"We can't imagine what you're all going through. Especially Haven County. The text messages we've sent back and forth aren't enough when I need to give you a big hug."

"Thanks, I agree. A big hug would be great. I'm at the hospital in the ICU now, keeping watch on Weber until Zubinski gets back."

"I heard you have lots of security there," Sara said.

"Like the old adage says, err on the side of caution."

"Have you talked to your mother?"

"Not today, but we've texted a few times," I said.

"Things will settle down again, Cork. Right?"

"They will."

"You want John to call you back after he's done burning the burgers?" she asked with a small giggle.

In the background I heard him say, "Not true." My brother was on the serious side and didn't always recognize when someone was kidding. And those times often made me smile.

"No I just wondered how the dogs were when he checked on them earlier."

She posed the question, and he responded, "They were good and I gave them fresh water."

"I heard that. Tell him thanks for doing that. I'll let you go so you can eat some burned burgers," I said.

Sara chuckled and disconnected. When I looked back at Weber, he had a small smile on his face. It was eerie, like he'd heard me. But even if he had been conscious, he couldn't hear me from the other side of the glass. Right?

18

Mandy returned at 7:38 p.m. with Smoke close behind. Her eyes were red and her face blotchy, like she'd cried the entire past two plus hours. I knew the red around Smoke's sky-blue irises was caused from lack of sleep, in addition to the stress he carried.

"Vince's still sleeping, huh?" she asked.

I didn't tell her he'd smiled a little because she hadn't been there to witness it. "Yes, and I know it's helping him heal. So what did you two find in his phone?"

Tears formed in Mandy's eyes, and she brushed them away. "I didn't think I had any left in me." She found a photo in her phone and held it up for me to read. It was a message from Damon Wilkins at 3:50 p.m. yesterday. *Hey, best buddy. You pull through this, okay? Heal up so we can do some serious fishing next summer. Love ya, man.*

"I'll be back." I was overcome with a wave of sorrow and headed to the chapel where I'd seen a box of tissues. Wilkins' words tore at my heart. It was the saddest I'd felt all day, even sadder than when I heard he was Weber's friend, and that he'd died. Vince couldn't send Damon a message back because Damon was gone and would never come back.

I soaked a few tissues with my tears as the soft, soul soothing music played. I said a prayer for Damon's family and friends, dried my face, and returned to the ICU. The deputy on guard duty gave me a curious look, and I gave him a slight shrug in return. Smoke had his arm around Mandy's shoulders as they kept watch on Vince.

"I'm back. Sorry but that message from Wilkins caught me off guard, and I lost it for a while," I said.

"Same thing happened to us when we opened it," Smoke said.

"Vince got messages from a bunch of other friends, including ones from Bart Johansen and Chase Loman," Mandy said.

My eyebrows drew together, "They're both safe, right?"

"As far as we know. The FBI sent special agents to their counties, but we haven't gotten any updates. As far as all the people who phoned and left voicemails and sent text messages to Weber, it's gonna take a while to track 'em all down. Many hours and a bunch of us, so Kenner told me tomorrow's another day," Smoke said.

"The last two days have been long ones, that's for sure. And they still haven't located the motorcycle?" I said.

"No. They called off the search for today. The sun went down just after four thirty, and it was dark by five. Made it difficult to search in all their nooks and crannies," Smoke said.

"Unless the shooter drove it somewhere outside that area. Or hid it in a utility trailer. Who knows? He's been all over the place." I pulled out my memo book. "I looked up some distances. It's over four hours from Oak Lea to Babbit, Wisconsin. Nine hours round trip. And two hours from Babbit to Sweden Township in Haven County."

"Yep, we came up with those same numbers," Smoke said.

"I thought about John Wayne Bauer and how he said he hated his brother. He lives in Waukon, Iowa, and it's only about an hour to either Babbit or Sweden Township in Haven County from there," I said.

Smoke nodded. "Good detective work, Sergeant. And I was able to check Bauer's whereabouts both yesterday and today; he was at his job at the Decorah Walmart from ten at night to six in the morning the last two nights. Also learned from his concerned father that his son's DNA *is* in the database. So that proves he was not the shooter."

My shoulders lifted. "I figured it was a long shot, but since the suspect had Iowa license plates, and since John Wayne Bauer had moved to Iowa a few months ago, he was someone we had to check out," I said.

"Of course, and now we know," Smoke said.

"How about Alexandria's school records?" I asked.

"After the debriefing, I phoned Douglas County and asked if we needed a warrant to get the records, or if they could get a hold of someone from the school. The dispatcher said she'd have a deputy call me when they were available, but I haven't heard back. We may need *our* sheriff to call *their* sheriff to take care of it.

"Reminds me, the Minnesota Sheriffs' Association advised all counties to be on high alert with the unidentified cop killer out there. We have a mediocre description of him at best. We know since his DNA's *not* in the system, either he hadn't committed a felony level crime before this spree. Or he didn't get caught if he had," Smoke said.

"Killing cops is a bad way to start a criminal career," Mandy said.

"And it will not end well for him," Smoke added.

We were silent a moment, then I asked, "How did the debriefing go?"

"It was a good start for our officers and other staff. They could verbalize their reactions and start their healing processes. Not get trapped in the recurring nightmare of it," Smoke said.

"It helped me a lot. Put things in perspective. Reminded me that although the memory of Vince getting shot—and the long minutes when we worked to keep him alive will always be in my mind and my heart—but like with other traumatic incidents, the debrief and therapy will help me heal," Mandy said.

I put my fist on my heart in response.

Smoke's phone buzzed. "Hello, Doug . . . . All right, let me know if you need anything. Thanks." He pressed the end button. "That was Matsen. The Ford Focus was delivered to our county and is in the evidence garage. He and his crime scene team will do a general overall check tonight, mainly to look for fingerprints on the door handles, the steering wheel, etc., and do a deeper dive tomorrow."

"It's after eight, and they've been on duty over twelve hours. It's hard to do a thorough job with details like that when your brain's fried," I said.

"I agree, and since I'm at fifteen hours myself, I know I need some shut-eye. We all do. Mandy, you agreed earlier that you'd go home for the night. If Vince wakes up before morning, a nurse or tech will call you the minute he does," Smoke said.

Mandy nodded. "Yeah."

Smoke and I walked out together. "I'm going to swing by the garage, take a look at the Focus," he said.

"I better get home. It's been a while since John Carl checked on Queenie and Rex."

"Sounds like a plan. Any thoughts for supper?"

"I know we've got pizzas in the freezer," I said.

"Good. Then I won't stop anywhere for takeout."

When I opened the garage's overhead door, the dogs yipped and barked their greetings. Coming home to them, and seeing how happy they were to see me lightened the heavy burdens of the past two days a bit.

"Hey, girl, hey boy." I closed the overhead door and opened the kennel door. They dashed out, Queenie faster than the older Rex. I bent over and uttered words of love they relished as I petted them. "Okay, time to run around the yard." I flipped on the outside light, opened the service door, and stepped outside with them. The air was still, and a crisp forty degrees. The crescent moon offered little light.

As weary as I felt, if it hadn't been dark, I would've gone for a short run, both to stimulate endorphins, the feel-good transmitters, and to reduce the stress hormone levels. I'd noticed, even when I wasn't under much stress, I felt crabbier when I hadn't exercised for a couple of days.

The dogs explored and sniffed around trees while I paced and drew in deep breaths of the cold air. Another good stress reliever. I heard the garage door lift and Smoke's vehicle drive in. When he closed his door, I poked my head inside the garage, and said, "We're out here."

Queenie and Rex saw Smoke and got even more excited. Or so it seemed, maybe because I was. We'd worked closely together on some major cases, like Weber's assault. But that wasn't always true, like in the more routine cases we often had. So I'd spent a lot of time with him on the job the past two days, but it was at work. We did our best to keep our personal and professional relationships separate. But when we worked on the same cases, our investigations, questions, and concerns often spilled into our private lives.

There were times I wished I could block out what was happening at work and concentrate on our personal relationship. When I looked at him, my heart melted. I wanted to hold him, show him how much I loved him, be distracted for a while, and concentrate on the positive things in our lives.

After the doggies had his attention for a minute, Smoke wrapped his long strong arms around me, and I stretched mine around him. "It'd be more comfortable for you without all the equipment on my duty belt jabbing into you," I said.

"I didn't even notice." He lowered his head, and his mouth found mine in a series of sweet kisses. "Mmm. Now that's what I'm talking about."

"Oh, yeah."

I felt his stomach rumble against mine.

"Let's go find something to eat," I said.

We went inside and the aroma of simmering pot roast filled the kitchen. My mother's slow cooker crockpot sat on the counter. "Thank you, Mother!" I called out, as if she could hear me.

"Be still my heart," Smoke said as he lifted the cover from the cooker. We knocked heads as we peered inside. Beef, potatoes, carrots, and onions floated in broth.

"I think there's enough here to feed us for three days," I said.

"Sounds like heaven to me."

"Go ahead and eat if you'd like. I need to lose twenty some pounds of equipment, and shower first."

"I'll shower myself, and meet you back here for dinner," he said.

Queenie and Rex didn't follow either one of us as we headed off in different directions. It smelled too good in the kitchen to leave.

I went through my routine in the bathroom laundry area off the kitchen, and was done in about ten minutes. Smoke wasn't back yet, so I phoned my mother.

"Hello, dear," she answered.

"Thank you, thank you, thank you. Even though you know you don't have to cook for us, we sure do appreciate it. And especially tonight because we just got home from work."

"You're very welcome. You've been putting in long days and need to keep your strength up, Corinne. You know I love to cook, and on a chilly night like this, comfort food like pot roast tastes good."

"Always delicious."

"I keep praying for Vincent, and all of you at the sheriff's office."

"Thanks, Mom. We're working through it."

"Your grandparents all send their love. I told Grandpa and Grandma Aleckson you'll call when you can. Gramps will be glad when you're able to stop by again." My Aleckson grandparents were in Arizona for the winter, and Gramps Brandt lived down the road.

"For sure. Thanks again, Mom."

Smoke came into the kitchen. He was in a track suit and held a duffle bag. I knew he wasn't headed to the gym, and tried not to sound accusatory when I said, "You're going home?" But it came out on the whiney side anyway.

He set the bag down, lifted my hands to his lips, and kissed them. "I need to check on things, and Queenie needs a night without Rex's loud snores." That meant he needed a night alone, and it hurt my feelings the rare times he did. "Corinne, I have to crash, and I still sleep the soundest in my own bed."

I gave him a sweet kiss. "I understand. So let's get some food in our stomachs so we can both sleep well."

The beef was so tender it pulled apart with a fork. We dished up our plates and ladled broth over the beef and vegetables.

"So tell me about the Ford Focus," I said.

"Back in Winnebago County without another scratch."

"How was Matsen and the team doing when you stopped at the garage?"

"Fine, but frustrated because the car seems to be wiped clean. They have the garage lit up like a Christmas tree to aid them in their search efforts," Smoke said.

"This time of year, and through the whole winter, we can't get too much light."

"You got that right."

"They're certain the same man who shot Weber shot Wilkins, given the evidence. And that he targeted the two of them specifically," I commented.

"Yes."

"The thing that eats at me is, why Babbit, Wisconsin? He hid his motorcycle in the woods there, then stole the Ford and drove four hours northwest to Oak Lea, where it's presumed he entered Vincent Weber's house, stole his bracelet, then likely sat in wait near Brookings Café for Weber to stop there for coffee, as he often did. But what if Weber had gotten a call and didn't stop there?"

"My guess is that was the shooter's Plan A. If it didn't work out, then I believe he had a Plan B and would've gone ahead with that," Smoke said.

"It seems he knew both Weber's and Wilkins' schedules and their areas of service."

"Sheriff talked to the FBI and Haven County. They came to the same conclusion but at this point nobody knows how he would've."

"You think he lives near Babbit, Wisconsin?" I said.

"It's possible, or he chose it because he lives nowhere near there."

"It's two hours from Babbit to Sweden Township in Haven County. Closer than Winnebago, but it's still a distance on a motorcycle. Given it could snow any time now, that would make for a more dangerous trip."

"That's a given," Smoke agreed.

"Vincent Weber and Damon Wilkins were friends, along with Bart Johansen and Chase Loman. The shooter may have had something against Weber and Wilkins but not against the other two. Could be there's someone else on the shooter's list," I said.

"That's why we need the class roster to check out every student. Find out who they are, where they are, and what they've been up to the last fifteen years."

Smoke dished up a generous second helping while I was still on my first.

"We need this recipe," Smoke said between bites.

"It's one even I don't need the recipe for. Put everything in a crockpot with a little garlic and beef or chicken broth. Set it on high for a couple hours, then turn it to low for another eight or more hours, and enjoy."

He raised his eyebrows. "Sounds like a good dish we could make with our often-unpredictable schedules."

"Like tonight?"

"Perfect example."

"Except we'd have to get up earlier to peel the carrots and potatoes," I said.

"Remind me sometime, and I'll do it."

I held up my fork as if for a toast, and Smoke clinked his fork against it.

Smoke and Rex left a short time after dinner. I went into the living room, semi-reclined on the couch, and patted the spot next to me. "Come up, girl. It's okay." Queenie jumped up and settled in. My thoughts moved from subject to subject then landed on Smoke. I respected his need to be at his own homey house, at least part of the time. But since he'd continued to dodge the conversation about setting a date to legally bind our commitment, we hadn't had a serious discussion about which house we'd live in when the time came.

I loved the property my grandparents had given me, and the house my mother helped me design and decorate. My one-and-a-half story with two bedrooms on the upper level, and another on the main level that I used as an office den, could serve as children's bedrooms if we were blessed with any. And living down the road from my brother and mother and Gramps was nice. But I loved Smoke more than my house, and would happily give it up if he asked me to.

"Right, Queenie? You'd be happy at Rex's house wouldn't you?"

Her ears perked up, she tipped her head to the side, and gave a single bark.

I scratched her head and laughed. "But don't tell them, all right?"

I was exhausted yet keyed up at the same time. In other words, ill at ease. I went to the kitchen in search of a beverage. The refrigerator held several choices. I mulled them over then pulled out a bottle of chardonnay. A lot of people preferred red wine during the cold months, but I had white on hand and it looked refreshing, late autumn or not.

I poured some in a tumbler and carried it back to the couch. Queenie had taken over my space and moved when she saw me. I took a sip of wine, set it on the end table, intent to learn more about Damon Wilkins. I'd avoided watching Haven County Sheriff Heller deliver his statement, and other news reports about Wilkins. The message he sent Weber gave me a glimpse of the person he was. *Love ya, man.* When I read it I was stricken and touched at the same time.

I lifted my phone, searched for Sheriff Heller's press conference, and clicked on the video. Middle-aged Sheriff Heller was behind a podium in what looked like a county commissioner board room. An American flag stood against the back wall. He was flanked by two deputies and a group of others gathered behind them. Every face displayed the great sadness, the gloom they felt. The backs of people in the audience were visible.

Heller nodded at the group then looked at the podium and read, "It is with great sadness I'm tasked to give you some tragic, unbelievable news." His voice broke and he cleared his throat. "We lost one of our finest this morning. Deputy Damon Wilkins was ambushed and gunned down while on routine patrol at ten fifty-four a.m.

"Deputy Wilkins was only thirty-three years old, and an eleven-year veteran with the Haven County Sheriff's Office. He served with dignity and pride, and his passing leaves a hole in our hearts, and in our office. Our thoughts and prayers go out to his fiancée, his entire family, and his friends."

Heller looked up. "Folks out there, please keep all of us here in Haven County in your thoughts and prayers. This is an active investigation with multiple law enforcement agencies involved, and we will find the person that committed this reprehensible crime. We will bring him to justice. Thank you."

Hands went up in the audience, but Heller shook his head and lifted his hands. He would not answer questions. Then he and the deputies filed out.

I finished the wine, set the glass down, pulled Gram's comforter over me, and fell asleep on the couch the second night in a row.

19

I spooned yogurt into my mouth as I watched coffee drip into a cup from my single server machine. It was 6:22 Thursday morning, forty-five hours after the dreaded call that Vincent Weber had been shot in Brookings Café. We'd launched an investigation that involved the Federal Bureau of Investigation, in both Washington D.C., and their Minneapolis headquarters, the Minnesota Bureau of Criminal Apprehension, and other law enforcement agencies in Minnesota counties and cities.

We'd joined forces with Vernon County when the vehicle Weber's shooter had driven was found there. Then after Deputy Damon Wilkins was killed by the same suspect, it brought in Haven County, and expanded the investigation.

My mother phoned as I reviewed details from the past two days.

"Morning, Corrine. You're up?"

"I am. Going on duty at seven."

"That's what I thought. Last night, I forgot to ask how Vincent is doing."

"We're still waiting for him to regain consciousness, but he looks comfortable, anyway."

"Well, that seems positive. Especially seeing how that poor Haven County deputy didn't make it. I try not to get caught up in social media, but a lot of people are saying they were shot by the same man," she said.

"That's what we need to find out. And if anyone else is in danger." I regretted the last words as soon as they'd left my lips. More for my worrywart mother to agonize over.

Her voice rose when she asked, "Like someone in your department?"

"No. But he is out there somewhere, and we need to find him in case he is after anyone else. Every agency in the state and beyond is looking for the suspect and don't worry, we'll find him."

"It scares me half to death someone like that is on the loose," she said.

Same here. "We'll get him, Mother."

"But on the bright side, someone posted a video of a special vigil they held for Vincent at the hospital last night on the Oak Lea Community site."

"I'll have to check it out. Have a good day at the shop. And don't worry, with so many law enforcement agencies looking for the shooter, we will catch him," I said.

"You tell me not to worry, but after you had that close call last month, when that bad man tried to drown you, we don't want anything like that to happen again. Ever again."

As I prepared for work, I did the usual three practice draws of my service weapon. Then added another three. Sometimes my mother's apprehension rubbed off on me. I got Queenie situated in her kennel with food and fresh water, and said, "See you later, girl. I just can't tell you how much later."

Smoke sent me a text on my personal phone. *Slept well, hope you did too. On my way to the office soon, will drop Rex off.* He ended it with three heart emojis. I sent him, *Leaving now, see you there,* and added an emoji of a face with three hearts on it.

When Smoke had left the night before, he'd pulled my squad car into the garage after he'd backed his own vehicle out. I kept the garage temperature at fifty degrees for the dogs, so it was pleasant to get into a warmish vehicle. I backed out and let Winnebago County Communications know I was 10-8. In service.

Sheriff Kenner was at his desk in the otherwise vacant outer office. The administrative assistants worked from 8:00

a.m. to 4:30 p.m. Monday through Friday, except for the occasional exceptions, like when Sheriff needed all-hands-on-deck.

Kenner tapped his pen on a report as he read. I knocked on his door frame. "Morning, Sheriff."

"Come in, Sergeant. Hoping today's the day we catch that you-know-what."

"Yeah. The sun's coming up, so when it gets light enough, Haven County can resume their motorcycle search. When they find it, they'll have the VIN and can track the owner down," I said.

"That'll be a start. Last night the FBI was able to obtain the list of students from Weber's class. So they will check out each one, find out who they are, where they are. And look for a connection and reason why two deputies from the same class were targeted. Yesterday, we gave them the names of the other deputies that Weber and Wilkins took that annual trip with. But would the shooter go after those two, Johansen or Loman? Are there others, or is he done? My head hasn't quit spinning in eight different directions since Weber was shot. Then with Haven County . . . all they're going through," he said.

"Dawes and I had a similar conversation. It's one long nightmare all right."

Kenner's office phone rang. "Mike Kenner. . . . Yes, hello." . . . A few seconds later he said, "What? Can you start over? I need to write this down."

Kenner's frown grew as the minutes passed. He listened and filled a page with notes on his legal pad. I resisted the temptation to try to decipher his scribblings upside down from the other side of his desk. The person on the other end delivered a ten-minute monologue then Kenner said, "Okay, thank you, Special Agent Maxwell. Let me know If you need us to send deputies up there to assist you."

After they disconnected, the strained look on his face made my heart beat faster. "What is it?" I asked.

Smoke knocked, entered the office, and took the chair next to mine. "What's going on?"

Sheriff shook his head like he needed to clear his thoughts. "Just got off the phone with Beth Maxwell. She's one of the assistant special agents in charge at the Minneapolis FBI headquarters. For starters, since we provided the FBI with Bart Johansen's and Chase Loman's names, and their connection to Weber and Wilkins, she wanted me to know that they haven't been able to locate either one of 'em yet."

Smoke's eyebrows drew together. "What'd she say about them?"

"Chase Loman works for Crow Wing, and had three days off that started two days ago, on Tuesday. But he called in yesterday afternoon, said he needed to add three personal days to his days off. Didn't say why. He lives outside of Brainerd with his family. Wife and two kids. FBI special agents paid a visit to Loman's house last night, but no one answered.

"They looked in the garage window and saw there were no vehicles inside. The Crow Wing deputies they got in touch with told them Loman hadn't said anything about leaving town. They'll talk to other family members and friends today, find out what they know, and keep checking. They did ping Loman's work and cell phones, but didn't get a location on either one," Kenner said.

"That is strange," I said.

"Seems to me that maybe after his two buddies got shot, he suspected something and left with his family, took them somewhere safe until the shooter was captured," Smoke said.

"The special agents considered that. But he's a deputy, so why wouldn't he work with law enforcement to find a safe house somewhere?" Kenner scanned his notes. "And then there's Bart Johansen. Single guy. Sounds like a real outdoorsman. He was supposed to be at his cabin this week for some deer hunting. It's an annual thing."

"Supposed to be? With a hunting partner, or by himself?" Smoke asked.

Kenner nodded. "Both. The FBI talked to his brother who said he was with Bart for the opener last Saturday and Sunday. Brother went home Sunday night. They didn't get a deer, and the brother said Bart planned to stay on through this Saturday, regardless. Like he does every year, and then would return home on Sunday.

"FBI special agents got both Bart's personal cell and work cell numbers from the Itasca sheriff, but he didn't answer either one. Brother said he's got bad reception out there in the boonies, drives to a bar about ten miles away to make calls and check messages.

"Long story short, the special agents drove to the cabin with his brother about ten o'clock last night. Bart's truck was parked next to the cabin but he didn't answer the door. They thought maybe he was sound asleep. His brother used his key to get in. No sign of Bart or the deer rifle he keeps in the corner when he's there," Kenner said.

It had started to feel like a horror movie. "What in the heck?" I said.

"To put a positive light on this: Bart may have left on foot, or got a ride from someone, a friend, somewhere," Smoke said.

"The special agents said they checked the area around the cabin and they only found two separate sets of tire tracks. They belonged to Bart's and his brother's trucks. Brother told the FBI that Bart likes to do some primitive camping, and thought he might've decided to do that," Kenner said.

Would Bart do that without telling his brother, or someone else?

"Did the special agents say what state the cabin was in?" Smoke said.

"Maxwell, the one who briefed me, didn't mention that. They're posting agents at Bart Johansen's house and cabin, and Chase Loman's house. At this point they don't know whether to consider them possible targets, or possible suspects," Kenner said.

"But they're Weber's friends," I said.

"We know that. But they have to approach their investigations without assumptions, one way or the other. Winnebago County's in the Minneapolis FBI's main office territory. Haven's included in the Rochester office area, Crow

Wing County's in St. Cloud's, and Itasca's in Duluth's. All over the state.

"Bottom line is, Special Agent Maxwell will have the class list from Alexandria Technical and Community College emailed to me this morning. We can have a look, see if we know anyone besides Weber, and his three fishing buddies. She also plans to set up a conference call this afternoon with the FBI and the four counties in question. They'll include the BCA too. We'll be apprised on what they know, and the rest of us can share what we know at that time," Kenner said.

"It'll be good to get everyone on the same page." Smoke turned to me. "Any updates on Weber?"

I shook my head. "Mandy hasn't called yet, but I have to say she seemed way better after the debriefing last night. Made me feel good."

"I agree. We had excellent participation. Mandy was able to unload a lot of the burden she carried, got to a better place by the time we'd wrapped up," Smoke said.

I smiled at that. "Sheriff, is Randolph having any trouble getting deputies to fill the hospital guard duty slots?"

"Not yet, and hopefully it won't be long before the shooter's caught and we won't need them to continue that detail," Kenner said.

"So Sergeant, you want to give me a hand, check out the list of unknown entities we got from Weber's phone calls and messages?" Smoke said.

"Sure."

Smoke handed me Weber's phone and the list of numbers to call. "If you use his phone, you might have a better chance people will answer."

I carried Weber's phone and the numbers list to the sergeants' office. The numbers weren't associated with names in his contacts, and that's what we were after. Of the first three I dialed, two had out-of-state area codes, and the other was from a southern Minnesota area code. I got messages that the three phones were not in service. Either blocked or robo-calls or prepaid phones that had used up the minutes.

I searched the numbers on reverse phone number lookup and got the same answer for each one. There was no owner name associated with those numbers. I added a question mark after each.

When I dialed the fourth number with a northwest metro area code, 763 that included Winnebago County, I got a surprise. A deep voice on the other end said, "Vince?"

"Hi, I'm phoning some friends for him. Who are you?" I said.

Click. He was gone. I jogged to Smoke's cubicle with Weber's phone and the list in hand. He looked over his readers at me.

"Smoke, we need to trace this number, identify the caller if we can. I called and a man answered. He didn't say 'hello.' He just said, 'Vince,' and the way he said it gave me the willies. Like creepiness surrounded his deep voice. When I told him I was calling Vince's friends and asked who he was, he hung up. It's in our area code." I laid the sheet on Smoke's desk and circled the number.

He stared for a moment, stood up, and rubbed his arms. "If he was one of Weber's friends, he would've identified himself, asked how Weber was doing. Someone phoned Weber from that number four times this week. Likely the same deep-voiced creepy person. He first called on Monday, the day before the shooting. When I looked at the details of that call, I noted it came in at ten thirty-eight a.m. Weber answered, and the call lasted two minutes.

"That same number showed up among the long string of missed calls on Tuesday and Wednesday. And again earlier this morning, before I got to my desk. It's reasonable to question if he's the shooter and is checking to see if Weber will pick up. If Weber's well enough to answer. The shooter's gotta be tuned in to the media, waiting for an update on Weber's condition, which we haven't given since the day of the shooting. It's someone Vince must've known well enough to talk to for two minutes, and up to three minutes, since it only lists the seconds if it's less than a minute," Smoke said.

"He didn't leave any voicemails or text messages?" I asked.

"No. And now that you've phoned him, he knows someone else has access to Weber's phone. He's smart enough to figure it's law enforcement, and not his girlfriend. And that we're searching Weber's phone, checking calls and messages, and contacts. He probably won't call again, not from that number anyway."

"I agree. When Vince wakes up, he can tell us who he talked to on Monday. And why he took a call from someone who's not in his contacts."

"I answer sometimes to find out who they are. If they tell me I've won a free cruise, or ask me to donate to an organization I don't support, I ask them to take me off their list," Smoke said.

"I do the same at times, not always."

"I need to tell the sheriff and FBI's Beth Maxwell; see how they want to proceed. Let's make the call in Kenner's office." He picked up Weber's phone and the list of numbers, and we headed to the sheriff's office.

When Smoke gave Kenner the report, he had Beth Maxwell on the line seconds later. I told Special Agent Maxwell about the phone call, then Smoke took her through the details, and our presumptions.

Maxwell cleared her throat. "If the alleged suspect used a prepaid phone, we don't need a warrant to ping it, of course. The seven six three area code is used in eight Minnesota counties, but that doesn't mean he's currently in any of them. My primary concern is that he was sharp enough to pull off monstrous crimes against two deputies—one witnessed by a number of people, and the other caught on the deputy's dash cam—and somehow managed to disappear. And is still on the loose. All that said, I would propose that he either ran over the phone, or threw it in a body of water somewhere."

"That's my fear," Kenner said.

"But we need to do our due diligence, try to track his whereabouts in case he still has that phone. We know where the shooter has been. Winnebago County, Haven County, and Vernon County in Wisconsin. We should also focus on Crow Wing and Itasca where Wilkins and Loman live. Pinging is iffy in rural areas where they don't have towers, much less microwave internet, but we'll still check," Maxwell said.

"What should we do on our end?" Kenner asked her.

"Sheriff, if your office can send an email to every sheriff in Minnesota, give them the number, ask them to ping it, hopefully we'll get a location. Sooner rather than later, in the event he hasn't destroyed the phone before then," she said.

"We will take care of that in the next minutes. What about counties in Wisconsin?" Kenner said.

"I'll contact the main FBI office in Milwaukee, ask them to check the counties there. We'd also like to talk to Amanda Zubinski, the one who was with Vincent Weber when he was shot. And who has been at the hospital with him the majority of the last two days," Maxwell said.

"I'm sure she'll be happy to do what she can to help," I said.

"Good. Oh, and I'd like you to check if the location feature is disabled on Deputy Weber's phone. If not, take care of that detail. It's possible the caller Sergeant Aleckson phoned is the unidentified shooter. And if he does call again—from that number or another one—if he's got a GPS tracker, he could get your location, Detective Dawes, since you're carrying Weber's phone," Maxwell said.

Smoke went to the settings on Weber's phone. "He has location services and tracking turned off. So it's taken care of."

"That's a relief. He wouldn't have known where Sergeant Aleckson was when she answered his call," Maxwell said.

"Thank you, Special Agent Maxwell. We'll be in touch," Kenner said.

"Thank you, Sheriff, Detective, and Sergeant. Keep fighting the good fight."

Kenner disconnected. "We have eighty-six counties to contact, not including ours. Good thing I've got Dina and her crew to handle that assignment for us."

20

"What are the chances they'll locate Deep Creepy Voice?" I asked Smoke as we walked to his cubicle.

"As Special Agent Maxwell said, we need to do our due diligence so we don't miss anything. We may think that guy's the shooter, but until we find him, ID him, get his DNA and compare it with what the lab identified from the black hood, along with other evidence, we won't know. So why don't you finish checking the rest of Weber's calls. I'm heading to the garage, see if Matsen and the team have uncovered anything, evidence-wise," Smoke said.

"Sure. See you later."

I settled back in the sergeants' office with Weber's phone and the list of unidentified callers, and started phoning. A furnace duct cleaning company, an Allendale city worker who was surprised when he heard my voice instead of Weber's, and a charitable organization he'd donated to in the past, answered my calls. The messages from the rest said they were not in service, and the reverse lookups led to more dead ends.

The task was completed up through the calls that came in before ten o'clock that morning. I carried the phone and notes to Smoke's desk. He'd returned from the garage and was jotting something on a notepad.

Smoke looked at me over the top of his readers. "Any more suspicious calls?"

"Nope." I held up Weber's phone. "You're still going to keep it with you?"

"Yep, until Weber wakes up. If a suspicious call comes in, we can check the number right away."

I laid the phone on his desk. "How's the search of the Focus coming along?"

"Per usual, Matsen's being meticulous, and it's a slow process. They've collected carpet fibers but weren't able to match them to fibers found in the café rug. Matsen said the suspect's boots likely had smooth soles, or any fibers rubbed off on the walk from the bar's parking lot to the café. Or both. There were a couple of beard hairs on the seat. Problem is, they're not real hair, they're a man-made fiber," Smoke said.

I raised my eyebrows. "Surprise, surprise. Or no surprise."

"Yep. If somebody saw the suspect, or he got caught on video, the beard would be something people noticed Like Pierre did, like Greg the car dealer did," he said.

His phone rang. "Yes, Sheriff? . . . Of all things, so the saga continues. . . . All right. No pings in any of the counties so far? . . . Thanks."

His eyes narrowed as he hung up. "Haven County found the motorcycle in a cave about five miles southeast of the shooting site. They said this time of year there aren't many spelunkers out there exploring caves, so no citizens had come across it. Plus it's something most of 'em do on weekends anyway. Not so much during the week.

"Back to the shooter. It appears he drove away in a pickup truck. The belief is the shooter transported the Honda in the pickup and hid it in a cave with a good-sized opening, likely on Monday. He then drove the Honda to Babbit, Wisconsin, hid it in the woods, then stole the Ford Focus.

"On Tuesday, he drove the Focus to Oak Lea, shot Weber, and returned to Babbit. Wednesday morning, he rode the Honda back to Haven County where he ambushed Wilkins. Then he returned the Honda to the cave, and drove away in the pickup. They're taking photos and casts of the tracks. Their detective said the tire pattern and width is consistent with factory tires found on a newer Chevy Silverado. Their office says he's a bit of an expert on tire tread patterns."

"The sequence of how he must've changed from one vehicle to the next makes my head spin. So we start looking for Silverados now?" I said.

Smoke stood and shrugged. "We'll see. There are a ton of them on the road, but it's not an insurmountable task. Here's the kicker. They got the vehicle identification number from the Honda. It belongs to a biker from Aitkin County. And when they contacted him, he told 'em to hang on while he checked. He'd put the Honda in his shed for the winter last weekend, like he always does this time of year. But when he looked, it wasn't there."

"Does he have any idea who took it?" I asked.

"No, he's trying to figure out who in the world it could be. His shed wasn't locked, but the keys weren't in the Honda, anyway. Aitkin County and the FBI are stepping in to see what they can figure out."

"Without looking at a map, Aitkin is by both Crow Wing and Itasca, right?" I asked.

"Yep, Aitkin borders both of them. South of Itasca and east of Crow Wing."

"Hmm. Well Smoke, you were right when you told Kenner the saga continues. We know how the suspect stole the Ford Focus, but now to find out how he stole the Honda. It makes you wonder who owns the pickup he's driving now."

"Maybe his own," Smoke said.

"Now that's a novel thought, and you could be right."

"The FBI, the BCA, eighty-seven counties in Minnesota, and at least one in Wisconsin, plus every PD in the state are looking for a man who brutally shot two cops. And he's still breathing free air." Smoke's volume increased with each sentence.

I touched his hand with mine a moment. "Some people go off the grid and turn up years later. Some never surface again, at least not with the same identity. Maybe that's what this shooter plans to do. Disappear. He's been good at that the last two days. He'd intended to kill Vincent Weber and Damon Wilkins, but failed when he shot Vince."

"The one good thing," Smoke said.

"He's scary smart the way he planned everything. Stole vehicles from places not connected to the locations where he shot either deputy. He disguised himself well—and in different ways—both times. It reminds me about our angel of death case, and all her disguises."

"Yes, she's come to my mind a few times after we saw the video of the way the suspect appeared as a biker when he killed Damon Wilkins, and like the grim reaper when he shot Weber."

I wouldn't doubt he's been by Oak Lea Hospital in the last couple days and noticed the security at all the entrances," I said.

"I agree. I also wouldn't doubt after he shot Weber—in that twenty some minutes he wasn't captured on video until Pierre spotted him—that he drove to the hospital and saw the ambulance when it arrived at the emergency entrance. If you take First Avenue instead of Highway Twenty-five, it's maybe three quarters of a mile from Harry's to Oak Lea Memorial. Nobody was looking for an old white Ford Focus at that time," Smoke said.

"True. Circling back to Bart Johansen and Chase Loman. It's been nagging at me where they could have disappeared to, and why they did that? It's very odd. I know the FBI has to consider them as possible suspects, but what reason would they have? They've been good buddies with Vince and Damon for many years," I said.

"Johansen and Loman, along with Wilkins, sent encouraging text messages to Weber after he was injured. If those two had wanted Weber and Wilkins dead, and I agree with you, I don't believe either of them did. But *if* they did, it would've been less complicated to arrange a boating accident when they were on their fishing trip."

"You're right."

"Meant to tell you, I spoke with Jonathan Bauer earlier. He asked how his son is doing. When Weber wakes up, as if he hasn't been through enough this week, at some point someone will have to tell him about his father. Somehow," Smoke said.

Yeah.

On my way to Oak Lea Hospital I kept an eye out for late model Silverado trucks. There were pickups all over Winnebago County, and I spotted three in the first five blocks, but none were Silverados. I hadn't been inside Brookings Café since Tuesday and decided to stop by, see if Pete was there and check out the signs he had posted. Pete had left right after the debriefing before I had a chance to talk to him. His vehicle, and two others, were parked in the lot. The sign on the front door read: "Closed until further notice. Sorry for any inconvenience." I pulled on the handle. It was locked, so I went to the east side door and knocked.

When Pete opened it he did his best to smile. A little. His gray eyes drooped and his jowls sagged. "Come in, Sergeant. We're having a little planning session."

Cleo and Ed were at a table with cups of coffee. They nodded at me. Both had wondered if they could ever set foot in the café again, and there they sat.

"Good to see you. All of you," I said.

It was quiet without customers eating and drinking and chatting at the tables and booths. I walked over to the booth where Weber had sat when he'd been shot. The back cushion with the bullet hole was still there.

Pete moved in beside me and pointed. "When the restoration company came in and cleaned yesterday, they asked me if they should remove the booth. I told them to clean it, but leave it there for now."

I didn't question his reason. "Okay." I studied the tile floor and area around the booth, and spotted no signs of blood. "They did a thorough job cleaning."

"They did. It's their specialty, you know," he said.

Pete and I joined Cleo and Ed at their table.

"Can I get you a cup of coffee?" Cleo asked me.

I shook my head. "I'm good, thanks."

It was a moment before Pete said, "I'm keeping her open. This café's been a big part of my life, especially after I took over ownership from my parents when they wanted to retire. It's been a good life and I've never been a quitter. And like Sergeant Matsen said yesterday, even a tragic event like we had here doesn't define who we are. Who any of us are."

Cleo waved her hand at the side entrance. "It was tough coming in here, but after I stepped through that door, somehow everything seemed normal."

"We've been talking about Deputy Weber, how he's been one of our best customers over the years. He was here nearly every day he was on duty. Either for coffee or lunch. When he's healed up, we want to be here for him," Ed said.

Pete added, "We don't know how he'll feel about eating here again, but we think he might want to. He's the kind of guy who runs toward burning buildings and has helped us out plenty with some of the weirdos that show up here from time to time. Vince has a way about him, able to calm most of the rowdies down. And the others? He'd escort them out without much ruckus. He even tracked down people who left without paying, got them to return, and take care of their bills."

Cleo smiled then drew her eyebrows together. "It's so hard with him being in the hospital and no one can tell us how he's doing. We can understand that. But we all believe that he will recover, and when he does, we want to have a little gathering here to thank him for all he's done. If he agrees to it, that is. And Sergeant, I hope you know that any time you deputies or police officers are here, it helps keep things calmer," Cleo said.

I smiled. "Thanks for saying that. We like to have that effect on people. I can't speak for Vince, but he has many fine qualities and one I admire most is his inner strength. So we'll see what he decides: party or no party."

Back at the hospital, I spotted Mandy on the other side of the glass from Weber in the ICU, her phone in hand.

"Hey," I said.

Her eyes brightened when they landed on mine. "Hey."

"Keeping up with your messages?"

"Trying. I didn't know how much the people I worked with cared about me."

I chuckled. "It's not like they all can admit to being touchy-feely, unless they have a good reason to be," I said.

She laughed too. "You're right. So what's new with the investigation?"

I ran through the details and she stopped me now and then:

"I'm glad they found the motorcycle, but now he's driving a pickup?"

And: "I wish you had a recording of that deep creepy voice."

And: "There's no way Bart or Chase, either one of them, could've shot Vince or Damon. No way. And it really scares me that they're both missing besides."

"Same here," I said.

We stopped talking when a nurse went to Weber's bedside. We watched him check Weber's IV bottles and vital signs. And we both stared at Vincent Weber, the sleeping giant.

"After Vince wakes up, he won't need to sleep for a week. At least," Mandy said.

"It seems like forever since he was shot, and it's only been two days. Not *only*, but you know what I mean."

Mandy sighed. "Yeah. It's like time doesn't mean anything right now. We're stuck in limbo."

"Feels like it." I gave her a gentle nudge. "Mandy, getting back to the investigation. One other thing we discussed is the time discrepancy from when the suspect left Harry's to when Pierre saw him on Highway Fifty-five. It was about twenty-five minutes. We wondered if he might've driven to the hospital, or found a spot where he could keep eyes on the café, and watch the activities for fifteen or twenty minutes," I said.

"No doubt in my mind he'd be sick enough to do that."

"Agreed. Anyway, the FBI got the list of students from Vince's class and will check out each one of them. As far as I know it's the only thing they've uncovered that connects Weber and Wilkins, and possibly Johansen and Loman. The FBI would also like to talk to you, pick your brain."

"Sure, anything helpful they're able to pick out of this muddled brain is more than I've been able to do," she said.

We were quiet for a while then my thoughts returned to something I'd pondered earlier: extreme survivalists. I'd heard stories about an occasional person who had been captured by one, or more. Or what some survivalists had done to protect their land, or their hidden caches of weapons and supplies. They certainly would need practiced skills to live those kinds of lives. What the shooter had accomplished with his crimes reminded me of a survivalist type of individual.

Smoke had described Weber's friend Bart Johansen as an outdoorsman who spent time alone in his remote cabin, and also liked primitive camping. I shook my head to dismiss the thought that he was capable of hurting Weber or Wilkins.

I asked Mandy, "So Vince didn't mention any bad encounters with a recluse at some remote spot he and his buddies were at on one of their fishing trips? Like they had accidentally wandered on to his property?"

Mandy's face contorted this way and that. "If you mean someone who threatened them to leave, or else? No. Even if that had happened, how would he know who they were or how to find them, and why would he care?"

"You're right, an out-there scenario I thought of. With so many unanswered questions my imagination has been more my enemy than my friend."

"I get that. Completely."

"How about someone in their class who'd harassed them, or maybe someone one of them had harassed, and the guy threatened him."

She shook her head. "No, just the two Vince mentioned when he told me it was a good thing they hadn't become cops. And then went on to something else without getting into any specifics about it."

"The FBI is emailing the class list to Sheriff Kenner this morning. They're having a meeting this afternoon with the counties where Vince and the other three deputies worked. Also, the two places the vehicles were stolen from. They can compare notes and make sure everyone has the same information," I said.

"I have to say it's a great big relief for me the FBI has taken a major role in the investigation," she said.

"They've basically taken it over, made it their own. With special agents all over Minnesota—and beyond—they have resources to get a lot accomplished in short order."

Mandy knocked my arm. "Look at Vince. His lips moved into a little smile."

We kept our eyes on him, and his smile relaxed after a moment. But I knew Mandy and I both had broad smiles of our own.

21

I convinced Mandy to go for a walk, get something to eat, do anything different than stare at Vincent Weber full time. I would be happy to take over the watch until she returned. I was checking messages when a gorgeous man in a sharp tailored suit joined me and held up his FBI badge. Special Agent Quincy Parsons.

Parsons favored Smoke in looks, more as a type, not as a twin. I drew a mental compare and contrast between them in seconds. Both were tall, lean, and fit, with angular faces, and dimples. Smoke's dimples were long and deep, Parsons' were round. Both had full lips, and Parsons had a small scar on his upper one. Smoke's eyes were sky-blue, Parsons' were brown. Both had dark brown hair, but Smoke's was sprinkled with gray.

I tried not to gawk then thought he must be accustomed to women's dumbstruck stares when they met him. So it surprised me when his eyes widened, his brows lifted, and his jaw dropped a bit.

It was the most awkward moment I had experienced in forever. I wanted to tell Special Agent Parsons I normally had a better poker face, but he was so darn cute, it had caught me off guard. As far as I was concerned, Detective Elton Dawes was the best-looking man in the world, and the last thing I wanted was to jeopardize our commitment.

Then to make things worse, Parsons glanced at my ringless ring finger, and said, "I'm married."

I glanced at his ringless ring finger, and said, "I'm engaged."

Then we both laughed and broke the moment.

"I apologize for being so unprofessional, but your beauty caught me by surprise. You look more like an actor than a cop," he said.

"Ditto. Truce?" I extended my arm.

He shook my hand.

"Sergeant Corinne Aleckson."

"I read your badge. So the C stands for Corinne," he said.

"Most people call me Corky. My mother *always* calls me Corinne and my fiancé usually does too." Did I have to tell him that?

"Most people call me Quinn, but my mother, and some family members, call me Quincy."

Were we long lost friends in the flash of a moment? "I'll call you Special Agent Parsons," I said.

He grinned. "And I'll call you Sergeant Aleckson."

We shared another short laugh, then Parsons cleared his throat and gave his head a slight shake. "A little unexpected levity we must have both needed."

"Sounds like a reasonable explanation. It has been an intense two days."

Parsons studied the motionless Weber asleep in the ICU bed for a moment. "Deputy Vincent Weber. We are committed to work around the clock to find and apprehend the man who shot him."

"Thank you. You're here to see Amanda Zubinski?"

"I am, yes. I was told she'd be in this ICU room," Parsons said.

"Mostly, but she's away for a bit. She's been camping out here probably fourteen hours a day for the last two, and we give her breaks here and there so she can do something else for a while. I'll text her, let her know you're here. Or better yet, maybe you two should meet in the chapel. It's quiet in there, without distractions."

Parsons nodded.

I sent Mandy a text and she responded with, *Be there in a few. Will you join us? Help remind me of everything I said later. We'll be close if anything changes with Vince. They have my number.*

The day was full of surprises. *Sure, see you there.*

I was curious what she would think of Quincy Parsons. Or was it just me? Because he was almost as striking as Elton Dawes.

On our way to the chapel, both women and men in the corridors took a second look at Special Agent Parsons. *No, it wasn't just me.*

Parsons stepped into the chapel and looked around. "Very nice. This would be a peaceful place to escape to in the middle of a tough case, to clear your mind, unload your angst."

"I agree. We have spent a fair amount of time here since Weber was shot. And you're right about unloading angst. Our debriefings help a lot, and if we took more time to decompress throughout a tough case, it would be beneficial."

Mandy came through the door, and when she spotted Parsons, her awed look was likely close to what mine had been. She stared, and I smiled.

Parsons stepped in close to her and extended his hand. "Amanda Zubinski? Quincy Parsons with the FBI, Minneapolis Office."

"Oh, for a second I thought you were an angel. Being here in the chapel and all," she said and shook his hand.

Parsons might question the professionalism of the female deputies in the Winnebago County Sheriff's Office, or the lack of it. He snickered anyway and pulled out a memo pad. "We've been brought into the expanding investigation of the unknown subject who shot two sheriffs' deputies, killing one. He also stole at least two vehicles that he used when he committed those felony crimes.

"He has been two steps, or more, ahead of multiple law enforcement agencies who are engaged in the manhunt to find him. It's apparent he's been planning these shootings for some time, down to the last details. We know how he stole the Ford Focus from a used car dealer in a small town in Wisconsin. We also have located the person he stole the motorcycle from in

Aitkin County, but don't know how he did it. We have a theory, but haven't found proof of it yet," Parsons said.

I raised my hand.

He nodded. "Yes, Sergeant?"

"Are you at liberty to share your theory?"

"Of course. Our common goal is to locate and apprehend the suspect, so the more information we share the better. Our thought is that the suspect knew, or knew of, the motorcycle's owner, Craig Erikson. Knew his habits. One thing we learned is there have been times when he'd leave the key in the Honda. Not overnight that he ever remembered, but a lot of times it'd be parked in the yard with the key in the ignition.

"Craig lives in the country, a mile from his nearest neighbor, and he said he'd leave for short periods of time and wasn't worried if the key was in the ignition, or not. When his motorcycle disappeared, at first he had no clue how it could have been stolen. Then he remembered an odd incident from a couple months back. In August. Craig had run an errand, been gone for less than an hour. When he got home the Honda was in his driveway where he'd left it. It looked like rain, so Craig thought he'd pull it in the garage but the key wasn't in the ignition.

"He'd lost the spare, planned to get another key made, but was busy with his construction business and never got around to it. Craig was sure he'd left it in the ignition, but started to doubt himself and thought he must've put it somewhere when he was thinking about something else. He said that happens to him once in a while. He looked everywhere for the key, more mystified about what happened to it than anything else. He figured he'd need to go to the dealer to have another one made.

"Long story, and I'm nearing the finish line. The next morning, Craig went out to take another look, see if he'd accidentally dropped the key in the back carrier, or somewhere else. To his big surprise, the key was in the ignition, and he was positive it hadn't been there the night before. He had to walk around for a while to calm down, tell himself he wasn't going crazy. He even called a few friends to see if one of them had played a trick on him. They all denied it, but Craig was convinced one had. Either that, or he was more absentminded than he realized," Parsons said.

"So the suspect took the key, had a duplicate made, and returned the one he had *borrowed*." Mandy made air quotation marks with her fingers when she said, "borrowed."

"Good supposition and the same conclusion we'd arrived at. Like I said earlier, we believe the suspect either knew Craig, or knew his habits. He may have thought when he returned the key that Craig would never have known it was gone in the first place," Parsons said.

"It does seem plausible. But last August? That means the shooter had been planning his attacks for at least two months. But it would take a while to put it all together," I said.

"Yes. And a thing to note. Law enforcement has eyes on Craig's property, and we're keeping watch on him also. Until we have the suspect in custody, we have no clue what he'll do next. We'll get into that more at the meeting this afternoon with Assistant Special Agent in Charge Beth Maxwell," Parsons said.

I nodded. "I plan to be there."

Mandy opened her mouth like she wanted to say something then closed it instead.

Special Agent Parsons homed in on Mandy. "Deputy Zubinski, I understand you have a close relationship with Vincent Weber, and the FBI is not interested in your private life together. What we are interested in is what you know about his friends, acquaintances, people he may not have gotten along with. Any comments he made about them.

"We know about his annual fishing trips with Damon Wilkins, Bart Johansen, and Chase Loman. But we're at a loss, a disadvantage, since none of them are available to tell us a solitary thing about their trips, like if something had happened that would've set this chain of events into motion. Weber is still in a coma, Wilkins tragically died, and Johansen and Loman have gone missing. Their disappearances cannot be coincidences," Parsons said.

Mandy sniffled. "I know, and I wish I had something helpful to tell you. I have wracked my brain for two days and the only thing I thought of, well, I don't know how it could be connected to what happened to Vince and Damon."

Parsons leaned in a couple inches closer. "What is it?"

"The guys went to Finland for their fishing trip this last June, stayed in a cabin up there."

"Finland in Lake County?" Parsons said.

She nodded. "Yes, about an hour north of Duluth. They try different spots every year."

"Do you remember the name of the resort?"

"Sorry, no. But Vince has photos. There might be one with the resort name sign on it. If not, maybe one of our deputies or Damon Wilkins' fiancée would know."

"Go on," Parsons said as he wrote that down.

"When Vince got back that last time he didn't seem as happy and relaxed as he usually was after their trips. So I asked him about it, and he said it was great to be with his friends again, but there was an annoying guy there by himself who wanted to hang out with them. They didn't want to be rude, but he was a stranger who acted a little strange besides. The four of them wanted to spend those few days together without a fifth wheel," Mandy said.

"I can understand that," Parsons agreed.

"Same here. They like to shoot the bull about their antics in training and skills, their jobs, their lives. Just spend time together, fish, go hiking, have a few beers. Vince said they ate at the cabin a couple nights. They grilled and ate food they had brought with them. They also ate at a place one night called the Trestle Inn someone had recommended. Vince said the strange guy even showed up there and sat at a table close to them," Mandy said.

"Did Vince mention his name?"

"Hunter."

"Last name?" Parsons said.

"He didn't say. I don't know if he even got it since they tried to avoid him. The thing that bugged Vince, and the others, is that there was something vaguely familiar about him, but none of them could figure out what it was. They couldn't place him and thought maybe he'd been at the same fishing place as they were at some point over the years."

"They didn't consider it might be someone from their class, someone who'd flunked out?" Parsons asked.

"Vince—well you'd think all of them, but at least one of them, should have remembered him if that was the case. Fifteen years later or not," Mandy said.

"You'd think, but they were eighteen, nineteen years old working on their academic classes, training exercises, skills, and maybe thinking about girls they had crushes on besides. A lot on their minds. A young male in his late teens, early twenties is suddenly an adult, ready or not.

"Plus the old birds-of-a-feather adage often holds true. People tend to befriend others with similar interests, similar abilities, and who share similar values. Did you know that the four of them were in the top ten percent of their class?" Parsons said.

Mandy and I both shook our heads. "Vince never mentioned that," Mandy said.

"I know how smart Vince is but figured he was an average student because he didn't say he wasn't. On the other hand, he doesn't brag or try to make himself look better than others, especially his friends," I said.

Parsons' eyebrows drew together. "The point I wanted to make about them being top in their class, *and* athletic, *and* friends is I can see how a person who isn't one of them would be jealous, become obsessed."

What were the chances that Vincent Weber had another person besides Darcie obsessed with him?

"Special Agent Parsons, the FBI has the student roster from their class. Is there anyone named Hunter on it?" Mandy asked.

"No, there is not. And from what you've told me about the friends' encounter with the man in Finland, it makes me wonder if Hunter was his given name or the name he gave himself.”

Every nerve in my body prickled. Mandy stood, did some back stretches, then rubbed her arms with vigor. We caught each other’s eyes and shook our heads.

“I’ll contact our assistant special agent in charge so we can set a couple of things in motion. We’ll check with Johansen’s brother and colleagues. Loman’s too. At least one of their contacts should know the name of the resort where they stayed. Amanda, do you have those dates?” Parsons said.

Mandy pulled out her phone. “I’ll check my calendar.” She pushed a button and scrolled back. “June twenty-second to the twenty-fifth. He left Thursday morning and came back Sunday evening. It’s about a four-hour drive from here.”

“Good. So when we identify the place we can check their guest lists, see who was in the other cabins. This unknown subject seems to know details about the four of them. He proved that with Vincent Weber and Damon Wilkins. He knew their work schedules. He knew about Weber’s bracelet and gained access to his house to steal it, in all likelihood,” Parsons said.

Mandy made a soft moaning sound.

Parsons focused on her. “This is not meant to scare you, but all that leads us to believe the suspect knows about you, that you’re a special person in Vince Weber’s life. He probably knows where you live and what you drive.”

I reached over and squeezed Mandy’s arm.

Parsons continued, “I discovered you Winnebago County deputies park your squad cars at your residences the six days you’re on duty, then leave them in the sheriff’s lot for the next deputies to pick up when they start their rotations.

“Even the least observant people notice law enforcement and emergency vehicles. Amanda, we noted your squad car is parked at your apartment building, and you drove your personal vehicle to the hospital.”

Mandy's brows lifted. "Yes. I'm on personal leave for the next days, and the sheriff's office hasn't needed it. They'll pick it up when they do."

"Okay. You have a garage space you park your personal vehicle in?" Parsons asked.

She nodded. "I do, yes."

"Good. I talked to other special agents, and we think it's important that you go to a safe location when you're not here at the hospital. The unknown subject has figured out it'd be next to impossible to get anywhere near Vincent Weber as long as he's in this facility. The bottom line is, given your relationship with Vincent Weber, we feel your life could be in jeopardy."

Mandy crossed her arms on her chest and bent over in the chair. "No."

I reached my arm around her shoulder. "No what?"

"No, I don't want this to be happening. Vince, his friends, and now me?"

"We presume Chase Loman either disappeared with his family, or sent them somewhere to keep them safe, and went to a different location himself. The same with Bart Johansen. After Wilkins was killed, if they weren't involved—and we don't have any indication they were—then they must have had reason to believe their own lives were in danger."

"Why haven't they sought protective custody themselves?" Mandy asked.

"We don't have that answer," Parsons said.

"Special Agent Parsons, back to Weber, I asked Sheriff Kenner if he should be moved to another hospital," I said.

"That's another thing we'd discussed. The suspect was very bold when he carried out those surprise attacks, but with the robust security in place here he couldn't enter with a weapon. And if he pulled a gun on a deputy or special agent, he would be dead before he pulled the trigger. We don't believe he has a death wish, given how much thought and careful planning he put into this evil mission. That said, we do hold the opinion that he's under the delusion he can kill and get away with it. And so far he has. But we will uncover his identity and stop him in his tracks."

Mandy's upper body twitched. "I'll do what you say because if that maniac killed me, Vince would never forgive himself. Plus, I don't want to die."

22

Special Agent Parsons and his team had put together a safety plan for Amanda Zubinski in short order. They didn't know what action the suspect would take next. But in the event he went after Mandy, they were prepared and committed to keep her out of the line of fire.

A youngish female FBI Special Agent who reminded me of Mandy entered the chapel. She had reddish-gold hair, was dressed in jeans and a brown corduroy jacket. She was there to help implement the safety plan. Mandy blinked several times as she eyed her, but made no comment. Parsons introduced us to Special Agent Tanya Elkin.

A special agent that resembled Smoke and another that looked a little like Mandy. With Parsons, it was happenstance. With Elkin, it was no doubt planned.

"Amanda, the FBI would like to drive your vehicle to your apartment building and park it in your garage space. And leave it there until we catch the suspect. Special Agent Elkin and another agent will take care of that detail," Parsons said.

Elkin nodded. "Yes."

"At some point we'll have someone collect personal items from your apartment, whatever you need. But first things first. If you'll agree to give Tanya your keys, address, and garage access code, we'll get that detail taken care of. Amanda, is there anything in your vehicle that you'd want retrieved before they do?" Parsons asked.

Mandy was still a moment then shook her head. I tried to put myself in her place, to imagine how she felt. Her boyfriend was unconscious in the ICU, and she was about to be banished from her home and lose access to her vehicle.

"Elkin will get a ride back here and hang around for the next four or so hours, and then someone else will take her place until you're ready to leave," Parsons said.

Mandy wrinkled her nose. "So this is what protective custody feels like."

"Could be worse," I said in an attempt to lighten the mood.

Mandy passed her keys to Elkin with a blank look on her face, then told her the vehicle model and where it was parked. Parsons handed Mandy a notepad. She jotted down her address and garage code, and gave the sheet to Elkin.

"I'll give you my number to put in your contacts," Elkin told Mandy.

"I meant to take care of that, thanks. We should all exchange numbers while we're at it," Parsons said.

With phones in hand, we tapped in each other's names and numbers. Then Elkin left on her errand.

"Amanda, one of our agents lives here in Oak Lea, and said you are welcome to stay with his family for a couple days. They have a guest bedroom, with an adjoining bathroom in their walkout basement for his in-laws, and other guests, when they're in town."

Mandy tugged her ear then rubbed her eye. "Protective custody and homeless," she uttered in a quiet tone.

Either Parsons didn't hear her, or chose not to react as he checked his watch. "Special Agent Maxwell scheduled the group Zoom meeting for two o'clock and it's almost one now. She asked me to join Sheriff Kenner in his office, and I'll stick around here until Elkin gets back."

"Mandy, what do you think about attending the meeting? I'm sure Sheriff Kenner would want to include you. They could send you the link if you're some place where no one can overhear you here," I said.

She shook her head. "I don't want to leave Vince, and wouldn't want to risk being overheard."

"That's fine. You're in good hands, so I'm going to take off." I gave her a hug and nodded at Special Agent Parsons. On my way out, I said a prayer for Mandy and all she faced in the latest upheaval.

I drove to Kristen's Corner, my mother's dress and accessory shop in downtown Oak Lea. Candy, mom's helper, was refolding a stack of jeans when I walked in. The bright smile she gave me lifted my spirits.

"Corky, it's so good to see you. Even if it always seems to be when you're in uniform." Her smile faded. "So how is Deputy Weber . . . and everyone else?"

"Hanging in there, thanks for asking. Mother around?"

"In her office. And by the way, when I told her I sort of organized the vigil, she gave me a hug. Wasn't mad at all," she said.

"What'd I tell you? It was a thoughtful way all you people showed how much you cared and supported Vincent Weber. And our whole sheriff's office. Thanks again."

Candy's shoulders lifted and her smile returned. "The least we could do."

I tipped my head toward Mother's office then headed down the hall. The door was closed so I knocked and called out, "It's me," before I stepped inside.

Mother jumped from her chair and was by my side before I took another step. She threw her arms around me and locked me in a death grip. "Corinne! I'm so sad about Vince but happy to know that he'll recover. Any changes in his condition?"

I was able to draw in enough breath to say, "Keep this to yourself. They've reduced his sedatives, and it appears his coma is getting shallower. They expect him to wake up soon, and we hope it's today."

She pulled back and studied my face. "That's a good thing. So why wouldn't you want people to know that?"

Oh boy. "It's not people in general. It's one person in particular. The suspect who's still at large."

She sucked in one of her "uh" breaths. "You mean you think Vince might still be in danger, that the guy will come back and try to kill him? Again?"

"That is a possibility, and the FBI has stepped in to help us. They are on top of things, no question. They have extensive intelligence and resources and know-how. There's a lot going on in this investigation, and I cannot tell you how relieved I am they've got our backs," I said.

"It makes me feel so much better to hear that."

"Mother, I hate to hug and run, but I have a meeting at two and should grab something to eat before that."

She gave my elbow a light tug. "I have some pot roast in the fridge here."

"Thanks, but that's what I plan to have for supper, the leftovers from last night. It's one of my top favorites that you make, Mom. And thank you again."

Back at the sheriff's office, I headed straight to the vending machine area and selected what I'd had the day before and the day before that: a chicken salad croissant. One at the hospital on Tuesday and one from the county's vending machine Wednesday. The county had changed vending companies, and staff continued to comment on how much they appreciated the healthier and tastier options over what seemed like mystery meat sandwiches—no matter how they were labeled—the former company had stocked.

I carried my meal to Smoke's cubicle. "I should have asked if you wanted anything," I said.

"Thanks, I had some soup a while ago." His voice sounded dull.

I sat down before I asked, "Mind if I eat here?"

He lifted his hand and blew out a big breath. "Please do. Corinne, any idea how many balls we've got up in the air?"

"I've lost count. I think in many ways it's the scariest case we've had," I said.

"No doubt about it. It started out as the most traumatic case we've had, given how our own Deputy Weber was having a cup of coffee, and turned into a sitting target."

"For sure. I've also lost count of the number of times I've had near panic attacks about it ever since. Whenever new information comes to light, it makes me hope it will lead to his capture. But on the flip side, it also makes me wonder what the suspect will do next."

"Same here. Where is he now, and what in the hell is he planning?" he said.

"I believe Special Agent Parsons will go in more detail about his interview with Mandy, but one question that came up is the name of the resort where the four stayed in Finland. We wondered if one of our deputies knew, or one of the other staff, maybe."

He picked up his phone and dialed. "Dina, will you do a blast email to everyone in the sheriff's office? Ask if anyone knows the name of the resort in Finland that Weber and his friends stayed at last June. Thanks."

"I hope someone's got the answer. Smoke, the FBI is worried the shooter might go after Mandy, and they'll be staying with her, and are putting her up at a special agent's house," I said.

"Yes, Sheriff advised me about that, and it's a big relief." He glanced at his watch. "Meeting is in ten, so you better eat your sandwich."

I'd lost my appetite and put it back in the box. "Maybe later. See you in Kenner's office." I carried my meal to the breakroom refrigerator and slipped it onto a shelf.

On my way to Kenner's Office, I spotted Special Agent Quincy Parsons as he made his way through the open area between the sheriff's assistants' desks. The assistant who had let him in trailed a few steps behind him.

Parsons smiled at me. "Sergeant Aleckson, you made it."

"Yes. Welcome."

The way each staff member ogled him, I felt it was only polite to introduce him to them. "Special Agent Parsons, this is the fine crew that works behind the scenes and gets things done. They've played a big role in this investigation."

Every assistant stood and smiled.

Parsons nodded. "An office is only as good as the staff that supports its efforts, so thank you. Why don't each of you tell me who you are."

As they did, Parsons repeated their names. I sensed from the awed looks and shy smiles they wore that Quincy Parsons would likely win the election for any position he sought. And given his personality and emotional intelligence, I figured those qualities also made him an expert interviewer and interrogator.

After they'd finished, Parsons flashed another million-dollar smile, and said, "Thanks again, and keep up the good work."

I waved my hand toward the sheriff's office. "Follow me."

On my way past Dina, she said, "I'll be there in a minute."

I spotted Sheriff and Smoke inside as I knocked on Kenner's doorframe and stepped into his office, with Parsons close behind. Sheriff Kenner's eyebrows lifted, and Smoke frowned a tad—not enough that most people would notice—when their eyes fell on Parsons then homed in on me. I smiled and made introductions all around.

They shook hands. Smoke and Parsons exchanged curious looks when they did. "Have we met before, worked on a case together?" Parsons said.

Smoke maintained his slight frown and shook his head. "I would have remembered."

Kenner had turned his computer and forty-three-inch monitor so we could view it from the five chairs arranged in a semi-circle, a few feet from the side of his desk.

"We appreciate you joining us for the meeting, Special Agent Parsons," Kenner said.

"Glad to do my part," Parsons said.

Dina appeared with legal pads, pens, and papers, and passed them to us. The paper was the student roster list from Vincent Weber's class.

Smoke took a seat on an end chair. I sat next to him, Parsons sat next to me, and Kenner sat next to him.

"Ready?" Dina said, then clicked the 'Join the Meeting' link with the computer mouse, and took the last seat. Faces in boxes appeared on the large screen, their names displayed at the bottom.

Assistant Special Agent in Charge Beth Maxwell had dark skin and gold-tinged hazel eyes that moved keenly from one room box to the next. There were five people in our room, others had multiples in theirs also. "Welcome everyone. Since individuals' names are not displayed on every agency's screens, we'll take a moment to go around and introduce ourselves." The 'This meeting is being recorded' message appeared on the screen the moment an audio voice stated the same thing. Maxwell went from room to room until we had all given our names.

It was nice to see Chief Deputy Clayton Randolph in uniform in his makeshift lower-level home office. Aitkin, Crow Wing, Haven, Itasca, and Winnebago were the Minnesota Counties represented. Vernon County was the Wisconsin County present.

"We'll do a recap of the chain of events that started when Deputy Vincent Weber was shot in Brookings Café, Oak Lea, Winnebago County, Minnesota on Tuesday, November seventh at nine twenty-six hours.

"Then Deputy Damon Wilkins was ambushed and killed in Sweden Township, Haven County, Minnesota on Wednesday, November eighth at ten fifty-four hours. Two of their close friends, Deputies Bart Johansen from Itasca, and Chase Loman from Crow Wing, disappeared yesterday afternoon. A note on that: the Itasca and Crow Wing Counties sheriffs' offices pinged their work cell phones. It was discovered both phones had been left behind at their residences. Johansen's at his cabin, and Loman's at his home. We have not been able to get their locations from either one of their personal cell phones. It is our presumption they felt they were in danger, and headed to a safe location, or locations.

"We'll review what the investigations have uncovered so far. This is meant to be interactive, so if you have something to add as we move along, please do so. Sheriff Kenner, if you and your team will start," Maxwell said.

"Sure. Some of you know I was in Hawaii with my wife when Deputy Weber was shot. I didn't return until the next morning. So Detective Elton Dawes will take you through the details of that morning, afternoon, and evening," Kenner said.

Smoke withdrew the memo pad from his breast pocket, and glanced at it as he recounted what the witnesses had said. That the shooter was tall, inches taller than the alleged suspect we'd captured on video. About the cloth hood the shooter had dropped that the Midwest Crime Lab had tested for DNA, but learned the shooter's DNA was not in the databank. About the videos we had of the alleged shooter, the search for Minnesota owners of the Ford Focus, that later turned up as stolen in Vernon County, Wisconsin, with Iowa plates.

That we'd discovered Deputy Weber's bracelet had gone missing from his home, and a similar, if not the same, bracelet was spotted by a witness on the shooter's wrist. Smoke touched on the search of Weber's home, that we checked for evidence the shooter had been there, but found nothing. That in the search through Weber's arrest records, his work emails, and both his work and cell phone calls and messages, only one phone number, one caller, had been deemed suspicious.

Smoke added that I had phoned that caller back, and the man had disconnected when he heard my voice instead of Weber's. All eighty-seven Minnesota counties had pinged that number, but none had gotten a hit, so he had likely destroyed the phone.

"Sheriff Heller, if your county hasn't checked to see if Deputy Wilkins got any calls or text messages from that number, it'd be good to do. It would be another evidence link between the shooter and the two deputies," Smoke said.

Sheriff Heller said, "Thank you, we'll do that."

"It's good for all of us to have that number. Detective Dawes, if you can share it for those who may not have it," Maxwell said.

Smoke nodded. "Sure." He recited the number, then continued. He said when our crime scene team went through the Ford Focus, they did not locate fingerprint evidence, but had found a couple of fake beard hairs. He talked about the robust security at the hospital, and the aid we'd gotten from other counties, the BCA, and the FBI over the past fifty-three hours. Throughout the lengthy recap, I noticed Smoke held peoples' attention as they jotted down notes.

He concluded with, "I'd like to add that despite the horrific event, and Vincent Weber's subsequent fight for his life, there has been a deluge of outpourings of support from the community, and people from across the state. Emails, phone calls, food deliveries.

"A group of citizens even held a vigil for Deputy Weber outside the hospital last night, on a very chilly evening. It gave our staff in the sheriff's office a huge boost when we found out about it. Lifted our spirits. Sadly, it had to be disbanded due to security concerns. But folks posted videos of it on social media, and I've viewed a few of them myself. I've got to say it had a huge, positive impact on me. Reminded me how much good people care. Truth be told, that's why we get up in the morning, and do what we do in this business. Because bad guys go after good guys, and it's up to us to track them down, and put them away where they belong."

I fought back tears, but a few escaped and rolled down my cheeks anyway. People on the call unmuted their mics, and clapped and cheered. All of them did from what I could see. We needed the encouragement Smoke's words had given us.

I slid my foot over to his and gave his shoe a discreet tap. Elton Dawes had given me reasons to admire and be proud of him on a regular basis, but that was a shining moment in my book.

23

"Thank you Detective Dawes for your detailed synopsis, and your sentiments. And you could see how much everyone appreciated your closing comments. Sheriff Heller from Haven County, if you'll go next," Maxwell said.

"Certainly." Heller held up a finger and swiped his nose before he did. "Well folks, you all know the horrendous day we had when our much-loved Deputy Damon Wilkins was on routine patrol, and was shot point-blank yesterday morning. The bullet struck his femoral artery, and despite efforts at the scene, and by the airlift helicopter crew, Deputy Wilkins had lost too much blood, and died. I hate the term 'bled out' but that's the reality of it. Almost seems like a lifetime ago, with all that's gone down since."

It looked like everyone nodded. They'd had the same feelings at some point, if not at that moment.

Sheriff Heller and the Vernon County, Wisconsin sheriff tag teamed through the next portion. They shared how the Ford Focus was stolen on Monday in the small town of Babbit and recovered on Wednesday in the same town. How the suspect's motorcycle had been hidden in the same wooded area. That the discovery had linked Vincent Weber's shooter to Damon Wilkins' shooter. They didn't know if it was a team of two, or one lone wolf who'd committed the crimes.

Sheriff Kenner cut in, "The videos we obtained did not show a second person in the Ford with the suspect. And the eyewitness who saw him leaving Oak Lea in that same Ford Focus said the driver was alone. Sorry to interrupt," he added.

Sheriff Heller waved his hand. "It didn't take long to put two-and-two together after the suspect shot Deputy Wilkins, and was caught on Wilkins' dash cam. It took us till this morning to locate the motorcycle, and find out who owned it. With all the caves and sink holes we got in our county, it made for a lengthy search. But it opened up a new search because the suspect left in a pickup. We took photos and casts, and they match Chevy Silverado factory tires, from the past two years."

Maxwell nodded. "Yes, we need to check those models, see what we come up with for numbers that are on the road. Certainly ask if anyone saw a Silverado in that area that seemed suspicious, or drove by with a motorcycle in the back. That would be valuable information."

Several people made muted comments to one another.

"Thank you, Sheriffs. Both of you. Now, Special Agent Parsons, if you'll share what we've learned regarding a probable scenario of how the motorcycle was stolen from the owner's shed. Along with the connection between Deputies Weber and Wilkins, and the two other deputies we have not been able to locate. Then talk about their school's student roster, and the new insight you gained when you spoke with Deputy Amanda Zubinski today," Maxwell said.

Parsons nodded, and referred to his notes as he went through each item she'd requested. "One thing we asked the motorcycle owner about is if he knew of anyone in his area that drove a Silverado. He said most of them drove Fords. We advised him if he got an odd phone call, or if he noticed anything suspicious near his home, to call us. We don't have specific reason to believe he's in danger since he didn't know who'd taken his motorcycle. Unless it turns out he does know the suspect after all," Parsons added.

Parsons' voice was firm and mellow at the same time. I was far from bored, so it surprised me when I had to stifle a yawn. I determined if he made relaxation tapes, people who had trouble falling asleep would be pacified in no time flat.

Maxwell raised her hand. "Thanks, Special Agent Parsons. Before we get into the student roster portion, let's take a ten-minute break. Walk around, grab a beverage, use the facilities," Maxwell said.

Maybe she'd felt a little lulled herself. We stood and stretched.

"My phone vibrated a couple times in the meeting, so I'm gonna see if I need to return any calls," Smoke said.

Sheriff Kenner went around to the front of his desk. "I need to do the same." He picked up his office phone receiver, held it to his ear, hit a couple buttons, and listened.

Special Agent Parsons, Dina, and I ambled into the assistants' office area.

"Can I get either of you something to drink, or eat? I know we have bottled water in the breakroom refrigerator," I offered.

"Nothing for me, thanks," Dina said.

"I'll go with you, if you don't mind," Parsons said.

"Right this way." We walked to the corridor, took a left, and passed the three interview rooms. The breakroom was the next left. I pulled out the waters and handed one to Parsons.

"Can I ask you a question I hope isn't out of line," he said.

"Go ahead, and we'll find out."

"I imagine you know Detective Dawes fairly well."

I felt my eye twitch against my will. "You could say that. Why do you ask?"

"We just met, and he acted like he was mad at me about something."

"The detective has a lot on his plate, for one thing. And for another, he's my fiancé, and you're the kind of guy that makes other guys jealous."

Parsons' eyebrows shot up. "I guess I was out of line. I apologize."

"No need to. Remember how we'd already established at the hospital that you're married, and I'm engaged?"

We both laughed, and Smoke chose that moment to peek his head in the breakroom. "Sorry to break this up, but it's time to get back to the meeting," he said.

Oh boy. I was both stunned and irritated. From shining moment to rude moment an hour later. When Smoke turned away, Parsons glanced my way, and lifted his shoulders a bit. I shook my head, and we followed Smoke to Kenner's office. When we'd sat down in the same spots, Smoke gave me a sideways glance. I turned to him and mouthed, "Grow up." The scowl he shot back told me there would be an exchange of words later that night. And they would not all be pleasant ones.

Everyone was back in place for the next portion of the meeting. "I hope you feel a little more refreshed after a few minutes away," Assistant Special Agent in Charge Beth Maxwell said.

As if, I thought.

Smoke pushed out a short breath.

Maxwell continued, "Special Agent Parsons, you have the floor."

"Thank you, Special Agent Maxwell." Quincy Parsons briefed everyone on the four friends in school who had remained so through the years, and took an annual fishing trip together every summer. He highlighted where they worked. That Johansen was not married and was a bit of a mountain man. Loman was married with two children, more of a family man.

The FBI believed, given the friendship the four shared, and the fact that Weber and Wilkins had been targeted, that the suspect would likely go after Bart Johansen and Chase Loman as well. The fact that they'd both disappeared the afternoon Wilkins had been killed, indicated they'd felt the same way. Unless one was the shooter. But which one, and why?

"Another thing is that we have not been able to locate them, pinging their phone numbers, anywhere in the state. The FBI presumes they turned off the location trackers, maybe so the shooter can't locate them, given the apps that are available to the public now," Parsons said.

Sheriff Heller raised his hand. "Johansen and Loman are both deputies, and from the sound of it, they disappeared about the same time. They must've been in communication with one another, so wouldn't they go to their sheriffs first thing, tell them they needed protective custody, somewhere to hide for a while?”

The sheriffs from Crow Wing and Itasca were on the call and they both agreed and had wondered the same thing. Neither could figure out “what in the hell had happened to them.”

The Itasca sheriff said, “Deputy Johansen’s pickup is still parked at his cabin. We’ve searched the woods all over the place, but no sign of him. I can tell you as a guy who’s hunted with him, been at his cabin, that if any one knows how to hide, it’d be Bart.”

The Crow Wing sheriff added, “What’s the most troublesome for us in Crow Wing is Deputy Loman is a devoted family man. And it’s not just Chase who’s missing, so’s his family.”

Parsons nodded. “Neither one was scheduled to work Monday, Tuesday, or Wednesday. According to Johansen’s brother who last saw him Sunday night, Bart planned to be at his cabin all week. Loman had requested that his office add three personal days to the three he was scheduled to have off. Didn’t give a reason.”

“Makes you wonder if Deputy Johansen went off the deep end and committed the crimes,” Sheriff Heller said.

The Crow Wing sheriff slammed his hand on his desk. “In no way, shape, or form would that have happened.”

The temperature in Sheriff Kenner’s office seemed to rise, like the tension between the two had crossed the airwaves.

Sheriff Heller held up his hands. “I’m sorry. I meant no offense. Just searching for answers.”

“I understand, and I might’ve asked the same question if our roles were reversed,” he said.

“The suspect shot Deputy Weber on Tuesday and Deputy Wilkins on Wednesday. Had he planned to kill Johansen or Loman on Thursday? Neither one of them were scheduled to work, so could he have managed to lure one—or both of them—to a remote area somewhere?” Sheriff Kenner asked.

Maxwell lifted her hand, and said, "That is a possibility, Sheriff. But a very slight one, and I'll tell you why. I'd planned to share this later in the meeting but now is as good a time as any. After Deputy Wilkins was killed, the suspect moved into the realm of serial killer. Unless he already was one, and his prior crimes had not yet been linked to these shootings.

"We contacted our profiler, asked if he had more specific info to help lead us to the suspect. He said the unknown subject needed a way to overcome his inferiority complex, to demonstrate that he has control over the best of the best: law enforcement officers who carry multiple weapons. He's motivated by the thrill of the kill, driven by the power he felt when he shot Deputy Weber in a public café with multiple witnesses.

"Then he killed Deputy Wilkins knowing full well his action would be captured on the dash cam tape, and viewed hundreds of times. And to add to his glory, he made sure both deputies saw him right before he pulled the trigger. Deputy Weber wasn't able to draw his gun, and Deputy Wilkins didn't have a chance to raise his from the ready position in time to shoot first.

"The suspect is driven by the delusion he has more power than law enforcement officers, and he wants the world to know that, to see that. After all, people witnessed one shooting, and the dash cam video would be viewed by others. As far as why he targeted the two—and maybe four—friends, we don't have the answer to that yet."

Maxwell paused a moment then said, "To address your questions, Sheriff Kenner. If the suspect was able to lure both Johansen and Loman somewhere remote, there would be no witnesses to what he believes shows off his great power, unless he had a camera set up to capture it. There are a few problems with that scenario.

"First of all, who would that person be? Someone both Johansen and Loman trusted enough to meet at a dedicated location? And say they agreed to it, the suspect would need to be well hidden, in an opportune spot, to kill them both before they could react. Plus if he was hidden, the deputies wouldn't see him before he shot them, like the other two had. Finally, he wouldn't be in the video when he shot them, so no one would see what his latest disguise was. Because he would no doubt think it was brilliant. We're looking for a narcissist, and an evil one at that."

"Wow. I sure can't argue with any of those points, Special Agent Maxwell," Kenner said.

What she'd reported made sense, but at the same time was difficult to process in one fell swoop. I'd made bullet point notes on my legal pad as she spoke. I tried to imagine who the killer was who fit that profile. If it was someone Vince knew, was it someone I knew as well? I rolled my shoulders to loosen them a bit.

"All right. With all that said, Special Agent Parsons, are you ready to continue?" Maxwell said.

"Of course. Okay, in our search for the suspect, since we presume he knew both Weber and Wilkins, we turned our attention to their fellow students in the Police Training Program at Alexandria Technical and Community College in Alexandria, Minnesota. You should have received the student roster from the college. Raise your hand if you didn't get it."

No hands went up, so Parsons continued, "We started the search on the students this morning. The seven females we can likely exclude, but it's possible one has changed genders, and is now a male, so we're checking everyone. Two male students did not make it past the first month, and we started with them. We've located one so far. He owns a shoe store in a small town in Douglas County. An agent verified he was at work every day this week, and was easy to rule out. We don't have a lead on the other one yet.

"Of the twenty-three students, we have verified employment and personal history on nine so far. No red flags. There was another student we are curious about. He had average grades, graduated, passed his Peace Officer Standards and Training board exam, but never applied for a law enforcement job. In Minnesota, anyway. Like the one who left the program after a month, we haven't been able to locate his whereabouts either. Did one, or both, move out of Minnesota? Don't know but we'll keep looking."

Maxwell raised her hand. "And I'll add that we've pursued different avenues in the effort to locate those two."

Parsons nodded. "We have. The next thing I have to share is that I had a fruitful conversation with Deputy Amanda Zubinski earlier. She has a close relationship with Vincent Weber. After some discussion, she remembered the four buddies had an encounter with a strange man who was at the same resort as them in Finland, Minnesota. Last June."

He went into more detail about the unidentified man then added, "Deputy Zubinski could not remember the resort's name, and thought Deputy Weber may have a picture of it in his photos. If not, Deputy Wilkins might. If he didn't either, another option is to ask both Weber and Wilkins' friends and colleagues. Or someone in Wilkins' family. Maybe his fiancée knows."

Sheriff Heller said, "We talked with Damon's fiancée, and asked her if she had any idea who would've targeted him but she didn't have a clue. Poor thing is in pretty bad shape right now besides. So's his family, but we can check with them, if no one in our office knows."

"It's incredibly sad for her, for his family, for all of you. Sheriff Heller, if you get an answer, let us know ASAP," Parsons said.

Smoke cleared his throat. "Two things. On our end, Dina sent a mass email to our sheriff's office personnel, and asked them that very question. Dina?"

"Yes, it went out shortly before the meeting. I phrased it that they should only respond if they *knew* the name, so I didn't get a hundred and fifty responses. I checked when we were on break and no one had replied by then," Dina said.

"Let's keep hoping. The other thing, I have Deputy Weber's personal cell phone. We got a warrant to search it, so we can look at his photos," Smoke said.

"Does that warrant include his photos, Detective Dawes?" Special Agent Maxwell said.

Smoke turned his head toward Kenner. "Sheriff?"

Kenner nodded. "When you wrote the warrant, it was inclusive. I interpret that to mean Weber's photos would be included as part of the investigation. Detective, you have his phone, go back to those June dates, see if Deputy Weber's got photos with the resort name on one of 'em."

Smoke withdrew Weber's phone from his front pants pocket, entered the passcode, and selected photos. He passed the phone across my lap to Special Agent Parsons. Parsons scrolled a minute, and said, "As far as the fishing trip photos go, he sure didn't take many. None with the resort, or its name, in the background. None of their cabin either. Just ones with his friends by a lake, holding up the fish they caught. That's about it," Parsons said.

"Sounds like Vince Weber. He wasn't much for taking photos, or having any taken of him," I said.

Parsons closed out of the photos and handed me the phone. I gave it back to Smoke.

Maxwell folded her hands, and said, "We'll do all we can on our end, talk to the Lake County sheriff, identify the resorts within a ten-mile radius of that restaurant. Shouldn't take long to get the names. The question is, how many remain open after Labor Day? I know some do, but most don't. A lot of resort owners head south for the winter. They love Minnesota during the summer, and Arizona, Florida, Texas, or another southern state over the winter."

Maxwell glanced down at her notes. "All right. This has been a productive meeting, and I appreciate everyone's input. Do any of you have closing comments?"

Sheriff Heller raised his hand. "You talked about the extra security at the Oak Lea Hospital, given the collective belief the shooter will do whatever he can to get to Deputy Weber."

"Yes?" Maxwell said.

"Well, it occurred to me that large commercial buildings have heating and cooling systems on their roofs. And they usually have a door up there to access them, in addition to ladders somewhere on the side of the building, from the ground to the roof. For maintenance and such.

"Well, a guy could fly a drone over the hospital, take a look at it to figure out how he could get inside. He could climb up that ladder to the roof access. Wear a shirt with an HVAC patch over his pocket. If he gained access onto the roof, he wouldn't need to go past security at the entrances. Once he was inside, if other deputies and special agents saw him, they'd likely figure he came in one of the other entrances. Had permission to be there."

My stomach was tied in knots by the time he'd finished.

Special Agent Parsons lifted his index finger. "Thank you, Sheriff. Good to have you on our team, to come up with a scenario like that. To let you know, in addition to the security at all the entrances, we have law enforcement officers sitting in vehicles in the hospital parking lots and nearby streets. We are doing regular perimeter checks but it doesn't hurt to add security so we have eyes on the roof access ladder at all times."

Smoke was next. "Sheriff Heller, we all know a person needs a license to fly a drone in Minnesota. But since our suspect thinks he's above the law, and beyond bold besides, he might try something like that. It's good to expand our awareness.

"We'll have security keep a look out for drones in the vicinity. And if they see one, they need to report it a-sap so we can take appropriate actions. Special Agent Maxwell, if we post someone on the roof itself, they would have a bird's eye view of the whole perimeter."

"Good suggestion, Detective Dawes. We'll coordinate that with our partners. All right, anyone else? If not, I see the chat feature is filling up with well wishes for Deputy Weber, and deepest sympathies for Deputy Wilkins' family and friends. Take a moment to read them before I end the meeting. Thanks again, everyone," Assistant Special Agent in Charge Beth Maxwell concluded.

24

After we had exited from the Zoom meeting, the five of us formed a ragged circle. I pretended not to notice when Smoke took a couple steps back. I wondered if he wanted to distance himself from me, or from Parsons, or from both of us.

"Special Agent Parsons, you and your agency have been a godsend to us, and the other counties in this expanding investigation," Kenner said.

"'Many hands make light the task' my mother said, at least once a week when we were growing up. Of course, if she hadn't had six children, and a bunch of pets, she wouldn't have had so many tasks," Parsons said with a chuckle.

We laughed with him. I even heard a genuine little "ha-ha" from Smoke, and that lifted my spirits.

"I'll check my email, see if anyone has responded to the email I sent about the Finland resort's name," Dina said, and excused herself.

The phone in Smoke's pocket buzzed. "It's Weber's," he said as he pulled it out and looked at its face. "Deep Creepy Voice." He held it up for us to read.

I withdrew my phone and snapped a photo of the number for Communications. Special Agent Parsons lifted his phone, selected his camera icon, and hit record.

It took Kenner another ring before he said, "Answer it, Dawes, with your best Weber impression. Everyone, turn down your radios. Sergeant, alert Communications."

Smoke followed the sheriff's directive. He answered with, "Yo." He must've hit the speaker button, because as I stepped from the room I heard Deep Creepy Voice say, "Vince, glad you answered. I heard you were injured—"

I shook off a shiver, rushed to Dina's desk, and picked up her phone. "Okay?"

"Sure."

When Randy in Communications answered, I relayed the number, said Dawes was on a phone call with him that minute. Then asked if they would try to locate it, said "thanks," and disconnected.

I stepped back into Kenner's Office, and shut the door behind me. Deep Creepy Voice had likely asked about Weber's release from the hospital because Parsons had jotted a note that Smoke rephrased to sound more like Vince. "Nah, prob'ly be in rehab for a while. Hope it's a place near here."

When I closed my eyes, I could almost imagine it was Vince talking, and not Smoke. Both had deep, yet different, voices. Weber's speech was faster, choppier, and his voice was on the raspy side. Smoke's voice was smooth. His words flowed at a slower, more even tempo.

Parsons held up another note. SAY GOODBYE.

"Yo. Well, gotta go, bro." And Smoke disconnected.

"I've never heard Vincent Weber's voice, but you spoke with such a distinctive speech pattern that I feared the more you said, the more the caller would grow suspicious," Parsons said.

"Good call," Smoke said. He sounded sincere, not like the jealous teenager he had earlier. "I'll check with Communications, see if they got a ping on that number."

Smoke spoke with Randy and shook his head as they disconnected. "Nope. That tells why he still has that phone."

"Yes it does. He'd disabled his location and tracking. And for added security, he may have a virtual personal network with a browser dedicated to encrypting his internet traffic, further blocking any tracking efforts," Parsons added.

"Boggles my mind how technology has advanced the last few years," Kenner said.

"It's like a second job to keep up with it. I need to let my boss know about that phone call," Parsons said, walked over to the window, and called Beth Maxwell.

After the few minute conversation ended, he turned to face us. "Special Agent Maxwell expressed her frustration. She agreed the caller is definitely a person of interest, based on a couple things. Namely, he phoned Deputy Weber on Monday and they talked for two minutes.

"When Sergeant Aleckson phoned him, he thought it was Weber calling, and answered. When she asked who he was, instead of identifying himself or even asking how Weber was, he hung up. Weber had been identified as the shooting victim, his name was made public, yet he failed to ask that question. When he called today, it was his first question. Now we need to figure out who he is before anyone else gets hurt."

Parsons held up his phone. "Detective, I don't have your number. Let's exchange numbers, and I'll send you the recording of the phone call."

After they'd done that, Parsons said, "We'll use our speaker, our voice, recognition software, see if that deep-voiced caller is in the system. If not, he will be after today."

Mandy's wish would be granted. She could listen to Deep Creepy's voice, and hear what he sounded like. Maybe it was someone she would recognize after all.

A second later, I got a text message from her. *I get to be inside the ICU room with Vince!*

That is awesome, see you later, I wrote back. "Mandy was approved to move into Weber's room, thank God. I know she's over-the-top excited. When she's able to touch him, talk to him, it'll boost her spirits. And I believe it'll help Vince recover."

Kenner clapped his hands together, raised them chest high, and moved them out and back a few times. "Very good news indeed."

Parsons nodded. "Over the years, I've spoken with assault victims in different cases that had been in comas. They had a variety of experiences. One young child, when she woke up, said she'd seen her deceased grandmother. A man reported he'd had horrible dreams, one after another, and it was the worst experience of his life. Some have no memories from the time they were unconscious. Others remember their vivid dreams.

"One young woman who'd been unconscious for five days thought she'd slept for a minute, and felt well rested when she woke up. Another who was out for two days said he thought he'd been sleeping for a long, long time, but could not wake up. When he did, he felt extremely tired. Some remember hearing their loved ones' voices, or other sounds. Some are pleasant and assuring, some are the opposite," Parsons said.

"I've gotten reports over the years myself. People have different experiences, all right," Smoke said.

"I have too," Kenner said.

"Let's hope Vincent Weber wakes up feeling well rested. I know his chest and ribs will be sore, but they'll help manage his pain, probably keep the meds in his IV drip," I said.

Sheriff Kenner's phone rang, so the three of us left his office. Parsons stopped in the outer corridor and handed Smoke his card. "I need to check some things before I leave town. But know that you can call me at any hour until we catch the killer."

Smoke accepted the card and extended his hand. "Thank you, Special Agent Parsons. I apologize for my behavior earlier."

As they shook hands, Parsons said, "No need, but thanks." He nodded at me and added, "Take care of your fiancée. She's a keeper."

I noticed a slight red flush creep up Smoke's neck. "You got that right. And I will."

I smiled. "Thank you." It was meant for both men.

"Detective Dawes, if that 'Deep Creepy Voice' as you call him phones again, don't answer. At least not for tonight. Let him wonder. If it drives him to do something he hadn't planned, it gives us an advantage."

"I agree, the less he knows the more he'll sweat," Smoke said.

We walked Parsons to the exit, and when he was out the door, I turned to Smoke. "I'm glad your skin color is back to its normal tone."

He scratched his neck, and I shook my head. "I didn't mean when you got a little red. I meant the hour you were green."

He glanced around. "This isn't a good place to talk but I need to tell you how sorry I am. I embarrassed you, and made an ass of myself in the process. Forgive me?"

"Of course I do."

"I don't know what got into me. When I saw you with that Greek god, I may have turned green but I saw red. It was an involuntary reaction."

"Smoke, you have no reason to be jealous. Yes, Special Agent Parsons is a very attractive man, but I'm in love with you. I'd never intentionally give you reason to be jealous."

His eyebrows drew together. "So how did he know we were engaged?"

"I told him when he asked if you were mad at him for some reason."

"Now I feel even stupider."

I gave him a gentle push. "The next time you see red, think about this conversation so you don't turn green."

His baritone laugh echoed against the corridor walls.

"My shift ended a while ago, so I'm going to take off, pay Mandy and Vince a visit. She wished we had a recording of Deep Creepy Voice and now we do."

"Yep. If Mandy recognizes the voice and can give us his name it will seem like miracle." He pinched the bridge of his nose. "Corinne, this case—these related cases—have me more on edge as the hours go by. When something new is uncovered, it sends us down a separate investigation paths instead of solving the original crime. I guess it's not that unusual, but it seems worse with these shootings.

"We're waiting to see how the FBI wants to proceed with the Silverado discovery, get the name of the Finland resort, and if anything useful turns up with the Alexandria students. To top it off, Weber's other two buddies are still missing. We've slipped into a tense holding pattern while we search for answers."

I nodded. "It's bad, all right. But with all the agencies working on this, especially the FBI, we'll find him."

"Gotta believe that. By the way, I plan to stop by the hospital at some point, if you're still there."

"If not, will I see you at home later?" I raised my eyebrows. "There's leftover pot roast."

His lips curved into a grin. "Comfort food two nights in a row is just what the doctor ordered."

When I entered the ICU area, I spotted Mandy's new shadow, Special Agent Tanya Elkin, seated across from Weber's bed, on the other side of the glass.

"Greetings," I said.

"Hi, Sergeant."

I sat down next to Elkin. "And it's Corky," I said.

She nodded. "Tanya."

"How goes it?"

"I've watched a lot of people in my career and I have to say Deputy Zubinski is the most patient one I can remember."

"She wouldn't have agreed with you a few days ago. She surprised herself she was able to keep watch hours on end."

"Love, huh? You do what you're called to do."

Mandy was inside, seated next to Vince. She waved and broke into a big smile when she noticed me, then got up and came through the door.

I stood, and we hugged for a moment. "For the longest time it's felt like Vince will wake up any minute, but hasn't. I've been reading about comas, and some people have been in one for years," she said.

"The medical staff don't think it will be long, do they?" I asked.

Her shoulders lifted. "No. So how'd the meeting go today?"

"It was good to hear from the different agencies, mostly the FBI. We got an updated profile on the killer." I filled her in then added, "The energetic effort to flush him out continues."

"I keep praying," she said.

"Mandy, I've got something for you to listen to. Deep Creepy Voice called after our meeting when we were still in Kenner's office. Sheriff instructed Dawes to answer in his best Vincent Weber impression voice. Special Agent Parsons recorded it."

Tanya stood, and it looked like Mandy's entire body went rigid. I touched her shoulder. "Are you okay, do you want to sit down?"

She shook her hands then her legs. "No, it just caught me off guard for a second."

I lifted my phone from its case, selected Parsons' message, and hit the play button. Both Mandy and Tanya looked down as they listened.

"Dear God, is that the killer's voice?" Mandy said, and turned her head toward Weber's bed.

"You recognize it?" I said.

"No, but play it again," she said.

When I did, Mandy said, "His voice is deep and creepy. Icky ick. And our detective sounded a lot like Vince. Makes me really want to hear Vince's voice again."

I laid my hand on her shoulder. "The FBI is going to put it in their voice recognition program, and we'll see where that leads."

Mandy nodded, and Tanya said, "Good. It's a distinctive voice so I would surely recognize it if I heard it again."

I nodded. "It'll be locked in my memory bank forever."

Tears formed in Mandy's eyes. "They'll find him, right?"

"They will. Mandy, do you want me to sit with Vince for a while? If I get the okay to do that?"

"Thanks, but I like being close by. The staff brings me food and beverages. And instead of going to the safe house, I'll stay here overnight, sleep in the recliner." It was close to Weber's bed.

I looked from Mandy to Tanya. "Is that okay with the FBI?"
They both nodded.

"This is a secure environment. We had planned to take Amanda to the house via one of the ambulances they park in the garage here, but this way we eliminate any potential risk associated with that. We'll see what tomorrow brings," Tanya said.

"I'm comfortable here, and my personal attendant is keeping watch." Mandy nodded at Tanya. "They packed a suitcase for me, so I'm all set."

"All right, I'll hang around a while before I head home."

Mandy gave me another hug. "Thanks for coming, and I'll call you if anything changes with Vince." She went back inside the unit, sat on the chair next to Weber, and slipped her hand under his.

Wake up and be well, Vincent Weber.

25

I sat back down. "Tanya, there are so many moving parts in these related cases, it boggles my mind."

"I get regular updates, and I'm with you on that. Whenever we have tough cases with devious suspects, there are times I have a deep-seated fear the killers we're after will flee to another country, or return to the holes they had emerged from—wherever they were in their lives prior to when they started killing people—before we're able to catch them. I think of famous serial killers here in the United States who were never identified, never caught. There's a list of them."

"Yes, quite a few of them."

"The Zodiac Killer, active in the late nineteen sixties and early seventies, is one that bugs me. He sent coded messages to newspapers until nineteen seventy-four, and claimed to have killed thirty-seven people. But they could only link him to seven victims. Five died. Two somehow survived, despite the brutal attacks," Tanya said.

"When I read about Zodiac a few years back—along with some others—I remember his profile cited that he was paranoid, a loner, a social misfit. He craved attention and recognition. Needed to feel powerful. In one message he sent, he said he loved to kill people. Made me sick," I said.

Tanya nodded. "A lot like the killer we're looking for here. Not sure about the loving- to-kill-part, but it's probably not too far off base. Add narcissist to the list, for both of them. When Zodiac killed the cab driver, three teenagers witnessed it from inside a house, and got a brief glimpse of his face from a ways away. But it demonstrates how bold he was, how confident he felt, committing a murder on a public street where he could easily be spotted. It's a shame the two victims who survived the attacks didn't see his face."

"Zodiac was deranged, like other serial killers," I said.

"No question about that. But instead of thinking about the ones who got away, we should think about the ones who didn't. Like Ted Bundy, Jeffrey Dahmer, Gary Ridgway, the Green River Killer, and Dennis Rader, the BTK Killer, to name a few."

"Yeah. Monsters who chose evil over good."

Tanya had gotten a number of messages, and we sat in silence while she checked them.

I sent a text to Mandy. *You are a champion. We'll be in touch.* I added a folded hands emoji before I sent it. She responded with a heart emoji. I smiled at the irony that the person I could barely tolerate, much less work with, a few years before had become one of my closest friends. A critical incident, when I'd helped rescue Mandy from cult members before they killed her, had mended our dysfunctional professional relationship, and boosted our personal one.

I thanked the deputies who guarded the hospital emergency exit. As I walked to my car, I took note of the unmarked vehicle with two officers inside. Teams were stationed in multiple locations and would soon be posted on the hospital's roof.

If the suspect showed up and tried to gain access, he would either be apprehended or dead in seconds. Waves of both reassurance and tension moved through me. We trained for different active shooter scenarios, and were prepared to implement whatever actions were necessary to stop the threat. In the heat of those anxious moments, when things could go sideways in a split second, we relied on repetitive training and muscle memory to carry us through.

On the drive home, I looked for Chevy Silverados and pondered the unknown suspect's identity for the umpteenth time. It was believed the shooter was the one we called Deep Creepy Voice. He knew enough about Vincent Weber to have his personal cell phone number, yet he was not in Weber's contacts. Whatever that meant. Vince had kept the same number with the northern Minnesota area code since his college days.

In any case, Deep Creepy Voice was someone Weber could identify when he woke up. If the suspect's game plan was to kill Bart Johansen and Chase Loman, but didn't know where they were, there was no telling what he would do next.

Neither Sheriff Kenner, Smoke, Mandy, nor I recognized Deep Creepy's voice, and it was possible he'd disguised it somewhat, as he had disguised his appearance. I wonder if he was someone who lived in the area among us. Someone I knew.

The toughest cases we had worked on over the years involved unlikely suspects that were guilty of the crimes, sometimes heinous ones. A successful veterinarian. A quiet woman who cleaned a facility. A personal care attendant. A University of Minnesota laboratory researcher. A pharmacist. And the list went on.

I parked in my driveway and heard Queenie and Rex's excited barks from inside the garage kennel. It was another long day, but shorter than the last two had been. I opened the kennel door and we greeted each other, then headed outside so the dogs could run around.

The sun had set an hour before. The temperature was brisk and the sky was clear. I breathed in the cool air and looked up at the sky for some mental energy. The moon was halfway to full, waxing gibbous. My eyes moved to the planet Jupiter. After the moon, it was the next brightest object in the sky, followed by Venus, visible in the first hours after sunset, and before sunrise. It was called the Evening Star or Morning Star, planet or not.

I was in my otherwise dark backyard when I heard a vehicle's tires slowly crunching on the gravel road out front. When it sounded like it had come to a stop, I glanced around the side of the house to check if I had an unexpected visitor. I felt some relief when I noticed it wasn't a pickup truck, much less a Silverado. Not that I was paranoid or anything.

The dogs also heard it, and barked as they ran toward the road. I hung in the background, and my heart rate sped up as I waited. A smaller black SUV that looked like a Buick continued slowly south down Brandt Avenue.

We didn't have much traffic on our township road, and it alerted me when a vehicle stopped near my house. The lights were off inside, but it was not an optimum time for a burglar to pay a visit anyway. The squad car in the driveway was a good warning sign to anyone with criminal intent. Unless someone with criminal intent had followed me, and had discovered where I lived.

Queenie and Rex returned to me, and we headed into the house through the garage. I had motion detection cameras, and they activated when a person or critter was eight feet from my home. Like business owners who didn't want to pick up highway traffic, I didn't need to pick up Brandt Avenue traffic. I attended to the dogs then stepped into a hot shower. The hot jet streams helped ease the tension in my neck and shoulders. After I'd soaped and rinsed and dried, I put on my usual flannel pajama bottoms, tank top, zippered hooded sweatshirt, and wool socks. All set to set up plates of leftovers, and wait for my love to come home.

I gave Queenie and Rex each a large milk bone. "Hey, let's go chill in the living room till our favorite man gets here." They ran ahead of me, dropped their bones on the rug, then worked their jaws as they crunched and chewed.

I sat on the couch, stretched my legs, and propped my feet on the coffee table. I answered a series of text messages, watched the dogs, then stared at nothing. Another day filled with events and information I needed quiet time to mull over. I tuned out the dogs' gnawing sounds, leaned back, and closed my eyes.

Deep Creepy's voice echoed in my mind. Everyone associated with Vincent Weber needed to listen to that recording. Mandy didn't recognize his voice. When Bart Johansen and Chase Loman emerged from wherever they were hiding, maybe they could identify him. If not, at least they could name the resort, and give the FBI more details about that Hunter character.

My heart ached again when I thought about Damon Wilkins' fiancée, family, friends, and his tragic, senseless murder. I heard the overhead garage door open, and the dogs were out of the room before I got off the couch. They always got Smoke's attention first. He smelled of woodsy eucalyptus soap and was dressed in sweat pants and a long-sleeved T-shirt. He'd hung his jacket on a hook by the door.

"You showered at the office?" I asked.

"No. I stopped at my place to check on things, seeing how I may be here all night. If that's okay?"

I gave him a kiss. "More than okay."

Smoke wrapped his arms around me, buried his head in my neck for a moment, then started nibbling. "How can you put up with a guy like me?"

"Let me count the ways," I said with a giggle; he was tickling me.

"I was thinking after another late dinner, maybe we could turn in a little earlier. Early to bed, early to rise. It's been late to bed, early to rise the last couple days," he said.

"It has, and your suggestion sounds like a dream come true about now. If you'd have given me a ten-minute warning, I would've gotten our food ready."

He pulled back, kissed the tip of my nose, and chuckled. "I think I can wait the ninety seconds it takes to warm a plate in the microwave."

I gave his chest a gentle push. "Good to know."

"Corinne, I have to tell you again how sorry I am for the way I acted around Special Agent Parsons, how I treated both of you. Especially you. I'm not pleased with myself when I act like a Neanderthal."

"Good thing it's a rare occurrence." I gave him another gentle push. "But don't let it happen again," I said with a grin.

From dinner until we finally fell asleep, it was the best night together we'd had all week.

26

The Friday morning sky was clear, and I got another glimpse of Venus before the sun rose. Another clear, sunny day. It helped elevate my mood, a little at least. I said another prayer for Vince and wondered how Mandy's night had gone in the recliner next to him, trying to sleep when medical staff made their regular rounds. I'd check on them in an hour or so.

After the dogs were fed and settled in the kennel, I headed to my squad car, climbed in, and started the engine. Equipment and buttons lit up, came to life. The variety of sounds they produced reminded me of when I walked into rooms where people with different voices talked at the same time. I radioed Communications I was 10-8, and let the car warm up as I ran through previous, and pending, calls on my laptop. I'd been on special duty the last days but still checked to see if any calls had been assigned to me. None.

When I got to the office, the sheriff's administration area was quiet. It was early, and no admin staff had reported for work yet. Sheriff Kenner's office was dark as well. I headed to Smoke's cubicle and found him at his desk.

He looked up and smiled until a frown replaced it seconds later. "The FBI can't seem to locate Craig, the motorcycle owner up in Aitkin County."

I sank onto the chair. "What do you mean?"

"Special Agent Parsons tried calling him several times yesterday, afternoon and evening. They wanted him to listen to the Deep Creepy Voice recording, find out if he recognized it.

But he didn't pick up, and Parsons left a couple voicemails that Craig didn't return. So he had the special agent from the Duluth territory office, who was watching his house at the time, knock on his door. Got no answer. Craig's pickup was still in the driveway, and the special agent never saw him leave.

"The agent looked in the windows in case Craig had a medical emergency and was unconscious. He didn't see Craig, but he couldn't see all the corners of the house. The special agent considered it exigent circumstances and let himself in. No Craig. He couldn't locate him anywhere. Not In his house, or garage, or shed," Smoke said.

I puffed out my breath. "Can the good guys quit disappearing, please? What does the FBI think happened to him?"

"They don't know. The FBI had told Craig they'd watch his place, and Craig said it wasn't necessary. A lot of people who live in rural areas develop special skills, ones that Craig likely has. He must have figured he could protect himself. But the FBI put a watch on his place anyway, without telling Craig."

"Hmm." It gave me a hunch about what had triggered his disappearance.

"The FBI thinks Craig left via his back door and headed into the woods. Where he went, and why, is to be determined," Smoke said.

"Let me take a stab at this. One of two things: Craig spotted the special agent and didn't like the way they went against his wishes. There are people who don't trust the government. If it's not that, then maybe after the FBI told him their plans, Craig thought more about it, got worried that maybe he knew the shooter—but not who he was—and went into hiding. So if the shooter came after him, he wouldn't find him," I said.

"You're saying Craig disappeared for reasons similar to those we believe Johansen and Loman had?"

I shrugged. "Seems like it. I don't know Weber's deputy friends. Or Craig, of course. But if I were in any of their shoes, I might take cover somewhere until the shooter was caught. He is the worst of the worst. I might turn my phone location tracker off and not tell anyone where I was."

Smoke's eyes narrowed. "You wouldn't even tell me?"

I frowned back at him. "Quit looking at me like that. If it was a matter of life or death, then yes, even you."

He pinched the muscles on the back of his neck. "I guess when you put it that way. Loman likely feared for his family, and either took them, or sent them somewhere to protect them. A helluva dilemma, all the way around. As far as phone calls and messages, Haven County has been searching through Damon Wilkins' arrest records, emails, and cell phones.

"Crow Wing and Itasca are going through their deputies' work emails and arrest records, looking for possible clues they could link to their disappearances. The FBI is still searching, tracking down fellow students, seeing what their work histories have been, where they're at now.

"And they got no hits on either the facial recognition— which was a long shot. Or the voice recognition. It's believed the shooter disguised his voice, anyway."

Smoke's office phone rang. He glanced at its face and shrugged. "Detective Dawes." His face tightened as he stood, hit the speaker button, and mouthed, "Chase Loman." I jumped up and rolled my shoulders. A lower, hoarse voice said, "Bart Johansen's with me. You might've figured that out by now. First off, how is Vince? There haven't been any updates posted since that first day."

"He's hanging in there, still in the hospital." I sensed Smoke didn't want to get into any details. It might be the killer on the other end, and not Loman.

"After what happened to Damon, it's a great relief to hear that about Vince," Loman said.

Smoke cleared his throat. "How about the both of you, are you okay?"

"We are, yes," Loman said.

"Good to hear that. Your counties, and the FBI, have been involved in the search to locate you two."

"After Vince was shot, and Damon was killed, we figured our deputy friends would've put two and two together, that we'd gone somewhere for a while, either because we needed to get away, or because we wondered if we were the next targets.

"But the FBI? We thought the BCA would be called in, and should've known the FBI would too. But we didn't see any reports on the news that they were looking for us," Loman said.

"No, and that was by design. I'm curious, why are you calling me and not your own sheriffs?" Smoke asked.

"You issued the statement about Vince. You're the lead detective working the case, and know more about it than our sheriffs would. And Haven County's dealing with Damon's death."

"Deputy Loman, do you have any idea who might've shot your friends?"

"No, or we would've let authorities know right away. It's been torturing us. When Vince got shot in the café, we thought it was a sick guy who wanted to kill a cop. A random act. Then Damon was ambushed on a rural road, about three hours south of where Vince was shot. Not random. We had no idea if it was the two of them the guy was after for some reason, or if he planned to kill all four of us," Loman said.

"An awful predicament," Smoke said.

"The worst. Bart was at his cabin, and I tried to reach him about Vince, but couldn't get through. He went into town for dinner late afternoon on Tuesday, and saw it on the news. He pulled out his phone to call me, and that's when he saw missed calls, from me and others. He phoned me, and we cried together, wanted to go see Vince, but thought we should wait a couple days. Both of us talked to Damon that night. And cried with him too.

"Then the next day, when I heard about Damon, I tried to reach Bart again. He finally got a signal when he was walking in the woods that afternoon, and saw my message. He called and we grieved together for a while. Then we started wracking our brains, wondering if we were next. We put a game plan together in about two minutes.

"I told Bart to grab a bag with some essentials, leave his truck at his cabin, that I'd pick him up in about two hours. He didn't want to leave any kind of trail, so he told me he'd walk out from the cabin, and meet me by a driveway outside of Deer River. He gave me the fire number."

Smoke said, "All right, I'm going to ask you to stop there, and give us the rest of the details when we can meet with the FBI, and your county sheriffs. Your safety is a top priority until we have the shooter in custody. Where are you now?"

"Here in Winnebago County—"

What?

Smoke's eyebrows shot up.

"—at the regional park north of Emerald Lake."

"Okay. I need to run this by my sheriff and an FBI special agent assigned to the investigation. I'm going to suggest we have you drive to our evidence garage and park your vehicle in there until we can come up with a game plan. One that ensures your safety. But I have a couple questions first. What's the name of the resort you guys stayed at in Finland last June?"

"Crooked Lake Resort."

"Okay. A man by the name of Hunter was there. We don't know if it's his first or last name. Did you get his other name?"

"No, just Hunter, and he was an odd duck. Why do you ask?" Loman said.

"One of the trails we're following. I'll get back to you shortly," Smoke said.

"Thank you, Detective Dawes."

As Smoke replaced the phone on the receiver, I noticed his hands trembled a bit. Like my insides. I touched his arm. "You okay?"

He moved his hands in and out of a series of fists. "Need to recover from the adrenaline rush. A shock, and a big relief, at the same time. I felt a little overcome for a minute."

I slipped my hands into his, squeezed them, and smiled. "You softie, you."

His shoulders lifted. "I'll see if Sheriff's in his office." When Kenner picked up, Smoke said, "You're never gonna believe this. We'll be right there."

When Smoke delivered the news, Sheriff Kenner stood and paced around his office throughout their conversation. "I think bringing the two here is a sound plan, Dawes. Let's see if we can get Special Agent Maxwell on the line. If not, I have Special Agent Parsons' cell number."

Maxwell didn't answer, but Parsons did. Sheriff Kenner gave him the lowdown. After a few-minute conversation, they disconnected. "Parsons will be on his way and estimates it'll be about thirty minutes. He wants to be here before Johansen and Loman arrive, so we'll wait until Parsons gets here. Detective, let the pair know we're making the arrangements, but it'll be forty-five minutes, or so."

"Will do."

Fifty minutes later, Special Agent Quincy Parsons and Special Agent Tanya Elkin waited outside the evidence garage dressed in coveralls, with brooms in hand. We had Johansen's and Loman's photos, and felt confident they were who they said they were. Nor should they have reason to enter a sheriff's evidence garage under false pretenses. But that sliver of doubt still existed until we'd seen the whites of their eyes, and had verified their identities.

Sheriff Kenner, Smoke, and I waited in the garage with Matsen and his team, Joel Ortiz, and Bruce Holman. Four cameras were mounted above the outside garage doors, pointed in different directions. We watched the live feed on the monitors that hung on the inside walls.

When a silver Ford Escape—what Loman had said to look for—pulled up to the garage overhead door, the special agents approached the vehicle. The two had been told they'd be checked before they gained entry. We watched as they handed their drivers' licenses, and sheriffs' IDs, to Parsons and Elkin. Parsons nodded, and gave Matsen a discreet thumbs up sign.

Matsen pushed the garage door opener. When the SUV and special agents were inside, he closed it again.

Loman climbed from the driver's side, and Johansen from the passenger's. They looked rough yet relieved, like they'd been lost in the wilderness, and had found their way back to civilization. Both extended their hands, and moved from one to the next, as they shook hands in our welcome home reception line. As we shook their hands, most of us added one-arm hugs.

"Your weapons are secured in the back of your vehicle, correct?" Parsons said.

"Yes," they said together.

"Good. It's not that we don't trust you, but it makes us feel more comfortable until we get things sorted out," he said.

"We understand," Johansen said. He was bigger than Loman, a few inches taller, forty or so pounds heavier, and had a higher, cleaner voice.

Parsons looked from Matsen to Ortiz to Holman. "We need to keep these deputies' identities under wraps. No other personnel in the sheriff's office, or anyone else, can know who they are until we catch the cop killer. If anyone asks, tell them they're with the FBI. Let them assume they're undercover agents."

They nodded, and raised their right hands like they were swearing to it.

"Of course, that applies to all of us," Sheriff Kenner said, then led the way for the deputies, special agents, Smoke, and me through the garage, down the back corridor, up the steps to the sheriff's office administration area, then into his office.

Chairs had been brought in to accommodate us, and arranged so we could all see Kenner's computer monitor for a Zoom meeting. Assistant Special Agent in Charge Beth Maxwell was not available that morning.

"All right, Deputies Loman and Johansen, your sheriffs will be mighty glad to see you. Take the seats front and center." Kenner pointed at the monitor. "You can see they're both waiting to be let in the Zoom meeting."

Parsons said, "And when we spoke to them earlier, we asked that they attend alone, and not yet discuss their deputies' reappearance with anyone, not even their command staff. As a side note, this office is about sound proof, unless you yell. So we'll keep our voices down, all right?"

Sheriff Kenner started the meeting, and let the other sheriffs in. He welcomed them, and asked that we introduce ourselves to Special Agent Elkin, who hadn't been with us the day before.

The Crow Wing and Itasca County sheriffs were indeed over-the-moon relieved their deputies were safe. Loman recapped what he'd told Smoke on the phone, then Johansen launched into more details.

"After Chase picked me up by Deer River, we headed to Duluth, got a room at the Canal Park Lodge, and holed up there. No real clue what the hell was going on. Still don't have one. But after what happened to Vince and Damon, we had a bad feeling one of us would be next. We're trained to respond to just about anything but the shooter's surprise attacks really put us on edge," Johansen said.

Loman continued, "So we decided to stay away from our families, our homes, our counties, in the event the killer came looking for us. I sent my wife and kids to her sister's house in Detroit Lakes. We followed the news, and since there was nothing about us reported, we figured people thought we needed a getaway. Or some might've figured we'd gone into hiding. We'd hoped the killer would've been captured before this. Of course. And since he hasn't, we knew we needed to do whatever we could to help track him down. And get word to our families and friends that we're safe."

Parsons nodded. "You did the right thing coming forward, deputies. We'd like to find out more about your encounters with the man in Finland. The one who called himself Hunter. Amanda Zubinski knew a little about him. But since Deputy Weber is still in a coma, he hasn't been able to tell us more."

Johansen and Loman both jumped up. One said, "*A coma?*" And the other said, "*What?*"

Smoke raised his hands. "I didn't want to get into details on the phone earlier, sorry. And I didn't think to tell you before the meeting. It's not public information, so we've kept it as quiet as possible."

"But he'll be okay?" Loman asked.

"The medical staff believe he could wake up at any time," Smoke said.

They nodded and sat down again. "So how is Mandy holding up?" Loman asked.

I raised my hand. "She's by his side, and the FBI, Winnebago County, and our partner counties are keeping watch to keep both of them safe."

"Good to hear," Johansen said.

Parsons recapped what Mandy had told him about Hunter, then Johansen said, "He acted weird, all right. Like he wanted to fit in but didn't know how. And we didn't encourage him, either. When we had a campfire, he would sit on a chair by his cabin and watch us."

"And when we went to the Trestle Inn, he showed up there too. Vince said, 'I think he followed us here.' We agreed with him," Loman said.

"One time Vince asked him, 'Should I know you from somewhere?' The guy looked at Vince, and said, 'I don't know. Should you?' It almost sounded like a taunt. An odd response for sure," Johansen added.

Special Agent Parsons said, "Now would be a good time for you to hear the voice recording we have of a man who called Deputy Weber a few times. Detective Dawes answered in his best Weber voice on this call." Parsons found the recording in his phone and played it for them.

They bent their heads to better concentrate, and shook their heads when it ended. "Detective Dawes, you sounded a lot like Vince, but I don't know who the other guy is," Johansen said.

"Me either," Loman agreed.

"Anything more to add about Hunter at the lodge?" Parsons asked.

"Maybe if I think about it some more," Loman said.

"All right. Detective Dawes, if you will give the deputies an overview of what has unfolded the last three-plus days, we can fill in more details later," Parsons said.

"Will do." Smoke spoke for about fifteen minutes and ended with, "Do you know a Craig Erikson in Aitkin County, lives outside of Hill City?"

Neither one did.

"He's the owner of the motorcycle the shooter stole. The FBI was keeping watch on him, and he managed to escape from his home last night, undetected," Parsons said.

Loman shook his head.

Johansen said, "And you have no idea where he is?"

"We're sending the best K-9 tracker we've got, and hope they locate him soon. At least we've got you two now," Parsons said.

"Sorry we panicked, instead of going straight to our sheriffs, or the FBI," Loman said.

Parsons looked from one to the other. "You did what you thought was best, given what had happened to your buddies." He paused, then added, "It may have saved your lives."

27

As Parsons and company started to put a game plan together, I got a text from Mandy, *Vince is waking up. He's mumbling in his sleep.*

It was more critical for me to be at the hospital with Mandy and Vince than at the meeting. I'd get briefed later. My fingers barely worked when I punched in, *Be right there.* I raised my hand. "Sorry, but I need to be excused. Weber's waking up!"

Everyone in Kenner's office stood and cheered. I noticed the other county sheriffs on the monitor clapping their hands. Smoke blinked his eyes a few times as he pulled Weber's phone from his pocket. "Give him this," he said.

"Reminder, no word about Johansen and Loman for the time being," Parsons said.

I nodded.

When I opened the door, and the sounds spilled out, Dina and the administration assistants sent me curious looks as I ran past them. They may have wondered why the group gathered in the sheriff's office cheered as I left.

It took forever to drive the two miles to the hospital, park, and get to the intensive care unit. Mandy was bent over Weber, and held his hand in both of hers. A steady stream of tears rolled down her face, and dropped onto his blanket. I nodded as I passed her FBI guard, and when I didn't see any medical staff to ask permission, I pulled open the door, and entered Weber's private room.

Mandy scooted over a tad, and we squeezed together on the chair. I more or less balanced on the edge as we stared at Weber. The hair on his head had started to grow, and it was evident from the sparse growth on the top center, it was the only balding area. And he had a good start on his beard. I reached over and laid my hand on his heart. It had been three days since I'd touched him in the effort to help save his life. To feel the steady beats of the heart that had stopped—not once, but twice before he got the hospital and twice more in surgery—made my own ache with joy.

"I've been talking to him, and he acts like he hears me. His eyelids flutter every once in a while," Mandy said.

"Vincent Weber, it's Corky. Time to wake up."

When his eyes opened, no one was more surprised than me. Mandy and I slid off the chair. She grabbed my hand for a second, then moved her hands to either side of Weber's neck. He closed his eyes and squeezed them together. When he opened them again, it was like the sun had risen for the second time that day. I'd never seen his face lit up like that, or his eyes so bright. He looked relaxed, and his smile reached halfway to his ears.

Mandy kissed his cheek. "It's me, Mandy."

I kissed his other cheek. "And Corky."

"Mandy, Sergeant Corky? We're in a hospital?"

"Oak Lea Hospital, for the past three days," Mandy said.

He lifted his arm a tad. "They got me all hooked up to IVs, huh?"

I glanced up at the FBI guard, smiled, and nodded. He gave me two thumbs up. I turned my attention back to Weber. "Do you remember what happened at Brookings?" I asked.

His eyes narrowed. "Not really. I remember that Mandy and me were there. But what happened next, I don't know how to tell you in plain English."

"What do you mean?" Mandy said.

"A lotta guys won't believe this, but I saw my body on a stretcher in an ambulance. An EMT we know, Lisa, was there with Mandy and me."

"Yes," Mandy said, and elbowed me.

Weber continued, "It shoulda seemed weird that I was somehow floating and watching Lisa work on me, but it didn't. You know how I'm kinda a control freak? Well, I didn't know how much until that instant when I heard someone say, 'time to let go.' And I knew I had no control over what was goin' on, or what would happen next. And the strange thing was, I was at peace with that. Hard to believe, huh?

"Then these large white light beams, I thought must be angels, were there with us, around us. Then I was moving a million miles an hour, with those light beams by me, and the next instant we were in heaven. And I realized I was outside the inner sanctum. It was like I knew things without being told in actual words.

"I was surrounded by light and magnificent colors. None like any we have on earth. Voices were singing, and humming, all around me. It must've been angels because I never heard human voices, or music, sound like that.

"An angel was there outside the entrance to the inner sanctum where I knew God was. The angel was communicating with me without talking, and I understood. I wish there were words to describe how it feels to be completely surrounded in love. Then my mother was with me. She looked younger and healthy again. Stacie was next to her. They both looked like they were illuminated somehow. Feelings of total joy and peace and love kept washing through me.

"My mother asked for me to forgive her so I could move on, and Stacie just smiled. Then I noticed a lot of beings behind them who all seemed to know me, but I didn't know any of them. Yet I knew they loved me, and cared about me, and even liked this ugly mug of mine. I felt accepted, welcomed, but those feelings were magnified by a thousand."

Vince paused, then continued, "I thought the angel was going to take me into the inner sanctum, but she said it wasn't my time yet, that my mission on earth wasn't over. My mother and Stacie both nodded and smiled, like they agreed with the angel. And then something happened I don't even want to tell you, because I don't want to believe it's true."

Mandy nudged him. "What is it?"

Tears formed in Vince's eyes. "My buddy Damon. He sorta floated past me. The last guy I would've expected to see there. Besides me, that is. 'Cause why would he be there? When he was at the entrance, outside the inner sanctum, he turned and looked at me. I felt all the love he had for me kind of spill out. And I knew he felt the love I sent back to him. Then Damon went inside. And here I am, back on earth."

Weber sniffed. I got a box of tissues from the table, and offered it to him. He pulled one out and dabbed his eyes. I set the box on his bed.

"It was an overwhelming experience. I felt elated for Damon 'cause he got to stay. But I had to leave, and I won't see him again until I die. Happy for him, sad for me, and the rest of us." He wiped his eyes and nose. "How did Damon die?"

"Let's talk about that later, Vince. For now, you need to rest as much as possible, regain your strength," Mandy said.

Vince wept over the loss of his friend. My heart hurt for him as my mind tried to absorb, to visualize what he had seen, heard, and experienced. And how he had seen Damon the day *after* his own heart had stopped.

Mandy pulled tissues from the box and handed them to Vince. Mandy and I cried with him. Vince stopped and caught his breath. We'd agonized over how to tell Vince the tragic news but he'd found out in a mysterious way instead.

The ICU nurse entered, and probably thought we were crying because Vincent Weber had awoken from his coma, but she didn't ask. When her own eyes filled with tears as well, she used a tissue to catch them. She left, and returned with a doctor and another nurse seconds later.

"Vince, the medical staff need to check you out. I'll take off so they have room to work, and go share the good news with Sheriff Kenner and Detective Dawes," I said.

Vince half-nodded. Mandy followed me to the door and we hugged. "Wow," was all she said before I left.

The FBI guard nodded as I passed by him. I headed straight to the chapel where I could talk to Smoke in private. But where to start? I sent him a text, asking him to call when he was clear. I was pacing the perimeter of the chapel room when my phone buzzed. "Corinne, good news?"

"Vince is awake, and medical staff are attending to him now. He looked very peaceful when he woke up. He's lucid. He had a near-death experience that he'll have to tell you about, because I can't. I will tell you something but you need to brace yourself first."

His voice was quiet when he asked, "What is it?"

"He said he saw Damon Wilkins go through the inner sanctum in heaven, before he came back to earth."

"The inner sanctum?" Smoke said.

"He'll have to explain. I'm still trying to process it all."

"Could Weber have overheard someone talking about Wilkins when he was in the coma, and dreamed about it?"

"Not that I know of. No one was allowed in the room with him until last night. Anyway, I'm feeling a little freaked out about things he said, what he saw. I know heaven will be my forever home, but I got pretty emotional when he was telling us about it. He saw his mother and Stacie. And his mother asked him to forgive her. For what, if she told him, he didn't say," I said.

"The whole thing is beyond curious, no question about that," Smoke said.

"A good way to put it. *Beyond* in a lot of ways. Smoke, I wasn't able to tell Mandy about Johansen and Loman yet."

"We'll have a lot to tell her, and even more to tell Weber. We had a productive meeting this morning, and I'll fill you in on the details when I see you in person."

"I'll check on Mandy and Vince, then will head your way."

"All right. Everyone's still in the sheriff's office. I just stepped out to call you."

28

I drove back to the sheriff's office filled with a range of emotions, but the strongest was gratitude. I wondered how Mandy felt when Vince talked about Stacie. She knew Stacie had been the love of his life, but Stacie was in heaven, and Mandy was on earth. With Vince. But life did not always boil down to the simplest levels of understanding. It was filled with complexities, especially in relationships.

The door to Kenner's office was closed. I knocked and Smoke opened it for me. The Zoom meeting had ended, and the other county sheriffs were not part of the next meeting.

"Welcome back, Sergeant. Tell us how our Deputy Weber is doing," Sheriff said.

"It's great that he's awake. There will be a lot to catch up on in the next days." I glanced at Johansen and Loman. "I didn't think to ask when he could have visitors."

Kenner waved his hand. "There'll be time for that. Special Agent Parsons, bring Sergeant Aleckson up to speed, if you will."

Parsons nodded. "Sure. A quick recap. We went through the class roster with the deputies here. It's the strongest link the four of them share unless they had a bad run-in with someone over the years. But it's our opinion one of their fellow students is the shooter."

Johansen shrugged. "We just can't figure out who it is. The FBI hasn't been able to locate three of them yet. One female and two males. It's not like we were mean to anyone, or ganged up on anybody."

"We were all on the same team and wanted everyone to make it. But two of 'em struggled from the get-go, and left after a few weeks," Loman said.

Parsons nodded. "Back to their encounter last summer. After Deputies Johansen and Loman gave Detective Dawes the resort's name, one of our special agents contacted the owner, asked him to look up the guests who were there over those June dates. Our agent added she was especially interested in a man named Hunter. She also gave the owner a brief description of the person of interest that the deputies had given her.

"Owner looked through his records, thought for a while, then told her it must've been Rudy Russell. Russell didn't have an ID, said he'd lost his wallet in a lake, and was waiting for a duplicate."

"The old lost it in the lake story," I quipped.

"Russell paid cash for his cabin. Our agent asked the owner if they had a record of the vehicle he drove, and the license plate number. Owner said they didn't retain that info. Deputies Johansen and Loman, you want to finish the story?" Parsons said.

Loman raised his eyebrows. "I remembered it was an older rust-colored Plymouth sedan, but didn't get the license plate."

"I noticed the car, but didn't pay much attention. We were on vacation, and try to take our cop hats off, leave our jobs at home. We didn't know who the guy was. We wondered if he started to seem familiar because he'd hung around those couple days. Now, if it turns out it was someone from our class, it'll seem like twenty-twenty hindsight," Johansen said.

Parsons lifted a hand. "Understood, yes. All right. Sergeant, we're all on edge with the shooter out there. As much as we feel driven to identify and apprehend him, we believe he's getting even more impatient with every passing hour, especially given the unfinished business he has with Deputy Weber who's been beyond his reach. Plus, if the suspect's checked out Crow Wing and Itasca Counties, he would've had zero luck locating Johansen or Loman.

Parsons checked his notes. "We haven't released any recent updates on Weber's condition, and we came up with this plan: Sheriff Kenner will hold a televised press conference in approximately three hours to announce the wonderful—albeit false—news that Deputy Weber will be released from the hospital tomorrow morning, and will spend a few days at a friend's house, at an undisclosed location to recuperate before he returns home."

"And what *friend's* house would that be?" I asked.

"Mine," Smoke replied.

My whole body tightened.

"Your house will be the trap?" I said.

Smoke's eyebrows lifted. "It's fairly remote, no close neighbors to get caught in any potential crossfire."

Parsons continued, "It's a good location for several reasons. Assistant Special Agent in Charge Maxwell is looking for a special agent to serve as Weber's body double. We'll make a big deal out of his fake release. One of our special agents will drive Weber's body double to Detective Dawes's house.

"We'll have an agent in the back seat for added protection. We'll keep close tabs on the streets and parking lots, from points where the suspect could keep watch on the front entrance. Special agents on the hospital roof was a great idea. We'll also have a vehicle follow at a good distance behind so it doesn't raise the suspect's suspicion, as well as law enforcement in civilian vehicles posted at stop signs along the way.

"Given the shooter's actions so far, we do not believe he would try anything while on the road. He'll want Weber to see him before he pulls the trigger, like he did the first time, and like he did with Deputy Wilkins. We'll have an army of law enforcement, in the house, and on the detective's property. Dawes says he has some pine trees that will serve as good cover," Parsons said.

The plan sounded both reasonable, and a touch unreasonable, at the same time. I lifted my hand to ask for the floor and looked at Smoke. "I forgot to tell you this earlier, Detective. When I got home last night and was outside with the dogs, I heard a vehicle come to a stop at the end of my driveway. My squad car was in the driveway. It was dark, and I peeked around the side of the house.

"The dogs ran out to the road to greet whoever it was, or to chase him away. Then the vehicle started moving again, and kept going. I had a bad feeling about it, and the question, 'did he follow me home from the hospital?' ran through my head. It was a smaller black SUV, maybe a Buick." I held up my palms. "Sometimes in the middle of a case I feel more paranoid than normal."

Smoke shook his head and gave me a "why didn't you tell me look?" then said, "The sergeant here gets hunches from time to time that have helped crack cases."

Parsons' brows lifted. "Doesn't hurt to keep a look out for smaller black SUVs around the hospital in the morning. All right, on to the next plan. Right now, aside from inside your jail, the most secure location we know of in Winnebago County is Oak Lea Hospital, and that's where Deputies Johansen and Loman will spend the night.

"One of the hospital's non-emergency transport vans will pull into one of the jail's garage sallyports, where deputies pull in with their arrestees, or pick others up. When they get to the hospital, the van will pull into their garage and a special agent will escort them to a patient room near the ICU. They'll remain there until the suspect has been apprehended. We'll announce that Weber will be released mid-morning, somewhere around ten. If we're too specific about the time, it might seem suspicious to the suspect. It would to me because I know that's not how it works. It all depends on when the doctor gives the final okay," Parsons said.

Johansen and Loman exchanged looks that told me they'd rather be at Smoke's house, and have a role in his capture, rather than hang out at the hospital.

"Special Agent Parsons, what about Weber's friends, his supporters who might be waiting at the hospital. Someone might recognize that the double isn't Weber." I said.

Sheriff Kenner nodded. "Yes, as part of the announcement, I'll say Deputy Weber needs to lay low for a few days. So to respect that, and the privacy of those who visit loved ones, we'll ask them not to be there.

"And no videotaping will be allowed. We don't want anyone within a hundred feet. The double will have a cap pulled down low, and keep his head down in his wheelchair ride, from the entrance to the SUV. We'll have deputies posted there in case people show up anyway. Because they will."

"Sheriff Kenner, for now, the only people in your office who know the details of this operation are the three of you here," Parsons said.

"Understood," Kenner said.

Smoke and I nodded.

"We all know what a critical operation this is. Everyone who works at the hospital knows about the security presence, and why they're there. No staff can answer questions about Deputy Weber's condition, per HIPAA. But the medical staff in the ICU who've cared for him, might question his release if they hear it on the news, or someone tells them that Deputy Weber will be released in the morning.

"I need to talk to the hospital administrator again, let him know I'll speak with the ICU staff. One of the things I admire most about doctors and nurses is they abide by HIPAA about a hundred percent of the time. Deputy Amanda Zubinski should be brought in the loop. I'm looking forward to meeting Vincent Weber, the man who refused to die," Parsons said.

If he only knew the whole story. But I had a feeling he was about to hear it.

Parsons looked at his watch. "It's just about noon, and after three hours of brainstorming and planning, I'm sure we've all worked up an appetite. Those rolls we had earlier hit the spot, but we should get something more substantial in our systems. Sheriff, is it okay if your guest deputies hang out here for the time being? I can pick up some food, go through a drive thru, or get whatever you all want."

"We've got some decent choices in our vending machines. Good deli options, like wraps, soups, salads," I said.

Loman shrugged. "Sounds good to me."

"It shouldn't be a problem, security-wise, for you guys to get something to eat here if you'd like. Special Agent Tanya Elkin, who's not always as quiet as she's been all morning, will hang with you until you go to the hospital," Parsons said with a smile.

Elkin shook her head, then smiled back. "I was here to learn, to get brought up to speed on this part of the investigation."

"She'll also leave with Weber's double, and be the backseat backup. From a distance she could pass for Amanda Zubinski," Parsons said.

I waved my hand at the door. "Let's go raid the vending machines."

When I arrived at the ICU after lunch, I stood by the FBI guard for a minute. Special Agent Quincy Parsons was inside, sitting next to Weber. The head of Vince's bed was elevated and it struck me how well he looked. I figured from the look on Parsons' face that Weber was sharing his near-death experience. Mandy was on another chair, rubbing her arms. I knocked on the door, then stuck my head inside. "Okay if I come in?"

"Sergeant Corky, you're back," Weber said.

"Hi, Vince. You're looking *really* good. Even better than a few hours ago."

"Yeah, they're gonna move me out of the ICU to a private room. Special Agent Parsons here asked if I felt well enough to answer some questions, and I gotta say I feel pretty darn good, 'specially since I'm getting rid of tubes, and can eat and drink again."

"That's awesome," I said.

Parsons stood and offered me his seat.

"Thanks, but I need to stand for a while."

"Deputy Weber shared his experience, about what happened after he was shot," Parsons said.

I nodded. "All I can say is, we're glad he came back."

"Yes. And he heard the recording of the deep voiced caller, the one he spoke with on Monday," Parsons said.

That's why Mandy looked so uncomfortable.

"Yeah, I don't always answer callers I don't know, but did it anyway. Didn't catch his name. Said his son was thinkin' of goin' into law enforcement. Said I'd stopped the kid for speeding but didn't give him a ticket. That made a good impression on him. He asked if we could get together sometime, and I said sure. He said he'd call back. I said that was fine. Extent of call," Vince explained.

"So you didn't know him?" I asked.

"No, but I shoulda had him repeat his name to know for sure."

"How'd he get your personal cell phone number?" Parsons asked.

"Good question, but a lotta people have it," Weber said.

"Another question, can you tell me what you remember about Hunter from the Crooked Lake Resort?" Parsons again.

"Hunter, yeah. It was weird 'cause I felt like I should've known him. And he seemed a little familiar to the other guys too. What's funny is, after I came to, woke up from my coma, a guy from our LE class came to mind. One who'd dropped out early. And I thought, that's why this Hunter guy seemed familiar, 'cause he kinda acted like him. But he didn't look at all like Rusty.—"

Rusty? Aka Rudy Russell?

"—That kid was scrawny, shorter than most, really thin, fine hair. Don't think he could've grown a beard. His eyes were a pale shade of blue, like almost white.

"And that guy Hunter was husky, taller than Rusty, by a few inches, at least. Had a full head of dark brown hair, a beard, brown eyes. But it was eerie the way Rusty came to mind as the one Hunter reminded me of."

"Rusty, as in Ruston Harris?" Parsons asked.

"Yeah, that's it. I knew it was kind of a different first name."

"He's one of your classmates we haven't been able to locate."

"Yeah? And if he's the guy I talked to on Monday, I know how he got my number. It's the same one I had in school. We got a list with everybody's names and phone numbers. He coulda kept it; I guess mine's filed away with my other school stuff," Vince said.

"So Hunter's voice didn't sound like that?"

"Nah. If it was Rusty who called, he musta used one of those voice disguiser machines," Weber said.

If that were true, when we captured the suspect, we wouldn't have to hear a deep creepy voice spew from his mouth. *Fine with me.*

"What would Harris have against you, against Damon Wilkins?"

Weber scratched his cheek. "No clue, unless it was 'cause we made it, and he didn't. And makes me wonder, did he just happen to be at the resort when we were, or what?"

"Your annual trips aren't a secret. He's probably kept tabs on the four of you for years. Maybe followed one of you up there," Parsons said.

That would be even creepier than his disguised voice.

After Sheriff Kenner held his press conference, our office was flooded with calls. Deputies and staff were happy with the positive news. Kenner made no mention of the FBI's involvement. The suspect may have seen special agents and suspected they were involved, but the report was focused on Weber's condition and not the investigation.

None of us wanted to put out false information, but in reality, Weber's medical team had determined he could be released from the hospital, and recuperate somewhere else. After they'd completed a thorough examination, they'd been impressed, and somewhat surprised, by his progress.

Weber's wound was healing well and showed no signs of infection. The area was tender to the touch, but he had little pain, and ibuprofen kept that under control. His color and vital signs were good, he was able to get in and out of bed without assistance, and had eaten and drunk for the first time since Tuesday morning.

Parsons had determined that when he told Mandy, Weber should also be apprised of the FBI's plans to lure the shooter to Smoke's house. Also that Bart Johansen and Chase Loman had laid low since they heard about Damon Wilkins, but were in Winnebago County, and would spend the night in the hospital under the guise of being patients.

Parsons had also coordinated a Zoom meeting with Johansen, Loman, and a sketch artist, to determine what Ruston Harris might look like. At least what he looked like when he called himself Hunter. Our office sent it to all law enforcement agencies in Minnesota, to be on the lookout for him. And each FBI Special Weapons And Tactics, or SWAT, Team member involved in Saturday's operation would get a copy.

Smoke and I planned to meet at the hospital before the hospital's transport vehicle left the evidence garage with Elkin and Johansen and Loman. They'd made a little fuss about spending the night in the hospital, not having a part in the suspect's capture. At least we hoped there would be a capture, that the FBI was correct in their presumption the suspect would swallow the lure. Hook, line, and sinker.

Vincent Weber was in a private room on a wing with only one other patient whose room was on the opposite end. Weber's deputy friends would stay in rooms on the same wing. When I rounded the corner, I saw an FBI special agent in a leather chair at the end of the hallway, about eight feet past Weber's room. I nodded at him, knocked on Weber's door, and let myself in. Mandy was at the window, closing the blinds.

"Hey," I said.

"Straw's cheaper," Vince cracked. And when Mandy groaned, it felt like we were getting back to normal. More normal, anyway. I smiled, and shook my head at his dumb joke.

Aside from the stubble on his head and face, Vince looked like himself again. Only better. Likely because when he was unconscious on the ICU bed, his face void of expression, he did not look like wisecracker Vincent Weber.

He'd been okayed to have visitors—besides Mandy, his almost constant companion—for short periods of time. They expected his friends to arrive any minute. I didn't want to be the fifth wheel in the room, but felt compelled to witness the reactions, and the expressions on their faces, when they reconnected.

Special Agent Tanya Elkin escorted Johansen and Loman into Weber's room. She said, "Welcome back, Deputy Weber." Elkin gave both Vince and Mandy big grins, then left.

Vince gave his friends a half smile, but the serious looks on their faces made his own mouth downturn in kind. As the two gave Vince gentle hugs, I mouthed, "let's go" to Mandy, and we slipped out.

Elkin sat in a chair by the other special agent and stood as we approached them. "The deputies are happy to see one another, I bet," she said in a quiet tone.

"Vince could barely contain himself before they got here. It's bittersweet for all of them, with Damon gone and everything. But it'll help heal their wounds a little." Mandy's voice was quiet, in turn.

"Mandy, you're staying again tonight?" Elkin asked.

She shrugged. "It's gotten to be a habit."

Smoke sent me a message, *I've been delayed, see you at the 5:00 meeting.*

I responded with a thumbs up emoji.

"Thanks, everyone. Well, I need to head out. Mandy, we'll talk later."

She smiled a little and nodded.

29

The late afternoon, into early evening hours, flew by. The county offices closed at 4:30 p.m., so the FBI set up a tactical meeting in Room 120 at 5:00 p.m. with their SWAT Team, and the two from Winnebago County—Smoke and me—involved in Saturday's operation. There was a mass exodus of employees from the building at 4:30, and most were gone by 5:00. The blinds on the windows had been lowered, and the shades on the two doors' glass side panels had been pulled.

Parsons stood in front of the whiteboard on the front wall. He logged on to his laptop, inserted a flash drive, and a map displayed on the whiteboard. It showed the streets in Oak Lea, from the hospital, south to County Road 35, the road Smoke lived on, a little over four miles west. It also included County Roads 9, 8, 7, and five other township roads, including mine, that ran north and south. Smoke lived just west of County Road 8.

Parsons looked over the group and nodded. "Before we start, I'd like to introduce our guest, Special Agent Justin Richards. We flew him up from Des Moines, Iowa and we were happy to find him, because he could be Deputy Vincent Weber's twin. His twin with hair, that is."

I nudged Smoke and nodded. A few others chuckled.

"Deputy Weber keeps his head shaved, although it's grown out a bit the last few days. But I assured Special Agent Richards that he'll be wearing a stocking cap so he doesn't have to spend all night shaving his thick hair, short as it is."

A few more laughs.

"Here's the plan. At around ten hundred hours, Detective Elton Dawes and Sergeant Corrine Aleckson will pull up to the hospital's main entrance in Dawes's SUV. Special Agents Tanya Elkin and Justin Richards will exit that door. Richards will be pushed out in a wheelchair because that's what hospitals do to ensure their patients don't fall on the way to their cars. Dawes will get out to assist Richards into the SUV. Front seat. Elkin will climb in the back with Aleckson. All will have their body armor on, of course.

"When they leave the hospital, they'll turn left on Highway Twenty-five, go south to downtown Oak Lea, turn right on County Road Thirty-five, and follow that to Detective Dawes's driveway, a tenth of a mile past County Road Eight, and to the north."

"We'll be watching to see if a vehicle starts tailing them. If so, when we run the plates, we'll learn his identity, and find out if there are any warrants out for his arrest. If there are, the special agent will call for backup to conduct a felony stop—and many will be close—and wait until they're out of city limits to stop him.

"Now that I say that out loud, we all know it would be safer to wait until he's exited his vehicle, since we know his destination. If he has no warrants, we'll wait until he pulls off the road, and is on his way to Dawes's home. There's a wildlife refuge to the west of his place that's public land, so we can't apprehend him until he steps on Dawes's property."

Parsons used his laser light pointer. As he called out street intersections, township streets, and county roads, he assigned special agents to position at those points. He also had a beacon shot of Smoke's property: a log home on forty wooded acres with a lake, and a duck slough.

"Our force of ten SWAT Team special agents will be on the Dawes property at oh nine hundred hours, and in position by oh nine forty. They'll have the four sides, and four corners of the house in their sight. There's an abundance of trees and shrubs, so it gives us an advantage in two ways: it provides good cover, and the suspect will be moving through the brush, so we'll hear him. He'll have to park his vehicle off the road somewhere, and walk in. The special agent following his vehicle will radio his position when he pulls off the road. In the unlikely event that the special agent loses the suspect, he'll alert us by radio.

"When the four arrive at the Dawes home, they'll park and get into the house as fast as possible. We'll have three SWAT inside. I'll also be in there,. The goal is to apprehend the suspect without firing our weapons. If we're close enough, and need to use our tactical spray, or tasers, or batons, that works.

"There is a very small—we believe less than a one percent— chance the suspect will not seize the opportunity, at this time, to go after the man he believes is Vincent Weber. He knows where Weber lives, and maybe plans to kill him when he gets home. He may follow the vehicle, find out where he is, and hang out until he sees someone leave, so he has fewer people to deal with.

"Or he may plan to return later, sometime after dark. In that case, our special agent will follow him to wherever he's staying, and we'll move and apprehend him there. That would be the slickest, least dangerous way to get him," Parsons said.

An agent raised his hand. "Special Agent Parsons, do you think he'd approach the house, knowing there are four cops inside?"

Parsons nodded. "It would be a surprise attack. He'll figure Weber's double wouldn't be armed, and Mandy's double probably wouldn't either. So that leaves Aleckson and Dawes. Detective Dawes's weapon will be concealed. Some cops carry when they're off duty, some don't.

"We believe it gives the suspect a big thrill when his victims look at him right before he pulls the trigger. And seeing four shocked faces quadruples that thrill. His mental state is compromised, so we don't know exactly what he'll do. But we'll be prepared to do whatever we need to."

He got into more details and answered questions. When the meeting concluded at 7:08 p.m., we were all committed to follow the plan, and do our part to the best of our abilities.

It was good to be home. Smoke had stayed at the office to attend to a few more details then planned to stay at his house overnight. His commitment, and part in the operation weighed on him. He needed to remove items he didn't want destroyed by bullets, in case. That included some wildlife prints and beer steins on his fireplace mantle.

I listened to Sheriff Kenner's press release a second time, and it rattled my nerves. I paced for a while, then put on a jacket, cap, gloves, and running shoes, grabbed a flashlight, and called the dogs to join me for a run around the backyard. I was grateful there was no snow on the ground as I ran twenty laps around my large lot. Not quite like five miles, but it helped relieve some tension.

The next day would be a big one. What would it feel like when we pulled up to the hospital, picked up our actors, and drove away? We'd be advised if a vehicle pulled out and followed us.

We'd had cases where we worked to flush out bad guys. Our last big one involved a man who'd posed as a drug dealer. We'd apprehended him, but the arrest had not gone as planned, and I still had an occasional nightmare about it. The old "expect the best, prepare for the worst," quote ran through my mind.

The worst. That's what we continually trained for. The FBI was the lead on the current investigation, and had dealt with high-risk incidents, far more often than we had. And they'd put together a sound plan, with lots of people power to successfully execute it. I thought of the one glitch that Parsons had referenced. What if the suspect didn't bite? I continued to run, and mentally went through the details of the meeting. The dogs explored and sniffed until it was time to go in.

When Smoke called early Saturday morning he said he hadn't slept a wink. I told him I'd slept two winks. Parsons had been there with some team members to be sure everything was set.

I took care of the dogs, and was ready when Smoke picked me up at 8:00 a.m. I climbed into his SUV, and leaned over for a kiss. "Mornin', darlin', he said.

"Morning. D-day, huh?"

"Yep."

The hospital transport van was set to pick up Special Agents Tanya Elkin and Justin Richards in the evidence garage at 8:30. Elkin had gone home the night before, and Richards had stayed at Parsons' house. The three planned to meet with Kenner that morning for any final instructions. When they arrived at the hospital, they'd be escorted to an office to wait, hopefully without being seen. The FBI didn't want them to arrive too early, but they needed to be mentally prepared, and ninety minutes was about right.

Smoke parked in the sheriff's lot, and we went inside to Sheriff Kenner's office. Special Agents Parsons, Elkin, and Richards were there with Kenner. Parsons was dressed in black tactical wear, Elkin and Richards in jeans and sweatshirts. They had their weapons strapped across their chests, concealed by their jackets. When I squinted, I could see Mandy and Vince.

Parsons stood. "Heading back out to your place, Detective. And praying for everyone on this operation."

We all agreed.

"We should get you two down to the evidence garage. Your ride will be here shortly," Kenner told the special agents.

Smoke and I went along and waited until they were on their way. My heart pounded as the transport vehicle backed out. The operation had been set in motion. The SWAT team was at Smoke's, our actors were en route to the hospital, and we'd be there to pick them up at 10:00, thereabouts.

Sheriff went to his office, Smoke to his cubicle, and I headed to the sergeants' office, and phoned Mandy. "Hey. And don't tell me straw's cheaper."

She laughed. "Where does he come up with that stuff?"

"How'd the night go?" I asked.

"Really well. His friends are with him now. I stepped out to take your call."

"I'm happy to hear that. I'll let you go. Say 'hi' to everyone, and I'll see you later."

"Later, and prayers," she said.

I checked work emails and some reports.

Smoke stopped by at 9:52 a.m. "Ready?"

"Yep."

The sheriff was waiting in the corridor and gave us hugs. "See you later. And I *know* I will," Kenner said.

His confidence boosted mine.

We climbed into Smoke's vehicle, and I called Elkin, told her we'd be there in about seven minutes. On the way, I scanned the streets for Chevy Silverados and black SUVs. No Silverados. But before we turned right onto the hospital's street, I spotted a small black SUV in a church parking lot, across from the hospital, on the other side of Highway 25. When we turned, there was another one at a chiropractic clinic, just south of the hospital, and still another in the main hospital parking lot, the one we entered to pick up the special agents. Small black SUVs were common.

The FBI had special agents in three separate vehicles to watch for the suspect, in case more than one vehicle happened to leave at the same time we did. One was at a financial building on the corner, one in the main parking lot, and the third on the hospital's south side street.

Sheriff had been right. People stood by their vehicles in the lot, with deputies nearby. Smoke parked in the patient pick-up spot, directly in front of the door, and stepped from his vehicle. He opened both the front and back passenger doors and went inside the hospital.

Within seconds, the group emerged. Smoke positioned himself in front of the aide who pushed the wheelchair, and it helped block the view. Elkin was bent over the wheelchair, like she was attending to her friend. They both wore sunglasses. When they reached the SUV, the vehicle further blocked the view.

A minute later, the three buckled in, and we were rolling. As we turned south on Highway 25, I saw the black SUV leave the church parking lot, and start down the drive. "Don't look now, but it might be our guy coming down the church drive," I said.

After we'd turned south on 25, I held up a mirror I had to see if he had followed us.

Bingo.

"Yeah, if that's our guy, he's behind us, and giving us plenty of room," Smoke said.

The FBI had provided radios for us, and we all got the call. "It appears a black Buick SUV is behind you. I'm calling in the plates," the special agent said. He was back seconds later. "Name's not Ruston Harris, or Hunter anything. It's Burton Beckett. Oak Lea address. And he's clean and clear."

Oak Lea address?

"There was no one on the Alexandria LE class roster by that name," Elkin said.

"Nope. Oak Lea address? Maybe another fake ID," Smoke said.

We continued down Highway 25, until we turned right on County Road 35, and headed west. The SUV turned also, but hung back a bit, and pulled over to let another vehicle pass before he pulled back onto 35.

The special agent said over the radio. "Is that some little trick he has, put a car between you?"

Elkin responded, "Looks like it."

Smoke turned into his driveway, and we saw that the black SUV continued west on 35.

"Buick turned into the wildlife refuge, and I kept going," the special agent said over the radio.

A succession of voices said they copied.

"Everyone in position. Unless he circles around, suspect will approach from the west," Parsons said.

Again, the special agents said they copied.

Smoke, Elkin, Richards, and I hurried into Smoke's house and joined Parsons, and the SWAT team who were positioned in different rooms. Parsons moved to the side of the front door, and the rest of us sat on the living room rug, between the furniture. We would lie flat if instructed to.

No more than six minutes later, we heard loud yelling and gunfire. Too many rounds to count.

"Shit," Parsons yelled.

"Suspect down, suspect down, unknown if anyone else is down!" the SWAT Team leader yelled.

We were off the floor, and at the front door in a flash. The SWAT team ran out first, and the four of us followed Parsons to Smoke's front yard. The suspect was lying face up about ten feet west of Smoke's attached garage. A Glock pistol lay on the ground near his right hand. His camouflage pants and jacket were riddled with bullet holes and stained with blood. His pale blue eyes—how Weber had described Rusty's—were open and stared at nothing. He fit the general description Weber had given for Hunter, minus the beard. A stocking cap covered his head.

As relieved as I was that Weber's shooter and Wilkins' killer could never hurt another human being, a part of me was disappointed he wouldn't be questioned, or hear from Wilkins' loved ones about the depth of their loss, or stand trial for his barbaric offenses.

The SWAT Team gathered around the body some distance away.

Parsons looked from one to the next. "None of you got hit?"

The SWAT Team leader took a step forward. "No, sir. He didn't get a shot off. When the suspect started toward the house, I saw his gun was holstered, and signaled the team to step from our hiding spots. When the suspect saw our force, his mouth flew open, and his eyebrows shot up to the sky. He didn't expect an army here. We ordered him to the ground multiple times. Instead, he pulled his Glock from its holster, and moved it back and forth, like he was trying to decide who to shoot. I yelled 'drop your weapon' a few times, then his finger moved toward the trigger, and we fired before he made it."

"Suicide by cop. Not the way we would've wanted this to end. But it's the way he chose for it to end." Parsons was silent a moment, then said, "And all of you are to be commended for your quick actions, the way you took down the threat. The fact that no one else got injured is nothing short of a miracle," Parsons said.

We had not been short on miracles in Winnebago County that week.

30

Smoke phoned Sheriff Kenner who told him he'd be right there.

I phoned Mandy. When I gave her the news, she yelped so loudly I had to pull the phone from my ear. We exchanged a few more words, then I said, "I gotta go but will touch base later," and disconnected.

Parsons made an announcement to the team. "We need to secure the suspect's vehicle to protect any evidence. He may have other weapons in there, besides. Someone could enter the refuge to look for geese, or other waterfowl, and decide to snoop around if no one is there. Volunteers?"

Many raised their hands. Parsons pointed at two, and they headed in that direction.

"I'll call the medical examiner's office, tell them what happened, that we need 'em here," Smoke said. After the call, he told us, "They'll be here within the hour."

Sheriff Kenner arrived, went over to the body, and shook his head. One of the times he'd had no words. His drawn face and furrowed brows were enough.

Kenner and Parsons determined the Minnesota Bureau of Criminal Apprehension should conduct the officer involved shooting investigation.

Parsons phoned the BCA, and had a several minute conversation. After they'd disconnected, he said, "Agents and scientists on the crime scene team will be out in about fifty minutes. Following protocol, they'll collect all weapons that were fired.

"I asked if it would be okay to check the suspect's pockets for his ID. They said it was fine, as long as we didn't compromise the scene. Also asked if we should fingerprint him. He said they'd do it when they got here.

"The BCA agent said we should have the suspect's vehicle towed to the Winnebago County Sheriff's evidence garage. Our three agencies will search it together."

Parsons called to Special Agents Elkin and Richards, and asked them to roll the suspect's body so he could check the back pockets. They put on disposable gloves. When the special agents had the suspect's body on its side, Parsons removed the wallet from one back right pocket and a ring of keys from the other. They rolled the body back, and Parsons patted the jacket pockets.

Parsons stood and held up the items. "Doesn't appear his cell phone's on his person, not in his pants or jacket pockets, anyway. When the BCA and ME get here, we'll remove his jacket, and check any inside pockets. Let's step inside, go through his wallet."

Kenner, Parsons, Smoke, and I trooped inside to Smoke's kitchen table. Parsons removed three separate driver's licenses from the wallet: one from Wisconsin and two from Minnesota, all with different names, and none were Ruston Harris. The one we were interested in was Burton Beckett whose address was 1506 Nelson Avenue NE, Oak Lea, MN.

"That's the apartment building across the street from the emergency area parking lot at Oak Lea Hospital," I said.

"He must've had a bird's eye view. That would explain why no one saw suspicious characters sitting in vehicles by the hospital for hours on end," Sheriff said.

"Tanya Elkin and I talked about famous serial killers who had hidden in plain sight, some for years," I said.

Smoke shook his head. "We'll find out when he moved here, how long it's been. We know he's been planning these attacks for months, maybe longer. But he didn't plan for it to end this way."

"No. Not until that last second when he decided to move his trigger finger," Parsons said.

"The guy was demented; thought he was smarter than any cop. After all, he committed two witnessed shootings, and got away with it. Until now. We can be grateful he was too impatient to wait for Weber to get back home before he tried to kill him again," Smoke said.

"Very grateful. Weber and Johansen and Loman and Mandy are gonna freak when they hear how close he's been, living right here in Oak Lea," I said.

"After we have his fingerprints, and run them through the database, we'll learn his true identity, and can look for his next of kin," Parsons said.

Smoke asked Parsons if it would be proper for our sheriff's office to search the suspect's apartment.

"Sure, you can team up with Special Agent Elkin for that detail." He checked the key ring, removed what he deemed was the apartment key, and handed it to Smoke.

Then Parsons turned to Kenner. "Do you want to give Sheriff Heller from Haven County the news, Sheriff?"

Sheriff nodded. "Be happy to do that."

Back outside, Smoke told Parsons, "I'm going to snap a photo of the suspect's face to show Deputy Weber and his two friends, see if they recognize him as the guy who called himself Hunter," Smoke said.

"I'll do the same," I said.

Parsons' phone beeped. He looked at its face, and said, "A message from Assistant Special Agent in Charge Beth Maxwell. She's planning to hold a press conference in about an hour to let everyone know the cop killer is dead."

The BCA team and medical examiner arrived within minutes of each other, and got to work. Parsons announced there was no reason for us to hang around, but to be sure we wrote our reports, and turned them in. Special Agents Elkin and Richards drifted our way.

"Sergeant, Special Agent Parsons said I should help you search the suspect's apartment," Elkin said.

"Yep. I'll give you a ride to your car, and we'll meet there," Smoke said.

Richards and I also needed rides. Me to my house, then Richards would go with Elkin. When Smoke dropped me off by my squad car, I said, "Detective, be sure to look for Weber's bracelet."

He nodded. "It's a priority."

"Richards and I will stop at the hospital after we've finished with the search," Elkin said.

"Yeah, I want to meet the guy who must be as handsome as me. I didn't think there were two of us in this world," Richards said with a chuckle.

That made me smile. He reminded me of Weber in more ways than one.

Before I stopped at the sheriff's office to write my report, I made a quick trip to the hospital to share a moment of celebration and joy with my friends, both old and new. Johansen, Loman, and Mandy were in Weber's room. All sat in chairs around a small table someone had brought in. All but Vince stood, and took turns giving me tight embraces. Then I gave Vince a gentle hug. Loman pulled up another chair for me, and we all sat down.

"It's over, huh?" Vince asked.

"It's over. I took a photo of his face to show you." I found it in my phone, and handed it to Vince.

His shoulders twitched. "He looks like Hunter, without a beard, and has Rusty's eyes. Ruston Harris. He grew a couple inches and filled out since school." He passed it around the table, and his friends got pained looks on their faces when they looked at it, and agreed it was Rusty. Mandy took a quick glance, and shuddered.

I gave an account of the events, from the time Smoke, Elkin, Richards, and I left the hospital until I got dropped off at my squad car a short time before. None could believe he'd lived in Oak Lea. The fact that his apartment was across from the hospital made us all uneasy, when we considered the advantage it gave him after Vince had been taken there.

We had been on a roller coaster ride all week. The hunt for the cop killer had ended in an abrupt way, and was difficult to absorb, fully comprehend. After I'd finished my report, I got a call from Smoke. "The good news is, we located Vince's bracelet," he said.

"Thank you, Lord," I said.

He continued, "Along with other items he may have lifted from people. And some things he used for disguises: different color eye contacts, wigs, beards, the long black gown, stilts, elevator shoes."

"He has maps, diagrams, and phone numbers the FBI will sort out. No personal photos of himself, or other papers. We also looked in his garage. Guess what was in there?"

"A Chevy Silverado?"

"And that answers that question. Shooter owned two vehicles, yet stole two others that couldn't be linked to him when he committed his crimes," Smoke said.

"When I showed Weber, and company, the suspect's photo, they said it was Rusty, so that's what his fingerprints should reveal. As for Weber's bracelet, I wish we could put it back on his dresser, not tell him it was stolen," I said.

"I see your point, but he deserves to know, and he'll want to read the reports, and would find out anyway."

"You're right. He's getting out tomorrow, so we can give it to him then."

"Tomorrow? Well, that's good news," Smoke said.

"Since Mandy's apartment is so small, I'm going to invite him to stay at my house a few days to recuperate, if that's okay with you," I said.

"Of course."

"Johansen and Loman are heading home later today. Johansen's brother's picking him up, and will drive him to his cabin."

"Ah. That reminds me, the FBI located Craig Erikson, the one who'd given them the slip. He'd hiked miles to another little town, and was sitting in a café there."

"Safe anyway."

"Yes, another relief. The FBI is planning a debriefing session, and a 'what did we learn from this incident?' meeting at our office later. Interested?"

"Interested, but I'd rather get your condensed version of it later," I said.

"Sounds like a plan."

I was home when Mandy sent me a video of Vincent Weber and Special Agent Justin Richards. It was fun to see the way they interacted, joked around, and seemed like two peas in a pod. Richards said they'd have to get together when Weber had fully healed.

31

Vincent Weber had spoken with his minister and asked him if he had a clue how he could've seen Damon Wilkins in heaven, the day before Damon died. His minister said the only explanation he had was time did not exist in heaven. Some people on earth had premonitions of future events. The minister's mother had experienced what she called, "whispers from God," several times, when she knew a loved one had died before she got the news. His explanation made sense to Vince.

Weber was released from the hospital Sunday afternoon. He'd agreed to stay at my house where he could rest in the den office, and sleep in the spare bedroom for a few days, until his doctor declared him strong enough to be on his own. Mandy was welcome to hang out there too.

It was the last day of my rotation, before my three days off. I signed off, and parked my squad car in the sheriff's lot, for the next sergeant to pick up for his rotation. Mandy and Weber picked me up there. He had shaved his head and beard. I'd gotten used to him with hair, and decided he looked good either way.

Weber expected company from three people who couldn't wait to see him. First, Jonathan Bauer—the father he had spoken with on the phone, but had not yet met in person—at four o'clock.

And his parents-in-law, the Wilsons, at five o'clock. We'd suggested he wait a few days for visitors, but Vince said it would be good for him, that he *needed* to see them.

Mandy carried Vince's suitcase to the guest room upstairs, then the two settled in the living room to wait for Bauer. Vince on a stuffed chair, and Mandy on the couch. I showered, put on leggings and a long shirt, released my hair from the rubber band, bent over, and brushed it out.

Smoke hoped to be there when Bauer arrived, but got tied up in another meeting with the sheriff and FBI.

My heart pounded when Queenie and Rex barked, and ran to the door to greet our guest. They obeyed when I said, "sit," and opened the door for Jonathan Bauer. "Welcome. Please come in."

His lips quivered when he tried to smile, and he stepped inside. Mandy hadn't officially met him at the hospital, and introduced herself. Then she took his hand, and led him to Vince, who had pushed himself up from the chair. Neither spoke, they just stared at each other until Bauer put his arms around his son. "We have a lot of catching up to do, Vincent."

"Yeah, we do. That's for sure, Pops."

Pops. "Why don't you go into the den for some privacy?" I said.

They had a *lot* to talk about, and I wondered what Bauer would think when his son shared his near-death experience with him. Because I knew he would, including what his mother had said to him. I had to wonder again if she'd asked him to forgive her because she'd lied about his father, or was it something else?

Mandy and I went to the kitchen and I handed her Vince's bracelet Smoke had retrieved from Rusty's apartment. "We can give it to him later and tell him the whole story when he's stronger."

"Good idea." She slipped it into her hoodie pocket.

Father and son were still in the den when the Wilsons arrived and returned to the living room when they heard them come in. I was fascinated the way the four gravitated toward one another. They sat in the living room and shared stories.

I wished I could have captured a photo of the looks on their faces when Vince shared his near-death experience. They all had tears in their eyes when he talked about his mother, and

Stacie, and Damon. Mrs. Wilson grabbed a tissue from the coffee table, and cried some more.

Weber touched his wrist. "Stacie gave me a bracelet I always wear, except when I'm on duty. I'll need to get that."

I smiled at him. "We have it for you. Mandy?"

She pulled it from her pocket and clasped it on his wrist.

There was not a dry eye in the house.

Vince was asleep in the upstairs guest bedroom when Smoke returned. Mandy had gone home to sleep in her own bed, reassured that Vince was safe from the shooter, as we all were. Smoke led me into the den where Vince couldn't hear us, in case he woke up. Queenie and Rex followed, then Smoke closed the door.

"I didn't want to tell you this over the phone. The suspect we're now certain is Ruston Harris, had a disturbing photo in a desk drawer. I took a picture of it." He held his phone up for me.

It was an enlarged photo of the four friends: Weber, Wilkins, Johansen, and Loman, sitting around a campfire. Their heads were turned toward each other, and it looked like one had told a joke, given the laughing expressions on their faces. None faced the camera, and it was doubtful they knew Harris had taken the shot. He had drawn a red X across Damon Wilkins' face, and half an X across Weber's.

After a quick glance, my stomach churned and I turned away. "That is sicker than sick. That monster planned to draw another line, complete the X, after he'd killed Vince?"

Smoke nodded. "Sicker than sick is right. We found out he moved to Oak Lea September first and subleased the apartment. We talked to the apartment owner who said the couple who lived there had to relocate, and the owner let them sublease it. Owner looked at the Burton Beckett license he produced, and asked if he had any references.

"Harris handed him three letters of recommendation he most likely wrote himself. Owner also looked him up, but didn't find anything suspicious. We did find a Burton Becket, now deceased, who lived in Aitkin County not far from Craig Erikson's place."

"Things are falling into place," I said.

"Yep. The FBI phoned Alexandria Tech. They looked back in their records and reported that Harris grew up in that part of Aitkin County. They'll take a deeper dive into his background, see if they can find family members, or acquaintances, or co-workers to try to figure why he did what he did.

"Like I said earlier, he had phone numbers and maps and drawings of the counties the four deputies lived, but there was no mention of their names. The FBI will interrogate his laptop and phone, and hopefully uncover more."

"I know people in the state, and four counties in particular, who will sleep more soundly tonight," I said.

"That is a given." Smoke pulled me into his arms and held on tight.

Over the next few weeks, the FBI positively identified the shooter as Ruston Harris. Harris had no prior criminal history. The fingerprints taken at the scene matched those taken at Alexandria Technical and Community College.

The FBI spoke with former students and teachers from his elementary and high school classes. He hadn't kept in touch with any of them. He was a bit of a loner, yet there'd been no indication he had a vengeful nature.

Harris had held a series of odd jobs over the years. The FBI contacted his former employers, and some co-workers, who reported he hadn't socialized much. He'd kept his nose to the grindstone, and had done his job.

They spoke with Craig Erikson who, as it turned out, had known Harris. They lived a few miles apart. Erikson said Harris was a quiet outdoorsman who liked to hunt and fish. He hadn't seen him since Harris's parents sold their place, and had moved to Texas some years back. Erikson struggled to come to grips with the fact Harris had committed those awful crimes.

When the FBI contacted Harris's parents, Mrs. Harris told the special agent their son did not have a close relationship with them, but they believed he loved them. He'd always dreamed of becoming a police officer, so it was a blow when he was asked to leave the program at Alexandria, but he would not give them any details. Their guess was, given his fierce independence, he likely had trouble with the training requirements. He'd struggled for a while, but found a job, and seemed to be okay.

Ruston Harris's heinous crimes left more questions than answers, as was too often the case in serial killings. It was presumed he was jealous of the top students in the law enforcement program he'd been expelled from, but they found no written rants about Weber, Wilkins, Johansen, and Loman—or plans to kill them—among Harris's things. Harris took all that with him to the grave.

Two weeks later, the Brookings Café crew threw a celebration party for their hero, and guest of honor, Vincent Weber. Owner Pete had invited the witnesses who'd been in the café when Deputy Weber was shot, along with first responders, and other guests: Mandy, Jonathan Bauer, Art and Joan Wilson, Bart Johansen, Chase Loman, Smoke, Sheriff Kenner, Matsen and his crime scene team, Carlson, Mason, other deputies, Oak Lea PD Chief Becker, and officers, EMTs Lisa and Max, and me.

Brookings Café was decorated with flowers, streamers, and balloons. And had a lavish food layout. Pete had contacted a caterer to make some special items, and they'd insisted on donating the prepared food, along with their help in serving it.

Grilled shrimp, slow-cooked ribs, broasted chicken, cheesy hash brown potatoes, asparagus, minted carrots, winter salad, Caesar salad, crusty French rolls. We were all in food-lovers' heaven.

Jonathan Bauer had provided a variety of craft beers and bottles of wine, both bubbly and non-bubbly. Mrs. Wilson had been a part-time professional cake decorator, and brought five 4-tiered stands filled with fancy cupcakes and looked too good to eat. Some had angel wings on the frosting, a heavenly touch. And they were scrumptious.

It was fun to mingle, and Mandy had the opportunity to thank Tony Edwards in person for his assistance after Weber was shot. I pulled Opal Reynolds aside, told her about the bracelet, and how it had been recovered. If she hadn't seen it on the shooter's wrist, we may never have known what happened to it.

When Pete asked Vince to say a few words, he walked over to the booth that still had the hole where the bullet had passed through him. There was a framed photo of his dear friend, Damon Wilkins, on the table with a banner on it that read, "Forever in our hearts."

Vince laid his hand on top of the back rest a moment, then clasped his hands, and said, "I'm not much of a public speaker, but I gotta tell you what happened after I got shot, and died. A lotta guys won't believe it. Scout's honor, it's true."

Eyebrows lifted among the guests, and I heard murmurs throughout.

Vince lifted his fingers in the scout's honor gesture, and shared his experience in heaven. Minus the part about seeing Damon, because it was the most difficult part to grasp. Most had awed expressions, whether they completely believed him or not.

"They sent me back because I have more to do here on earth. But I tell you what, I'll never be afraid to die again." Vince touched the infamous booth. "So Pete there asked what I wanted him to do about this booth, with the bullet hole, and all.

"I thought for about two seconds, and said, 'why don't you have people donate money to sit there, and give the proceeds to a good cause? Maybe one month it's the food shelf, another month it can pay for hotel rooms for homeless people. The list goes on. We could have a suggestion box, and come up with all kinds of ideas.' What'd ya think?"

If the cheers and claps and hoots were any indication, everyone thought it was an excellent idea.

"The Vincent Weber Worthy Cause Booth," someone yelled.

"Nah, just call it the Worthy Cause Booth," Weber said with a broad smile.

Winnebago County Mysteries

Murder in Winnebago County follows an unlikely serial killer plaguing a rural Minnesota county. The clever murderer leaves a growing chain of apparent suicides among criminal justice professionals. As her intuition helps her draw the cases together, Winnebago County Sergeant Corinne Aleckson enlists help from Detective Elton Dawes. What Aleckson doesn't know is that the killer is keeping a close watch on her. Will she be the next target?

Buried in Wolf Lake When a family's golden retriever brings home the dismembered leg of a young woman, the Winnebago County Sheriff's Department launches an investigation unlike any other. Who does the leg belong to, and where is the rest of her body? Sergeant Corinne Aleckson and Detective Elton Dawes soon discover they are up against an unidentified psychopath who targets women with specific physical features. Are there other victims, and will they learn the killer's identity in time to prevent another brutal murder?

An Altar by the River A man phones the Winnebago County Sheriff's Department, frantically reporting his brother is armed with a large dagger and on his way to the county to sacrifice himself. Sergeant Corinne Aleckson takes the call, learning the alarming reasons behind the young man's death wish. When the department investigates, they plunge into the alleged criminal activities of a hidden cult and the disturbing cover-up of an old closed-case shooting death. The cult members have everything to lose and will do whatever it takes to prevent the truth coming to light. But will they find an altar by the river in time to save the young man's life?

The Noding Field Mystery When a man's naked body is found staked out in a farmer's soybean field, Sergeant Corinne Aleckson and Detective Elton Dawes are called to the scene. The cause of death is not apparent, and the significance of why he was placed there is a mystery. As Aleckson, Dawes, and the rest of their Winnebago Sheriff's Department team gather evidence, and look for suspects and motive, they hit one dead end after another. Then an old nemesis escapes from jail and plays in the shocking end.

A Death In Lionel's Woods When a woman's emaciated body is found in a hunter's woods Sergeant Corinne Aleckson is coaxed back into the field to assist Detective Smoke Dawes on the case. It seems the only hope for identifying the woman lies in a photo that was buried with bags of money under her body. Aleckson and Dawes plunge into the investigation that takes them into the world of human smugglers and traffickers, unexpectedly close to home. All the while, they are working to uncover the identity of someone who is leaving Corky anonymous messages and pulling pranks at her house. An unpredictable roller coaster ride to the electrifying end.

Secret In Whitetail Lake The discovery of an old Dodge Charger on the bottom of a Winnebago County lake turns into a homicide investigation when human remains are found in the car. To make matters worse, Sheriff Twardy disappears that same day, leaving everyone to wonder where he went. Sergeant Corinne Aleckson and Detective Elton Dawes probe into both mysteries, searching for answers. Little do they know they're being closely watched by the keeper of the Secret in Whitetail Lake.

Firesetter In Blackwood Township Barns are burning in Blackwood Township, and the Winnebago County Sheriff's Office realizes they have a firesetter to flush out. The investigation ramps up when a body is found in one of the barns. Meanwhile, deputies are getting disturbing deliveries. Why are they being targeted? It leaves Sergeant Corinne Aleckson and Detective Elton Dawes to wonder, what is the firesetter's message and motive?

Remains In Coyote Bog Bodies marked with religious symbols are recovered from Coyote Bog and send Sergeant Corinne Aleckson and Detective Smoke Dawes on a quest. Who buried them in the bog? They pore through missing persons' files, consult an FBI profiler, and are soon in pursuit of an angel of death. Their investigation leads them into unchartered and dangerous territory, but they'll stop at nothing to end the death angel's reign.

Death To The Dealers When a man finds his deceased wife's secret phone, her list of contacts sends him on quest to uncover who caused her death. As he navigates his way into the dreary, drug-dealing world, danger holds a constant presence. The one bright spot in his life is his growing attraction for his canine patient's owner, Sergeant Corinne Aleckson. It's a relationship that will not blossom as he had imagined.